# Luci:
## *Rhoades to Hell*

By Anna Rose

Dedication:

To the creators and cast of the show LUCIFER, He Who *Is* "Dear Old Dad": the brilliant Neil Gaiman, Tom Kapinos, Ildy Modrovich, Len Wiseman, their amazing stars, Tom Ellis, Lauren German, Lesley-Ann Brandt, DB Woodside, Kevin Alejandro, Rachael Harris, Aimee Garcia, and so very many others in front of and behind the camera, who make the show possible.

All their brilliant work got me interested in the character of the Devil beyond the centuries-old Biblical stuff, but then I went in a completely different direction with the other bits. I hope you are okay with this. Believe it or not, your opinion really does matter to me.

I also want to extend a heartfelt "thank you" to Netflix, who picked LUCIFER up when its original network, FOX, decided to be monumentally stupid and cancel the show. Over eight million fans of the show made themselves known online and Devilishly delightful goodness manifested.

Yes, I am pathetic that way. Unapologetically pathetic.

So there.

Also, thank you to my beloved family and friends. You have always been amazingly patient with me and have (usually) listened to my ranting and raving about whatever has been on my mind at the time. Thanks for not committing me, although I suspect that possibility has not been far from your thoughts at times.

The delightful Ekaterina, who puts up with all of my nonsense. My Mom, who, while she may not read my stuff, *does* support me in everything I do. My son of the heart, Rowan Green, with whom I can discuss virtually anything in the multiverse. The brilliant, hilarious, and delightful Uno Bubba. My wonderful friend Caoimhe Kelly. My late-night chat buddy James Cole. The witty David McCoy. The impish and awesome Tracy Brown. And my beloved sister from another set of parents, the wildly fun Michele Roger-Beresford, who is also an author.

I swear I will keep my promise to you, Michele. Just a few more years from now (2020) – and it will be far better than fast food.

To my cousin Paul, who passed from cancer during the writing of this novel, I love you so very much, and I will miss you always. We may have been nine years apart in age, but I always enjoyed spending time with you when I was a kid. I will remember those joyful times for the rest of my life. I look forward to seeing you again when I also cross the Bridge. Hopefully Ivan is already there and making your afterlife special, but in a good way.

And last, but not least, I want to thank the woman who gave me my love of the written word when I was all of five years old, Mrs. Betty Cowan, from the bottom of my twisted little black heart.

I have not stopped reading (and writing) ever since you were my tutor and taught me to read using phonics, and it is all your fault. I truly wish schools still used phonics, because for me, they were a window into a much broader and interesting world.

To the **Sumaire Pressmen**: Hector, David, James C., James L., NJ, Mary, and Geoff, I thank you from the bottom of my twisted little black heart for all you have done to help make this book the very best it can be.

Other Works by Anna Rose:

TALES OF THE DRAGONGUARD:
Aya's Dragon
Sara's Fire

Audiobooks:
Aya's Dragon

THE SUMAIRE WEB:
Siofra
Fiach Fola
Droch Fola
Féasta Fola *(short story)*

## One

"Remy, what are my appointments for the day?"

Across the large room, sitting at a dark antique wooden desk, a voluptuous woman with what seemed to be impossibly-pale blue eyes looked up from the computer screen she had been reading and directed her gaze to the speaker. That luminary, a slender, well-dressed young woman with carefully coiffed long dark hair and blue-hazel eyes returned that gaze with the barest suggestion of a smile and a raised left eyebrow.

"The Governor wishes an audience at two this afternoon. He was firm about the time. Councilman Anderson is looking for donations for another term, and there is a university professor who would like to speak with you at your convenience," was the prompt reply. "As per usual, Ms. Sheffield would like to invite you to lunch at her restaurant at 12:30pm, but only if you are absolutely available then, was how she put it."

"Ah, yes, dear thoughtful Myra. I suppose I'll be feeling a bit peckish about then. Please let her know that barring unforeseen circumstances, I will be there. Her chef is above reproach, but I believe she knows that already."

"Of course, my Lady," Remy responded crisply. "And the other three appointments?"

"Anderson did not follow through with his promises to me after his last donation campaign, so I believe he can do without my assistance this time around. We'll see what his chances are when he doesn't have all that money to throw around on re-election hijinks. Tell him the well has run dry, and I don't see anyone striking oil again there anytime soon." She took a breath and tapped a fingernail on her desk. "Oh, and send an anonymous donation to his opponent. Nothing spectacular, but reasonably generous."

"And the Governor? He seemed quite determined to see you today. He let slip something about a time constraint," Remy said. "I'm not certain he realized that he had done so."

"The nerve of the man! I told him no before, and he doesn't seem to understand that my answer will not change, and then trying to dictate an appointment time? Beyond the pale!" She fumed. "Tell the Governor that my schedule is full, but if I have an opening, you will contact him with an appointment date and time. Then don't."

"Very good, ma'am."

"I really need to find a way to impress upon him that his continued pestering is unwanted," she muttered. "You said one more petitioner is waiting on an audience? Who is he or she?"

"The professor? His name is Dr. Hector Rhoades. He teaches comparative religion at UCLA."

"Comparative religion," she snorted. "Why on Earth would he want to see me? Well, I suppose I could use a bit of amusement. It's been a dull week after all. Let him know that if he can be here by 10am, I'll find a way to fit him in…and his lyrical name."

"Yes, ma'am. I should tell you that he's been waiting outside, at least since I unlocked the front doors at six-thirty this morning. I've no idea what time he actually arrived. He seemed to me to have been waiting a long while."

Luci looked at the ornate brass clock that hung on the far wall. If one looked closely enough, one could see the faded letters TI  IC, still barely visible, etched on the bottom of its frame. That it continued to keep proper time after the travails it had endured was one of those miracles of which others spoke, but which very rarely existed.

The clock's weathered face indicated that it was now 9:33am. The brass pendulum's steady ticking off of the seconds was almost hypnotic, and it was difficult for her to pull her eyes away from it and back to the matter at hand.

"Indeed? Has he given you any inkling of what he wants of me?"

"He has not, but he has what seems to be an ancient leather and oiled canvas book bag full of texts, journals, and spiral notebooks, along with some sort of tablet device in his possession. It all appears to be quite heavy."

"Interesting," she noted. "So, no bell, book, or candle in that collection?"

Remy's face betrayed no hint of a smile.

"No, my Lady."

"Whatever could you want of me, Dr. Rhoades?" she murmured under her breath, tapping immaculately lacquered red nails on the top of her ironwood desk. Whatever he wanted, it might be fun to play his unannounced game. Things had been boring for a long while now, and it might do her some good to spend some time poking the theological bear. If nothing else, it might improve her frame of mind.

After a moment's thought, she made her decision.

"Visit the kitchen for a couple of cherry Danish pastries, fresh fruit in season, coffee, and tea, and bring them to the Red Office," she instructed. "After that, collect our little bird from his perch outside and bring him up there. I'll meet with him shortly after that."

"Yes, my Lady."

"And be sure to let him know he's free to partake of what he finds there. Also tell him that if there is something he prefers, it will be made available, if possible."

"Immediately, my Lady," but Remy waited, knowing there was more coming. Their long association had instilled in her an even deeper knowledge of her employer than most long-married couples possessed of one another.

A pause.

Half-closed eyes.

A raised index finger.

"And a bottle of that whisky I've been keeping for special occasions."

"*That* whisky? Are you certain?" A rare appearance of surprise suffused Remy's normally serene face. Her Mistress did not often share *that* particular beverage with just anyone.

"I wouldn't have mentioned it if I was not certain, Remy. Just do it. Please. If he has any inkling of who I am, he might as well have some liquid courage available, eh? Don't bother to wipe the bottle down, however. It's earned its dusty shroud, I think."

"Of course, my Lady. It shall be as you say," Remy replied and rising gracefully from her seat, the blue-gowned, pallid-skinned woman slipped from the room to complete her appointed tasks. Loyal to a fault; trustworthy beyond measure.

After Remy left, Luci sat back, a thoughtful expression on her face. She rubbed her chin with the tips of her left hand.

"So, Dr. Hector Rhoades, will you be some sort of fanatical true believer intent upon my banishment, or is there something else on your mind? What impossible boon will you ask from me? A longer life? Immeasurable wealth? I suppose I'll find out soon enough."

## Two

When she entered the Red Office, so named for the antique cordovan velvet wallpaper that comprised the upper walls, from chair rail to ceiling, Luci found Dr. Rhoades dabbing absently with his fingertip at the final crumbs from his plate and washing them down with a deep swig of what appeared to be coffee.

Remy, who had been standing near the door, inclined her head to Luci and slipped outside, shutting it behind her soundlessly. She had work to do and this interruption of her routine was not welcome, though one would not know that to look at her.

As Luci walked in, Rhoades rose and turned to face her, giving her a slight, stiff bow. Whoever he was and whatever his mission, he had had good manners drilled into him to the point they were second nature.

He was of slightly above average height, maybe six feet, but well built. Dark hair, dark eyes, tanned. A scar marred the skin over his right eye, describing something that looked like a capital T. Whatever had caused that scar had very nearly taken his eye as well. Luci was certain there was an excellent story to hear about that, but whether the story she heard would be true or not was something else again. Human males seemed prone to the telling of so-called "tall stories" when attempting to impress others.

"Thank you for taking the time to see me, Ms. Inferi," his expression was odd, but nothing she had not seen before. She had found it to be a common malady among those who sought an audience with her. She knew she had developed a reputation over the years and humans all seemed to be taken aback at her deceptively slight figure.

"Please, Professor, no need to stand on formal address! You may call me Lucinda, but Luci is also fine, Dr. Rhoades," she interjected smoothly. "What was it you wished to see me about? My assistant was not clear on that when she told me you were here."

The Professor waited until Luci walked around to her seat. He observed it was a quite substantial chair of dark timber, upholstered in grain leather. It reminded him of his childhood; of the furniture in his father's office, which was all perfectly matched and was made of French oak, as he recalled. It was a good choice if you were going to spend long hours sitting.

She sat gracefully, and pulled the tray of Danish pastries, fruit, coffee, and tea closer to where she sat. Ignoring the fruit, (Remy had, perhaps playfully, included a perfect bright red apple in the assortment) Luci selected and then tore a small piece from the side of one Danish. She poured herself a small cupful of black tea from the ornately wrought silver teapot that occupied one corner of the tray, and sat back in her chair to nibble and sip, waiting for the Professor to explain his presence.

Rhoades sat down again and bit at his lower lip. His eyes were slightly downcast, but not in regret, more as though trying to resolve his thoughts.

"You seem to be in the throes of some sort of conundrum, Professor. What is it," she asked. "Don't be afraid. I don't bite. Usually."

The man took a deep breath, then looked her in the eye.

"Please call me Hector," he said. "I have answered to that all of my life. Might as well keep it in practice."

*Hmmm...dissembling,* Luci thought, trying to decide whether he really wanted to say whatever it was that he was thinking. It was one thing to plan things in your head and quite another to actually follow through on those plans.

"I thought your name was Paul," she murmured, watching for his reaction.

"Oh, all of my names are far too common in my unimaginative family. Too many people were already using Paul, so I chose Hector when I was still a child."

He did not even blink when she spoke his first name. Perhaps he had somehow suspected something like this would occur. There was more to this man than met the eye.

"I see, so Hector it shall be then. Now, please tell me what it is that is trying so hard to get out of you, if you will let it. I have a busy schedule today and my assistant had to work in order to find a way to fit you into it. No easy task."

No need to let the Professor know she would have deliberately made the time to speak with him even if her schedule had been tighter. Better to have him believe his visit was an imposition.

"I apologize for intruding and for my forward attitude in coming here uninvited today, Ms. Luci, but I believe it is not completely out of the realm of possibility that you are the one commonly referred to as the Adversary."

Rhoades tensed up when he finished speaking, eyes darting to one side in nervous fear she could smell. He seemed to have expected a violent reaction from her.

Instead, she laughed.

That only increased the delicious scent that rolled from his body and into her nostrils. It left her tingling from her fingertips to her toes.

"I suppose that *is* one of my titles, Hector. What is it to you?" She took another nibble of her Danish, looking him in the eye as she licked her fingertips clean.

"I have some questions that I believe only you would be able to answer," he replied, appearing to ignore the sexual innuendo. The scent of fear was now diminishing, but to her astonishment, no lust replaced it. "If you are of a mind to do so, of course."

This was different, she thought. No demands. No expectations. No threats? What was the world coming to?

"Very well," Luci said. "Ask your questions. I may or may not answer them."

Sitting forward, the man held his arms close to his sides, his hands on his knees. The scent of fear was now entirely gone, replaced by—anticipation.

"I know who and what you are, but I thought the Devil was male. Is this some sort of shapeshifting thing?"

Luci laughed again. She laughed until blood-red tears ran down her cheeks, and her laughter dwindled to choked giggles. Rhoades never so much as blanched at the sight. A point for him. Once he had conquered his fear, his bravery had increased.

She hoped it was not mere foolhardiness on his part. Or worse, insanity.

"Leave it to the Church to depict Angels as male," she told him. "Angels are female, Hector. Every one of us. If you recall your New Testament, the answer is in there. It was the male-dominated Church that decided females couldn't be trusted with celestial honors."

"Does that mean that God is—"

"*God*, as you refer to that Entity, is whatever gender that Entity decides to be, if any. In fact, last I heard, They were using a whole range of pronouns to refer to Themselves, some of which are not even comprehensible to human ears." Her expression became thoughtful. "It should rightly be 'Our Parent, Who art in Heaven,' I suppose."

"Really, I—"

"They aren't actually in Heaven, though," she said lowering her voice to a conspiratorial whisper. "Last I heard, They were vacationing in Rio."

"*God is in Rio!?*" The Professor blurted out, face draining to a deathly white that then flushed red. His mouth opened and closed like a koi begging for food at the surface of a decorative pond.

Luci laughed again. The man was perfectly delightful. If he had not had his introductions made here, it might have been amusing to have some sport with him at the Club. A minor disappointment when compared to the hilarity of his current apoplexy. She was glad she had taken the opportunity to invite him in for an interview.

"That's something you should probably keep to yourself, Professor," Luci smiled at him once she stopped laughing. "They like to keep things as private as possible, after all."

Dr. Rhoades still appeared to be a bit green and wide-eyed. How delicious. She had managed to shake his outward calm. A nice start to her morning, after all!

She opened the slightly dusty bottle of whisky that sat on the antique carved credenza behind her, took a deep, dramatic sniff of the contents, and then poured two fingers of the clear amber fluid into each of two engraved crystal tumblers. She held out both, allowing him to choose which one he wished. No reason for him to suspect her of anything untoward, after all.

"Care to join me in a wee dram?"

After only a half moment's hesitation, Rhoades grabbed the tumbler from her left hand, tossing back the contents without even wincing and depositing the empty glass on the edge of the desk in front of him.

"God takes vacations?" he finally managed once he had collected his thoughts, his voice a little calmer, but still a bit hoarse. "*Vacations?*"

"*You* take vacations, don't you? It seems only fair to me that the Divine gets to take one occasionally, as well," she smiled sweetly, saluting him with the hand that held her own tumbler before downing her drink in one go. "Or do you think They don't deserve a rest every so often?"

"But—"

"So, the Divine gets only one day in all of Eternity to take a break? You humans expect Them to pay attention to your exhortations on Fridays, Saturdays, and Sundays and whatever other holy days the Abrahamic faiths recognize? They don't even get weekends off. Tell me how that's fair? Not to mention all the other religious faiths out there and their own holy days."

Consternation. Realization. Was that shame? All of them flashed across his face. Guilt over something which was entirely out of his control.

Interesting.

"No, Ms. Luci, you're exactly right. I should have realized—"

"All gods take vacations. Often. Putting up with mortal nonsense is draining. How do you think humans got the Black Death?" She could not resist the urge to play with him a bit more. The temptation was simply too great.

Silence. She poured him another shot of whisky, thought about it a moment, and added another generous splash to the glass before handing it back to him. Luci was amazed to see the man down the entire contents of the tumbler without pausing for breath.

"Quite so. Goes on a break. Overstays. Forgets to feed his pets. Fourteen million die of famine. It's a lot of responsibility, being a god."

This time, Rhoades held out his empty tumbler, which was refilled without comment. Luci realized the human had seemed to have acquired remarkable resistance to the effects of ethanol. Not uncommon, with this species, but it rarely ended well for them. She wondered at the condition of his liver. Had it become so pickled over time that it just did not care anymore? The man's eyes remained clear and sober, his manner regaining some of its previous certainty.

"As you know, my assistant went through your bag to verify that it contained nothing potentially dangerous," Luci stated. "She noted that there was no Bible or other holy object in that collection. As a professor of theology, why is it that you do not have one or the other with you? I find that most religious sorts tend to carry a holy book of some sort with them on a regular basis."

"I thought about bringing something with me," he admitted, "but then I decided that it might be offensive to you, and so I decided to leave anything like that behind."

"Offensive?"

"You're the…uh…Devil, Ms. Luci," he said, quietly explaining the obvious. It amused her that while he had had no apparent qualms about visiting her in her domain and asking if she were 'the Adversary", as he had put it, there remained something about referring to her by her classic designation. "Everything I have been taught since I can first remember suggests that you would spurn such a thing and perhaps react badly if and when confronted with one."

"Did you think me some variety of vampire, then? That if you were to brandish a holy object in my direction, I'd be driven from your sight? Be rendered helpless against you, perhaps? Beard me in my lair and all that rubbish?"

An unexpected snort of mirth came from the suddenly squirming human. He appeared embarrassed and maybe even a little relieved at her good-natured sarcasm.

"I'm not really sure what I thought, ma'am," he replied, reddening. "This is all so very new and unexpected for me. I didn't want to make a bad first impression."

"A bad first impression," she said, rocking back in her chair just a tiny bit and raising an eyebrow. "Really."

"Yes, ma'am."

Ma'am? He could *not* be serious.

"You said you had more than one question. Is there still another or are you finished here?"

"I have a sabbatical coming soon, and I would like to offer my services to you for that year," he responded. This time, he sipped at his drink. Considering its extreme age, it was a more respectful way to address the stuff. He looked down into his glass at the pool of amber liquid that waited on his attention. "This whisky really *is* rather good, you know."

"It should be, it was laid down in French oak before the Battle of Culloden, as I recall. I took it in consideration for a favor, almost three hundred years ago or so. After three quarters of a century, with some of the whisky having been kept in bourbon barrels and the rest in sherry barrels, I finally had it bottled."

The chastened human blanched, and sipped at his drink delicately, suddenly a careful connoisseur. Perhaps he knew more about whisky than the average human.

"Please, don't waste it on me," he told her. "I'm sure you have more worthy visitors on occasion."

"Oh, don't worry, I've got an entire warehouse full of the stuff. There's plenty more. I've been very careful to monitor how much of it I drink. I have certainly existed long enough to have learned forbearance."

Stunned silence. Perhaps her true identity was becoming more *real* to him now.

"Now, whatever services could you possibly offer me, Dr. Rhoades?"

"If my research is correct, this is about the time you go on an expedition of some sort," he explained. "At least that has been your habit for the past century or so. You vanish from your headquarters of the moment and resurface somewhere in the world around ten to twelve months after that. I would like to request the opportunity to accompany you on your upcoming travels. I would embrace the opportunity to be your secretary and traveling companion. If this offends you, I apologize for my temerity."

Luci was surprised. She had thought she kept her activities as circumspect as possible, but this human had figured at least one of them out. The thought that she could be in any way predictable was somewhat offensive, but his request was not. It had brought this situation to her attention, which was important.

"Y—yes," she replied. "I *do* have plans to travel in the very near future, but I'm not sure you would necessarily enjoy being my traveling companion during that time. My route and destinations are not necessarily for the faint of heart. None of them would be anywhere you would know."

"I would find the opportunity fascinating, Ms. Luci," he protested. "If I decided I didn't like it, I would be happy to return. At my own expense, of course."

Luci laughed. She could not help herself.

He looked so earnest.

So young.

So naïve.

A perfect storm of possibilities to exploit.

"When I go on these 'expeditions' as you label them, they are not always to places that one may return from easily. You really have no idea what you are proposing here."

"All I ask is that you give me a chance, my Lady!"

An interesting change of address, that. He did not truly sound desperate, but there was something in the tone of his voice that also let her know that he was not actually insane. That was something, anyway. The insane, she had discovered over the millennia, were boring, the perfectly sane potentially dangerous. Anyone who would challenge the Devil in her lair had to be at least half a bubble off plumb.

There had been more than a few humans, or rather the souls of damned humans, who had been rather fun to almost push over that ephemeral edge from sanity into something different and far more terrifying. Since the dead could not actually *be* driven insane, as the soul is in an unchangeable static state, it added to the torture of the condemned.

Dying and entering the afterlife wrenched even the most demented souls back into sanity, no matter their ultimate destination. For the damned, that mental recovery was a curse. For the blessed—well, that was not the Devil's concern.

Luci sat back into the leather upholstery of her seat, steepling her fingers under her chin, turning his proposition over and over in her mind. It had been a long time since she had taken a human along with her on one of her jaunts. Perhaps this one would provide a little amusement before he begged to be returned to his boring little world. So far, the longest a human companion had lasted was an entire fortnight before pleading for rescue. Taking another look at Rhoades, she wondered if he would make it through half that record-breaking time.

Dr. Rhoades sat back just a bit, his presence exuding an air of patience as he waited for her answer. It struck her as being an almost military bearing. The "Hurry up and wait" attitude that served professional soldiers so well, whilst their political masters decided their immediate fate or tried to negotiate an advantage from the opposition, without committing their forces, exhorting them to keep training, to keep them out of trouble.

"Give me some time to think about it, Dr. Rhoades," she told him, finally. "I wasn't planning to leave for at least another month, so there is time between now and then."

"That's all I can ask, I suppose," Rhoades agreed, a slight smile on his lips. "Thank you for considering my request."

"You said you were about to embark on a year's sabbatical?" She asked. "When does that begin, Hector?"

"Officially, it begins in late August, but as the school year ended last week, I actually have some time before then to make arrangements for things during my absence." She was back to using his first name again, he realized. Informality was good.

"No lease agreement to fulfill, no pets to board? Loved ones to kiss goodbye?"

If he caught the double meaning of her last question, he did not react. In her short acquaintance with the gentleman, she suspected very little escaped his notice. Lucifer wondered what it would be like to play Poker with the man.

"None of that, in fact. My residence can easily be closed up for whatever period of time I am away. I own it."

Luci nodded her approval. Personal baggage could be such an inconvenience, whether her own or anyone else's who might come with her. This made his proposition more possible, though he did not need to know that just yet.

He had only just begun to sit for this exam, after all. There would be some time before the bell rung its end.

"So, your schedule is, as they say, open at the moment?"

The Professor looked a bit startled, but he nodded. She saw the hint of anticipation that brightened his eyes and smiled inwardly.

"Do you already have plans for lunch today?"

Confusion played across the man's face. From interrogation to an invitation to break bread, as it were. Luci could tell this was something for which he had not planned.

"No," he replied cautiously. "I do not."

"I have a standing appointment for lunch at Virgo, and I would be happy to treat you to a meal there if you have nothing else to do today."

"I did not realize that—you—ate, Ms. Luci."

She snorted.

"I have no *need* to eat, Hector, but I find I enjoy doing so. The more exquisite the meal, the better." She saw him make a face. It was good to know that his knowledge of her and her abilities still contained gaps.

"No, nothing weird, I assure you. At least nothing weird for your human palate," she said. "At the moment, I'm into more contemporary Earthly cuisine. The chef won't be serving me anything he knows I would not enjoy."

The man's eyes brightened. Few in this city had not at least heard about Virgo. It appeared that he, too, was aware of its existence. He was not a complete savage, then. All the better.

In her experience, those who subsisted on anything resembling fast food had other annoying habits as well. His physical condition suggested that he made a practice of making healthy food choices, at the very least.

"I have it on the highest temporal authority that the chef will be making something special for the afternoon meal, so perhaps you would care to join me in enjoying its expected excellence." 'On excellent authority' meant that Myra had spied on Roger's meal plan while he was not looking, which, if the temperamental chef discovered, would cause him to storm out of 'his' kitchen in frothing fury. "I would welcome the chance for a more relaxed conversation with you, Professor."

The human, no fool, immediately accepted Luci's invitation. His excitement at the opportunity was immediately dashed when he looked down at his academic clothing, worn to the point of obvious comfort. He knew without being reminded that Virgo had a dress code and that his current attire was everything they would look down upon.

Another point in his favor. So many academics of Luci's acquaintance seemed oblivious to their personal failings. This one, at least, did not appear to have been born and raised in a ramshackle and abandoned barn.

"I believe I see your dilemma, Professor," she said. "The reservation is for 12:30, so if you hurry, you can get properly cleaned up and arrive at Virgo in plenty of time."

He looked at his watch, a nice, sturdy analog device instead of one of those electronic monstrosities, and she saw his surprise when he realized how long the interview had gone thus far.

"I took the bus," he told her, a bit shamefaced. "My own vehicle is in the shop at the moment."

"The bus? Why ever for, when there are so many car services out there," she frowned, then brightened. "I have just the solution for you!"

She reached for the black antique phone that sat on one corner of her desk, pushed a button, then rattled out something too quickly for him to understand, then set the heavy receiver back in its cradle. Luci noticed the Professor looking at her curiously.

"Yes, I know, cellular telephones are the thing these days, but there is something about a wired receiver that appeals to me. At least when I'm in my office. Call me old-fashioned."

"Ah, I don't think I will," Hector replied. "What was that call all about?"

"Oh, yes, well, I've arranged for a driver to take you to your home, wait for you to wash and primp yourself, and then deliver you to the doorstep of Virgo just in time for lunch," she explained.

"Really, you needn't go to all that trouble," he began, looking just a bit uncomfortable. She found it a little charming that a man who would visit the Devil in her lair would think about good manners. "I don't wish to intrude further on your day."

"Nonsense! You are my guest, and I will do as I please," she scolded him. "Now get yourself down to the front lobby, and Sean will be there waiting for you. He's a small man with an enormous — smile. He'll take care of you. Now, scoot! I have things to do before lunch!"

Once the Professor had tottered out the door and was making his way downstairs, Luci called Remy back into her office. She wanted to know what other secrets this Professor Hector Rhoades might hold.

Three

Remy, anticipating her Mistress' request as always, placed a pristine manila folder down in front of Luci and stood back, waiting for her Mistress to look. It was not long before Luci opened it to do so, picking up the top sheet to read it, then put it down again with its fellows.

The Devil took a long sip of her drink as she began her digestion of its contents, rubbing her chin with the fingers of her free hand as she considered what she had just read. Luci gave a nearly inaudible sigh and then looked back up at Remy.

"Hmm, Dr. Paul Ambrose Hector Montague Rhoades, 17th Baron of Darneer Bottom, M.A. (Archaeology), Doctor of Divinity, Maj (ret.) British Army, LLB. Tell, me, Remy, was there a partridge in a pear tree included in that voir dire," she asked with a sideways grin. "Our unassuming-appearing Professor has far more under his bonnet than he indicated in our earlier discussion."

"There *is* more, my Lady, and it does not paint a pretty picture," Remy said. "He is widowed, no children. His wife, Amelie, died ten years ago under rather unfortunate circumstances, and he has buried himself in his work since then, eschewing both entertainment and relaxation in order to continue his studies."

"Additionally, while he claims that he has another term forthcoming, from I was able to unearth, his contract with the University was not renewed past this most recent term, and surprisingly, it appears he did nothing to avoid that. To be fair, I do not believe he is necessarily being untruthful in what he told you, as I could not find anything that officially terminated his association with the University. He simply may not be aware of his lack of situation as yet."

"Unfortunate circumstances?" Luci prompted. She poured herself another drink. The now-empty whisky decanter was replaced with another that was full. The Devil could count on only a single hand the number of times Remy had not kept up with her alcohol consumption, and she would still have more than one finger left over.

"A drunken driver, my Lady. Unfortunately, the Professor's wife was the passenger in the vehicle, and it went over a bridge in the Cotswolds, near Bath. There were no survivors."

Luci looked at the drink in her hand, shrugged, and tossed its contents back to follow the earlier swallow. Bad news, but no sense in wasting good whisky, especially stuff as old as this was.

"What was the former Mrs. Rhoades doing in another person's vehicle? Was she unfaithful?"

"No, it appears the driver was her younger sister, Pernille. They had been at an office holiday party until late at night, and, according to all accounts, both were more than a little inebriated when the party came to an end."

Luci sat back and absorbed all she had been told. She tapped the fingernails of her left hand on the outside of her now-empty tumbler, her expression thoughtful.

"Something tells me there is more to this sad tale, Remy. Out with it."

"Indeed, there is, my Lady. Our Hector appeared to love his wife to the ultimate end, and her passing devastated him."

"As one might expect when one's spouse passes. There is nothing unusual in that."

"This was far more than that, my Lady," Remy continued. Was that a note of remonstrance in her tone? "From all accounts, his grief came very close to breaking him. Once a happy and gregarious sort, in the decade since her passing, he has become a veritable hermit, when one discounts his career as a University professor. There are those who question the decisions he has made in the time since her passing."

"Decisions?"

"His hobbies have taken an extreme turn, my Lady. Extreme to the point of mortal danger."

"I see. What else?" Luci refused to become caught up in mortal drama. Except in certain circumstances, she was not interested in such things.

"His wife was the moneyed heiress to a racing stable fortune. She left him a pile of dosh that is being doled out on a monthly stipend, by a firm of chalk-striped London lawyers. Amelie knew him well enough to avoid leaving him the cash to dispose of in one lump. That money allows him to do pretty much as he pleases whilst providing for a comfortable future."

"So, our dear Professor is more than he appears but isn't forward about it. I'm not accustomed to such examples of humanity," she observed. "I'm much more familiar with the humans who appear to possess a need to wave wads of filthy lucre under one's nose to 'prove' something. I'll admit to being more than a little intrigued at this additional information."

She pursed her lips.

"Which firm?"

"My Lady?"

"Which—how did you put it—chalk-striped London lawyers—are managing his money?"

"Huntley and Cherish."

"Even better. Sir Ian owes me a favor," Luci said, her voice thoughtful. "So, have him give me a call. He and I have something to discuss."

"When do you wish him to call?"

"When would be the most inconvenient time for him?"

"He takes a massage at three o'clock our time, my Lady."

"I really don't know how you pick up all this information, my dear Remy. You are surely a treasure trove of knowledge."

"I have no need for sleep, so I spend my time learning what I can to be able to serve you more ably."

"You certainly do. Please have him call me at 3:10pm this afternoon. I'm sure I'll be back from my visit to Myra by that time," Luci said. "Thank you once again for your excellent assistance and information."

"It was my pleasure, my Lady."

"I really don't know what I'd do without you, Remy," Luci opined. "If I haven't mentioned it to you recently, thank you for befriending me, all those many years ago."

"Those thanks should come from me, my Lady. Without you, my execution would have been a far more permanent affair."

"Nonsense, child," Luci protested. "However, you are of far more help here in the living world than seeing to things in Hell, so there is that."

There was relative silence as Remy picked up the two empty tumblers and set them on the platter with an empty cup and plate. She paused a moment in her ministrations before she spoke.

"Sean is taking the Professor to Virgo?"

"Yes, once he's made sure the man is presentable in public," Luci snorted. "Why is it that academic types always appear to be so woefully unprepared for dealing with the rest of the world? If I'd looked closely enough, I'm sure I'd have seen worn elbow patches on his coat."

"I looked, my Lady," Remy told her. "You are correct. They are there."

The Devil sighed and took a drink of fresh hot tea from the Ming Dynasty Chenghua teacup Remy had just poured for her. Noting that the level had diminished appreciably, Remy topped it up again. It helped that Luci enjoyed an exclusive blend of Chinese Pu-Ehr tea, that Remy somehow managed to acquire for her.

Luci looked at the cup, with its handsome cockerel delicately painted on the side, reflecting that Sotheby's of London had recently claimed there were just seventeen of these teacups left in the world. Luci herself had ten, which were not included in their count, and the matching teapot, and a range of other Ming Chenghua dinnerware. She mused internally that the last sale price for only one of these cups was thirty-six million US dollars. It was amazing what some people offered her to allow them to escape eternal damnation, apparently unaware that she had no say in where they ended up after their demise. It did not seem to matter...they still offered.

"Anyhow, I've a few things to take care of before lunch with Myra," she said to Remy. "I wish I could take you as well, but as you don't eat— "

"Such excellent food would be wasted on me." Remy finished for her Mistress. "It doesn't bother me in the least. At this late date, I don't really miss it anymore. It's a faint memory of a long-ago time."

"Are you certain you aren't saying that to make me feel bad?"

"I could never do that, my Lady," Remy gently scolded her Mistress. "You know that perfectly well, too!"

"I wonder, sometimes, if I should have left you there and allowed you to move on as you had been intended at that time."

"I'm quite pleased that you did not, my Lady," was the reply. "If you had, I would have missed the adventures which you have shared with me in the time since."

"There have been a few that put even you in danger," she began.

"Indeed, my Lady, but as you can see, I managed them quite well enough!"

Luci looked at Remy and made a face.

"I know you wear those ridiculous gowns to cover up as much damage as you can, Remy."

"This is true, my Lady, but were that damage to be out in full view, it would cause far more trouble than good, so, with your generous permission, I will continue to conceal myself this way."

"Very well, Remy," Luci allowed. "At 11:25, remind me that I have a lunch reservation. I have a stop to make before I arrive there just before noon."

"As you wish, my Lady."

Four

Dr. Rhoades' hair was still slightly damp when he arrived outside Virgo at 12:20pm, but it had been brushed into a tidy sort of style, a few unruly curls breaking ranks along his neck. It appeared he had brought his knapsack with him once more, and Luci wondered if it was a habit, or if there was something important inside of it. Either way, it really was not an appropriate item to bring along on a lunch engagement. This was not a trip to a school cafeteria, after all. This was fine dining!

"Good afternoon, Dr. Rhoades!" Luci greeted the man and opened the front door of the restaurant for him, ushering him inside. "I trust Sean made your trip as smooth as possible?"

"I'm not sure how he managed to drive as fast as he did without getting pulled—" he blanched as he remembered to whom he was speaking. "I suddenly feel pressed to ask if he's even human."

"No, he isn't, but I wouldn't worry too much about it, Dr. Rhoades," Luci replied. "My local arrangements make things much better for everyone involved."

"What is he?"

"Luchorpán, albeit a fairly tall one, for the race."

"A lepre—"

"No, not a leprechaun. A *Luchorpán*," she corrected him, enunciating the word carefully. "He needed a place to be, so I took him in. Don't bring it up to him, though. If he wants to talk about it, he'll choose to do that on his own."

Hector simply nodded his acceptance of her explanation, quietly hoping the faerie creature might someday do just that.

A very attractive young woman who must have been the hostess approached them, her nearly-ebony face bearing a warm smile that appeared genuine, rather than business-appropriate. The floor-length blue silk gown she wore draped her body like something one might see depicted on a classic statue, suggesting curves without being overtly sexual.

"Welcome to Virgo," she told them, her voice matching the warmth of her smile. "Madam, sir. I am Linda, and I'll be taking care of your personal needs while you are here."

"New here, are you, Linda," Luci inquired. "I don't believe that we've met before."

"Indeed, Madam," the young woman gave a single nod. "I started here only a few days ago."

"Where did you work before this?"

"I moved to Los Angeles from Seattle, Madam," the young woman responded, an odd look on her face. "Miss Sheffield was kind enough to give me a chance."

"Does Miss Sheffield know you're welcoming us here today?"

"Yes, Madam," Linda replied, "She encouraged me to do so, in fact."

"I see," Luci said, pursing her lips.

Not seeming to notice the discussion, Dr. Rhoades seemed out of sorts as he stared at the pleasantly helpful young woman. She held out a slender, graceful hand.

He noted that her fingers had been given a splendid manicure of French tips, her nails filed to a curve, rather than flat, which added to their graceful appearance. In Hector's opinion, flat-filed nails tended to make their wearers' fingers look stubby.

With a pang of grief, he thought of his wife's hands, when she was not involved with horses, and racetracks and the inevitable dirt of those places. They had been exquisitely manicured, when that served her purpose.

Hector wondered, idly, whether she had ended up under Luci's purview. He sent out a private prayer to Them that wherever Amelie was, she was at peace.

*Them.* What a surprise.

"Sir, if you will allow it, I will take your bag and keep it safe in the cloakroom until you are done with your meal and are ready to leave," the young woman suggested. Rhoades' expression grew a bit stubborn.

"Really, Doctor, your bag and its contents will be perfectly safe in Linda's capable hands," Luci reassured him, placing a hand on his shoulder. "I promise you that. Myra only hires the most capable individuals."

Hector watched as the young woman in question unconsciously preened under the compliment.

With a sigh that only Luci heard, Rhoades placed the bag in the care of the hostess, making it clear that he was in no way happy with the situation. He knew his request was still being considered, so he also knew that he should display only his best behavior.

"All of my important papers are in that bag," he said in a low voice. "Some of my things in there are irreplaceable."

"My dear Dr. Rhoades, no one would dare violate the safety of an item having anything to do with me," she reassured him. "I promise you that it would not end well for the perpetrator."

A sigh of relief.

"And they know it," she finished, her voice an otherworldly deadly, flat sound. Although she was several feet away, Hector could see the young woman who bore his belongings away give the barest pause before continuing on to whatever storage area she guarded.

She felt a faint shiver run through Rhoades' body and then slipped her hand from there to the middle of his back, guiding him toward the dimly-lit dining area. A gentle push propelled him forward.

A ginger-haired young woman burst out of the kitchen and half-ran to Luci, a broad smile lighting her face like a burst of sunshine. Luci returned the smile, and gracefully enfolded the full-figured woman in a warm hug, kissing her soundly as she did so.

"Myra, may I introduce you to Dr. Paul Ambrose Hector Montague Rhoades, 17th Baron of Darneer Bottom, M.A. (Archaeology), Doctor of Divinity, Maj (ret.) British Army, LLB? Dr. Rhoades, this is Ms. Myra Sheffield, the proprietor of this fine establishment."

Rhoades looked not a little bit taken aback and surprised. Luci delighted in his discomfiture, and she took advantage of the opportunity to play with him.

"Our relationship shocks you, Professor?" She already knew his answer from what she had seen earlier in Remy's research, but wanted to hear his response.

"No, not that, my Lady," he replied. "My brother and a few of the men and women with whom I served were gay, lesbian, and bisexual. All excellent individuals. It's only that you seem to have gathered quite a lot of information about me in a truly short time. I had no idea."

Luci snorted.

"Did you really think I wouldn't have you investigated at my earliest opportunity? Don't forget that I have far more extensive resources at my disposal than perhaps any human in this reality," she said loftily. "I'm going to want to know everything I possibly can about you. Unlike my Parent, I don't know everything there is to know without doing a bit of footwork to ferret it out. Does my thoroughness offend you?"

"No, I can't say it does," he allowed, nodding. "To be honest, I think I would expect no less of you."

Another point in his favor. Where had this treasure been until now?

"Wisely spoken."

"And honestly intended."

Meanwhile, Myra was holding out her hand to Dr. Rhoades.

"I'm pleased to meet you, Dr. Rhoades. I'm Myra Sheffield, the proprietor of this overblown establishment. But you may call me Myra," she told him, her expression open and welcoming. "Luci rarely brings anyone along with her, so I feel honored to have the opportunity to meet you."

"A pleasure, Ms. Myra," Rhoades said, taking the proffered hand, and bowing over it, his lips not quite brushing the skin there.

"No, just Myra, please, Dr. Rhoades," the young woman insisted. "Please, come this way."

"Very well, then, Myra," the man agreed, the tone of his voice implying that this was something irregular for him. "Thank you for including me in the lunch invitation for today. It must be a terrible inconvenience to you."

Myra shook her head and then laughed, a blush coming to her dimpling cheeks. She stopped at what appeared to be a side room and after knocking on it twice, opened it to reveal a single, linen-draped square table, three places already set.

She stood back, directing with a graceful gesture for her two guests to enter, which they did.

"Oh, I'm happy to have you here, Doctor. It's nice to meet other people who are here for more than the food. I don't get many opportunities to meet real people, instead of customers," she said after they had all chosen their seats.

"Hey, now, if I cannot address you as Ms. Myra, you must address me as Hector," he insisted. "Fair's fair, after all."

An actual sommelier came into the room with two bottles of wine, interrupting their playful conversation.

"Oh, I'm so sorry, Hector," Myra exclaimed, raising a hand to silence the sommelier. "We *do* have a most excellent bartender who would be more than happy to provide you with a harder libation if you wish. Would you like me to have Jina come to take your order? She's quite gifted, actually."

"I may have had enough of the hard stuff for now, but I will most definitely keep her in mind, Myra, thank you," Hector replied.

Questions about the wines were asked and answered. Another bottle was procured, and then, after a bit of show, two of the three were approved of, and portions of the white poured into waiting glasses.

Taking a sip, Luci pronounced it acceptable.

"Hector, then," Myra agreed after taking her own sip of wine, her eyes crinkling as her smile grew even broader. "Your parents were into the classics?"

He made a face.

"Actually, no. More acceding to the demands of grandparents. It's a family name, and there was no one willing to carry it as their first name when I was born.  I really did not want to be just another John, Robert, Paul, or Henry, so I chose it when I was four years old. Best of a bad lot, really, you might say. Family duty and all that is how it was explained to me when they realized I was old enough to express an opinion on my Christian name." His face went red as he must have realized what he had said, but Luci let it slide. It was a common enough description for a first name in Western culture.

"Oh. I'm sorry, I suppose," Myra murmured, patting his upper arm in sympathy. "I'm sure you've found a way to rise above it, dear Hector."

"Oh, well, if you must know, I was named after a horse, of all things. Well, not strictly true...I was named after my father, grandfather, and great-grandfather and so on, back to somewhere in the early seventeenth century, who was named after a horse that could run and jump particularly fast whilst carrying a tiny man around an oval track. I just hope it was a good horse. I really don't know much about the beasts," he explained. "That's the family lore, anyhow."

"Of all those first names, my friend, which was the horse?"

"I'll let you wonder, dear lady," he riposted with a light smile.

Luci allowed herself a tight little smile at that revelation. She wondered if that was what had brought he and his now-deceased wife together in the first place. Not for the first time, she was reminded that there was something about Myra which made people want to open up to her. It was a skill she possessed, and she wondered yet again if Myra had perhaps been here before.

She stood a little back as she watched Myra distract Dr. Rhoades from his previous distress and get him thinking about something else. As a professional, she had learned well the art of removing someone from the stresses of their normal day and taking them into the rarified atmosphere of her restaurant, called Virgo. Myra seemed a Western version of a geisha in that way, taking away the cares of the day to enable the guest to relax and perhaps forget, if only for a few precious hours.

Luci remembered her own introduction to the place, and Myra, six years earlier.

Luci was new to this city and was looking for a suitable building in which to set up her headquarters, the previous location having been demolished by misguided religious fanatics.

Her main choices being New York, Chicago, and Los Angeles, she eventually settled on Los Angeles both for the rather predictable weather and the fine foods available there. It had been a simple choice, really, when it came right down to it.

She had tried several of the finer eating establishments in West Hollywood, Burbank, downtown, and the like, but had not found anything that had resonated in a voice that sang to her. A connoisseur of fine foods for the majority of the time she had spent on the Earthly plane, she had standards, and so far, the driving force behind the establishments she had visited were primarily based upon exclusivity and price, which did not mean much when the fare really was rather basic.

A negotiation for a particular building had not gone well, and, feeling peckish, Luci had decided to stop by a nearly unseen doorway in the neighborhood near where the building she had set her sights upon was located.

Going inside, she was greeted by the aroma of fine cooking going on in the kitchen. Intrigued by the tantalizing scents, she had wandered back toward that kitchen, wanting to know what sort of wizardry existed within those magical confines.

It was only the fast reflexes of a plump ginger girl that stopped the chef from plunging his carving knife into Luci's forearm as she entered the swinging doorway. She swatted at the chef to move away, unfazed by the sharp and pointed weapon he wielded. Instead, she pointed him at his workspace and told him to get back there and finish whatever it was that he had been working on before he flew off the handle once again.

That "once again" had caught Luci's attention, and she filed it away for future reference.

"I'm so very sorry about that, Miss," the girl had burbled at her. "Chef Rogers is very particular about who has access to his kitchen!"

"His kitchen? You mean that refugee from a bad movie owns this place?"

"No, no," the young woman corrected her with an effervescent laugh. "I own the place. He makes the food that keeps people coming back for more!"

Luci could not help but instantly like the young woman. There was something about her that was pleasantly infectious, and the next thing she knew, she was having drinks with the young woman at the otherwise empty bar. She had no idea how that had happened, but it was part of the natural magic the human possessed that caused it to come to pass.

"I think he worries more that spies might invade his kitchen and try to steal his secret recipes."

"Ah, like Orochon in Little Tokyo," Luci suggested, expertly shelling the salted edamame pod she'd plucked from the snack bowl in front of her, before tossing the small handful of crisp beans into her mouth.

If one wanted to set one's guts on fire, the noodle place was an excellent choice, but internal combustion was not really what the Devil was looking for this day. "I visited there two days ago and thought the Special Number Two looked good."

The young woman stared at her, shocked.

"How much of it did you have?"

"All of it, of course!"

"All of it?" The young woman appeared skeptical. She leaned forward, grabbed a fresh bowl of edamame pods from behind the bar and set it down between them.

"You seem surprised."

"The Special Number Two is more of a challenge than anything else, usually attempted by those with more arrogance than common sense. What made you feel up to that challenge?"

"Testing myself."

"Yourself?"

"I do foolish things at times, and this was one of those times."

"So, did you like it?"

"I did," Luci replied. "I've always been quite fond of very spicy foods."

"Then you have chosen the perfect place to live, as the Korean restaurants in the downtown area known as Koreatown have some of the very best Korean food around."

"That's good to know. Perhaps you'll consider offering some recommendations."

"Indeed," the young woman replied, and then she began laughing, her cheeks dimpling. "I'll see if I can think of anything in particular, since I now know you enjoy setting fires in your belly."

Once her burst of laughter was under control, Lucifer introduced herself to the young woman who introduced herself as Myra Sheffield, a native of the area, although well-traveled. In point of fact, she had finagled the Rogers fellow out of a restaurant in New York a few years ago with the promise of his own kitchen and then opened Virgo to the public once that kitchen had been built to his specifications and the Health Department declared it free of any violations.

In the time since she opened, several restauranteurs had tried to tempt the mercurial Chef DeShay Rogers away and into their own kitchens, but, for whatever reason, the man stubbornly remained, even when offered far more money than Myra was paying him. That thought intrigued Luci, and she wondered what it was about the young woman that made the man do that.

"Are you and Rogers a couple, then?" Luci asked her. "I am surprised that he stays with you when he has so many other opportunities open to him."

"I've asked him the same thing, but he refuses to give me a straight answer," was the answer she received. "And no, we're not a couple. Not in the least."

She blushed a little.

"What?"

"Let's just say that I don't swing that way, and Rogers knows that very well."

"Really?"

"Yes, really. I think Rogers feels a bit protective of me," Myra conceded. "He is old enough to be my father, after all, Luci!"

So, a paternal thing to it all. How interesting that was.

"You say you don't 'swing that way,' as you put it," Luci said. "Does that mean what I think it means?"

"If you're asking if I'm a lesbian, yes it does," Myra told her. "All my life, in fact."

"All your life? Wasn't that a bit precocious of you?"

"Somehow, I think you know what I mean," Myra told her, making a funny face. "Do you—um—swing the same way?"

"I've swung many ways over the centuries," Luci replied with a light chuckle.

"Centuries," Myra started to laugh, then stopped abruptly, staring at Luci. It seemed she was seeing the woman next to her for the first time. "You're not kidding."

Luci was shocked silent. No one took her that seriously unless they had been introduced to her true nature, and Myra certainly had not seen any of that at all in their short acquaintance. It was not something that she regularly revealed, although she had never made a secret of who she was.

She was impossible to destroy by mortal means, after all, though literally thousands of attempts had been made against her in her very long existence. Sometimes she was amused and others more than a little annoyed. The fools who made such attempts never ended well.

"Ah, no, I'm not," Luci admitted. "Not in the least. Does that bother you?"

"No, I can't say it does," was Myra's reply, and almost as though to prove her point, she leaned forward and kissed Luci on the cheek.

Then, before Luci knew what was happening, Myra had grabbed her hand and squeezed it firmly. She could almost feel the warm regard the young woman felt toward her flowing out from her fingers and into her own body. It made for quite the experience, really.

"Chef Rogers has some wonderful soup on the back burner that he only allows certain folks to have if you're interested," she grinned, her voice lowered to a conspiratorial whisper. "Let's just say it's not on the menu."

"Soup? What's so special about soup?" Luci blurted. She had never been much of a fan of soup. It seemed best suited for dealing with smaller portions of leftovers that probably shouldn't have been kept around in the first place, but to keep her new acquaintance from losing that lovely smile, she decided to follow along to see what might happen.

"Oh, you'll see," Myra promised her new friend. "Come with me, and we'll sit down to a bowl."

She nearly dragged Luci from the barstool, and the Devil remained stunned that she was allowing this to happen. Remy was the last human who had given this much freedom to touch her, and that was many centuries ago.

"Oh, and it's on me," Myra told her with another squeeze of her hand.

All these years later, and Rogers still had the great grand-offspring of that soup slowly simmering on that back burner. At least he no longer tried stabbing her to death when she entered his domain. That had been a happy achievement for her.

He would probably have made an excellent demon if he had not been born on Earth, but she did not share that thought with anyone else. He might not take that knowledge very well at all. Or worse yet, he might consider it a challenge of sorts.

Chefs could be a bit spiky that way. There were a surprising number of them taking up space in Hell, or perhaps not so surprising. One rarely hears of quiet, thoughtful food creative types, after all. A common aspect of their personal Hell for that sort was one where they were the minion with a temperamental chef lording it over them, in addition to whatever it was they were being punished for doing.

Luci rather enjoyed that sort of irony.

Chefs everywhere were a bit strange in her experience, all the way back to the first one to take a real interest in preparing food short of eating it dripping raw or nearly setting it on fire. She wondered who the first cook had been to take a swing at an unwelcome interloper.

Today's offerings included shallow bowls of that most excellent soup, an expertly cooked piece of very tender beef delicately spiced and prepared exactly the way she liked it, some sort of steamed, but still slightly crunchy seasonal fresh vegetable medley. Luci knew the dessert would be something her sisters would have loved to eat, had they lowered their snobbery to the point they could discover that human food could surpass even Heavenly ambrosia.

Not that they had to eat in the first place, that is.

Dr. Rhoades somehow managed to keep his mouth full and hold conversations without even once committing the social faux pas of having anything in his mouth except his teeth and tongue while he spoke. Watching them interact, Luci could see that Myra approved of the man, as she and he were discussing Luci's true nature as though it was the most natural thing in the world to discuss such a thing.

"How did you find out about her?"

"It's not as though she's ever really made a secret of who she is," the Professor explained. "It's just that most people think it's some sort of poppycock, so they think she's having them on."

"I am sitting here with you, you know," Luci said a bit icily. "I can hear every word you are saying."

"Oh, come on, Luci," Myra chirped. "You know perfectly well that you don't like talking about any of this. I'm glad you brought him here so someone could answer the questions you normally don't."

Myra got away with things no one else did. It was the boon Luci had granted to only a very few in her exceptionally long existence. There was something about the woman that made you trust her because you simply knew your secrets were safe with her. Perhaps four other beings in her existence had possessed that rare quality.

Luci noted that during the friendly question and answer session, Myra never volunteered information about her to the Professor. She would only answer direct questions. She was not blatant about it, either. She smoothly deflected some of the questions if they could be too personal, and indeed some of his questions fit that bill, but overall, she answered all his questions to the best of her ability.

A little over an hour and a half later, the sumptuous meal consumed, and the dessert and aperitifs being considered with the respect and reflection they deserved. In that time, the conversation had become more evenly split between the three of them.

As they had used a private salon within the restaurant for lunch, their privacy was assured. While the staff had some inkling that something was up, none of them truly knew what that might be. Those too new to know better were kept busy elsewhere in the restaurant.

"Now, Doctor, I must ask—how is it that you are not afraid of me? Your attitude around me is oddly balanced, and that is something to which I am unaccustomed. What makes you so different?"

"Don't misunderstand me, my Lady. I am most definitely disturbed to find my research has proven to be true," he replied with a wry smile. "I would guess that my apparent calm is due to your attitude in response to my coming to you."

"I suppose that makes sense," Luci said thoughtfully. "Keep in mind, my friend, that most humans would not even attempt contact in the first place, should they suspect my true nature. Most who have confronted me, and I use that word in exactly the manner it should be, tend to think I must be banished back to Hell."

"I can imagine," Hector murmured. "Over the millennia, you have garnered quite the reputation. I doubt that all that reputation has been rightfully earned. I have found throughout my life that misunderstandings seem to be the stuff of which Creation is constructed."

"It's a bit simpler than that, actually, Doctor. They don't understand that where I am, or even any of my siblings are, has no bearing on whatever their religion says," she continued to explain. "Our Parent has moved on to other things, and doesn't really care what goes on here, as long as They aren't bothered by minutiae."

The Professor looked a bit stunned.

"So, the whole Second Coming— "

"Not a real thing, my dear Professor. Made up out of whole cloth, as it were. Their 'only begotten son' was here that one time, and once he got his walking papers, he went off to do his own thing. It was not the first time, nor will it, I think, be the last."

"Walking papers? Own thing?" Hector echoed. Luci enjoyed his confusion.

"He's a serial Messiah, Professor. I consider him to be more than a little unsavory, if I am to be honest about it. Last I knew, he was off in some alternative universe where he's started some new cult religion, lording it over intelligent creatures you might consider to be some sort of insects. They have ten limbs, and five sets of internal organs inside a metallic exoskeleton. They are also less than what you would call an inch long but have managed to colonize several hundred planets in their region of the universe. They also smell absolutely terrible. Anyway, he's got them believing in virgin birth, miracles, all that crap. It seems to be something he likes to do. He's done it countless times since he was made, and will, I'm sure, do it again. Ultimately, he gets himself martyred, on purpose, and then moves along to some new game. My own thought is that he set up that 'Second Coming' nonsense in the unlikely event he decided to come back and play with humanity once again. If he was not also an immortal, he would have ended up under my tender care in Hell at some point, of that I am certain."

Silence. Luci gave one of her knowing smiles. At what point would the man jump up and loudly denounce her? Thus far, he was showing remarkable forbearance, which was a surprise.

"What, you thought that humans killed his earthly form, and he just tamely went to Heaven, and that was it? Heaven is boring, Professor. No one in their right mind hangs around there unless they absolutely must."

Luci watched as years of religious study was soaked in the wave of disappointment her words brought him. Humans could be so attached to things, and sometimes it was fun to burst their pompous little bubbles.

"Then all I have been taught—all I have learned—and passed along to my students— "His eyes were as wide and wounded as those of a child discovering that a cherished fantasy was not true.

"Come now, Professor, surely with all of your traveling you have become familiar with belief systems from all over the planet. Better than most, you should understand that nearly all faiths believe they are the one true path. You're smarter than to believe in infallibility."

Hector's expression changed, and he looked a bit rueful and perhaps not a little embarrassed as well. Had he had some sort of breakthrough?

"I suppose there is that part inside me that would like to think there is one only one right and true way. But you are correct in your assessment. Even those religions who claim that they are accepting of others tend to feel theirs is actually the 'best' way. I wasn't always a religious man but I found myself attracted to it when I was a soldier, suffering under the crushing weight of futility and loss of some of my men and, of course, the loss of my wife."

"I can't say I'm sorry to burst that bubble. There should really be a lot more bubble bursting out in the world, but it is sadly lacking."

Myra put out a hand and laid it atop Hector's where it rested on the tablecloth. Its warmth was a bastion of reassurance for the man, and for that, he was grateful. If this sweet young woman could sit calmly with the Devil herself, knowing what and who she truly was, then he had to trust that he was in no real danger.

"Imagine my own surprise when I discovered she is who she is, Hector," she said to him softly. "I didn't want to believe it, so she had to prove it to me."

"I didn't want to do that, you know," Luci said, sadness in her voice. "You forced it on me."

"Yes, I know I did, but it all worked out for the best, didn't it?" She smiled at Luci, then put her hand over the Devil's, her smile full of nothing except love.

"How did you prove it to her?"

"She showed me her true form," Myra explained. "Boy, was I surprised, too!"

"You didn't even scream," Luci noted. "I thought I might have broken your mind when I did it, but for some reason, you were fine. Or you started out bent, and so it made no difference."

Myra laughed and thumped Luci on one shoulder.

"What is her true form?"

"You'll have to ask her that, sometime, when there's no one else around. It's not for the faint of heart."

"You seem rather loose with these invitations, Myra," Luci commented, making a face. The Professor noted to himself that there was no actual malice or disappointment in the Devil's regard for the rather remarkable young woman who interacted in so familiar a manner with her. Her attitude was more of an amused acceptance.

"If Remy could handle learning the truth of who you are, then why not me? Why not Hector here?" she asked reasonably. "I don't know that we're any stronger than anyone else. Maybe we're just more open-minded and accepting. Whatever the reason, I'm glad that you showed your true self to me."

"It had been a long time since I did something like that, Myra. It's not something I do lightly." There was a reason for that, too. Usually, when she did reveal her true form to mortals, it was right before they discovered something else that was worse, in its own way.

"I know that, Luci," Myra said, her voice soft. "I glad you did, though."

And then there was more hand-holding and tender touching, and then even a bit of kissing. All things that had never been addressed in Hector's religious studies. In the books he'd studied, the Devil was about absolute control and power, and what he was watching was something far different than that. The young woman did not appear to know how much power she possessed over the one so commonly referred to as the Prince of Darkness.

Perhaps that was for the best.

Hector knew he was witnessing something very personal, so he kept his mouth shut. If he was honest with himself, it was fascinating to watch. So much had been written about the Devil, Satan, Lucifer, or whatever other names, but nothing seemed to ever have been written about the chance of personal relationships. Much less the idea that the Devil might want them, or even actual friends, in the first place.

All this consideration opened doors in his mind that he never knew had been closed and until this moment, had remained firmly locked. Misinformation, what amounted to educational garbage, was discarded and new information lovingly filed away in the spaces that unexpected mental cleaning created. He was only saddened that this was information he would be unable to share with any of his contemporaries. He had essentially promised to keep the Devil's secrets, and he was a man of honor if nothing else. He was only as good as his word, and that was important to him.

Several minutes later, Luci and Myra seemed to remember there was a third person in the room. Myra looked as though she felt a bit guilty, but Luci displayed no regret at all. In fact, her expression was a bit proprietary, when one got right down to it.

"Ah, well, Professor, you probably want to go and do things before it's time to leave town," Luci suggested as she stroked Myra's silk-clad back. Rhoades recognized lust when he saw it and stifled a smile. "Keep me posted on what's going on. I will assume that Remy has your contact information in the event she or I need to get in touch with you."

"So, you've decided that I may come along?" The barely-concealed delight in his tone and face were amusing. The human's response reminded Luci a bit of human children anticipating a long school holiday.

"Provisionally, yes, Professor. You've shown some good sense, and that counts for something," she told him. "Oh, and when you're packing, leave clothing and toiletries behind. I will be taking care of that for you. No sense in bringing things that will be redundant. That said, this isn't one of those Merchant-Ivory costume drama English caravans, so keep those items you *do* bring to a bare minimum where possible."

"Of course! I prefer to travel light whenever I am able," he assured her. "I learned to pack light while I was in the service."

Luci thought about the ever-present backpack and wondered at the truth of his statement.

"All evidence to the contrary," she replied, one eyebrow raised. After only a moment's apparent confusion, the Professor seemed to get the gist of her comment.

"The things I have in that bag are important, Luci, and I dare not lose track of it!'"

She gave him a look that questioned that assertion but said nothing more about it. He appeared to be becoming comfortable with the more familiar form of address she insisted upon his using with her.

"Indeed. Remy will contact you about one week before our departure date. She'll give you any necessary details then. So, you go and do those needful things to get ready, and I'll—" she glanced at Myra, a wicked smile playing about her lips that the young woman returned. "I'll get some things taken care of here.

Once Hector had gone and it was just Luci and Myra, the tone in the room changed. The human woman sat back in her chair and looked Luci straight in the eyes.

"I know you don't have playtime in mind, Lucifer," Myra told the Devil. "I know you've got a busy day ahead. What's really going on?"

"This new girl you have, Linda. What's her story? I can feel that it's more than it seems. She was a little squirrelly when I asked her about her background."

"Leave it to you to pick up on that, my love," Myra replied. "Yes, there is a lot more."

"So, spill it. What's up?"

"Linda's not her real name. It's Rianne."

"And?"

"She was an escort up in Seattle and had to make a quick exit. She was in the wrong place at the wrong time and saw something she should not have."

"Do tell."

"A drug deal gone sideways. She was shot and left for dead, but a friend of mine found her," Myra explained. "Once she was well enough to travel, Cary sent her down to me to lend a hand."

"So, you're playing the guardian angel now, are you? What inspired that sort of altruism on your part?"

"I owed Cary a favor."

"You did this because you owed someone a favor?"

"You're someone to point fingers," Myra pursed her lips. "I know you've helped out humans who needed it, Luci. I was able to lend a hand, so I did."

"We agreed long ago not to talk about that."

"Indeed," Myra agreed. "You have a bad reputation to maintain and all that."

"Send Remy the particulars on this young woman's unfortunate incident and I'll see what I can do to help out. Maybe make it safe for her to return to Seattle if she wishes."

"Thank you, Luci," Myra said, smiling, and then leaned forward. "Are you sure you can't spare me a few minutes?"

Lucifer looked at her watch and nodded.

"I'm expecting a phone call in about twenty minutes, but I suppose I can dawdle until then."

"Good."

# Five

While Hector was an expert at "official" waiting, when left on his own, he was far more openly impatient. Not a very social person to begin with, he was, perhaps, a bit terser than he normally was when dealing with others.

He had been ready to leave even before Luci had accepted his proposal. He was done with his mundane life and was ready for whatever new adventure awaited him. Mundane life hurt entirely too much, and he was done with it.

His wife's death had torn him asunder. He had loved her more than life itself, and her loss had viciously wrenched a part of him away. It was as though his soul was incomplete, torn, even raw, and that left him with a dark hunger that could not be sated, even all these years later.

For now, that hunger had expressed itself as a drive to do things that might not be "safe." Rhoades' sense of self-preservation was currently almost non-existent. Whilst he might not actively attempt suicide, it being against his beliefs, choosing adventures that stood a better than average chance at fatality had drawn his attention and eager participation.

He had tried so-called "extreme sports," but with the safety protocols required of those activities, that hunger for danger had remained unsated. Sky diving, bungee jumping, outrunning bulls, motorcycle racing and more that consumed his life in the first few years following Amelie's death.

More than one provider of some of those services had firmly told him he was no longer welcome, as he was a serious risk to their insurance policy, no matter what waivers he might have signed. Even they seemed to recognize his death wish, though none came out and said so.

Perhaps some part of him had hoped the Devil would destroy him for his temerity in approaching her, but that had not occurred. Instead, after teasing out more information, Lucifer, or Lucinda, or "Luci", as she seemed to prefer to style herself these days, had accepted his suggestion of being a traveling companion.

He did not understand why she had agreed to his proposal but was grateful that he was being given the opportunity he had requested of her. Who knew where it might take him?

Would it end in him being reunited with his beloved?

Or had he sinned enough in his life that he would instead become a permanent resident of the Devil's domain?

To his thinking, either outcome would be better than the Hell he experienced living without her on Earth.

The note, when it finally arrived, came via private messenger. The envelope was a formal-sort of thing, with a stylized ragged edge at the flap, which appeared to have been sealed shut with a wax stamp. Aware that he was being observed, Hector made a point of carefully opening the envelope and slowly reading the handwritten words in the folded note it contained.

The messenger waited with a given level of patience while Hector read the message and then a bit longer as he composed a handwritten reply. When a substantial tip was offered, it was declined.

"No, thank you, Professor," was the curt reply. "I have no need for a gratuity."

"I apologize if I have offended you, Ms. Remy," Hector told her. "I don't know how your relationship with Luci works."

The deathly pale woman's expression softened just a little, and she allowed the ghost of a smile to curve the very edges of her lips. It seemed to Rhoades to be an unfamiliar feature on her face.

"Just Remy, please, Professor. As for your generous offer of a gratuity, I have no needs at this point in my existence and have no desire for anything more than what I have now," she explained. "I genuinely appreciate your kindness, but it is not necessary. I am happy as I am."

"As you are?"

"You may not have noticed, but I am not mortal," she explained. "In fact, I have not been mortal for several centuries now. That said, unlike my Lady, I am not entirely immortal, either. I can be damaged, and my wounds will not heal over time. There will come a day when I will cease to be, may that day be very long in coming."

"That sounds a bit scary, if I was being honest. You're sharing an awful lot of information with me, Remy," he noted. "Of course, all sentient beings do what they can to survive, and I understand that completely. I will not betray that trust."

"As my Lady Lucifer is trusting you as a traveling companion, I will trust you with my own secrets," she said, then smiled. "Well, some of them, anyway. I admit to being unaccustomed to the level of trust she appears to be placing in you, but I have known her long enough to know that such trust is generally not misplaced."

"How did you come to be like this? If my question does not offend you, that is," he asked, and then gestured at a nearby chair. "Please, sit."

"You worry entirely too much about offense, Professor."

"Please, if she is calling me Hector and I am calling her Luci, please call me by my given name. It's what I'm accustomed to, anyway."

"As you wish, *Hector*," she replied with an emphasis on his name. "I admit to be in far more used to formalities, but if you desire an informal form of address, I will accept that."

"You're making this far more involved than it needs to be, Remy," Hector admonished her. "Just try is all I ask."

She made face.

"Anyway, as I was saying, I was tried, convicted, and executed for consorting with the Devil," she explained further, then sat in the indicated seat, her expression matter-of-fact. "When she discovered what had been done, my Lady grabbed my soul and thrust it back into my corpse. By some strange alchemy that she has not been able to replicate since, I reanimated much as you see me now. I am neither alive nor dead. I do not feel hunger or thirst, and I am happy as I am, overjoyed to be able to continue to serve my friend and Master. Those who murdered me have long since taken up accommodations in their personal cells in Hell."

"So, they were condemned for what they had done to you?"

"And for any number of others who met the same or similar fates. Murder is one of the very highest crimes, and trust me when I tell you that those who murdered me, and so many others did not do so for any noble purpose. Ultimately, it was all about greed and the desire for money and fame."

"Are you happy they're in Hell?"

"I feel it is justified," she said with another slight smile. "When I say I was put on trial, that examination did not involve an actual courtroom as it would in a modern setting. No, for me the word trial speaks more to the torture to which I was put during my interrogation, to get me to confess to things that never happened, and to incriminate any other possible future victims of their monstrous behavior."

Rhoades felt a bit sick to his stomach at her explanation. It was odd to know he was speaking to someone who had endured something like the Inquisition and had not survived the encounter. Not really, anyway.

She appeared to notice his discomfiture.

"My apologies for sharing quite so much of my experience with you, Doctor. I sometimes forget that such frankness can be disturbing for some. Perhaps my extended removal from the ranks of humanity has affected me that way."

"No need for apologies, Remy," he countered with a weak smile. "I'm honored that you have shared so much of your history with me. It's just not one of those things you expect someone to be able to share with you after the fact, as it were."

"Indeed, that is quite true," Remy replied, smiling. "I'll leave now and take your return message to my Lady Lucifer. She expects you to be ready to travel within the next few days. You may take no more than what will fit in your bag. My Lady noted that you seem quite attached to the thing, so you might as well continue to guard it so ferociously. She will provide anything else you might require for the journey. Be sure to wear serviceable clothing, and I would suggest including a sturdy leather jacket of some sort. Preferably with some sort of warm lining or a thick sweater."

"I'm already packed and have only one more thing to address before I leave, so I am at her service at a moment's notice," Rhoades assured the Devil's majordomo. "You have my cell number, so don't hesitate to call me at any time, day or night."

"That may end up being the case, Professor, but let us hope it is the day, for your own comfort. Until then, Dr. Rhoades," Remy said, rising. "I wish you a speedy and painless resolution to whatever that 'one more thing' might be."

And with that, she was out the door before Rhoades could say another word.

He stared after her and wondered if she would have accepted tea and biscuits, had he offered them. Then he recalled that she was Undead, and decided that tea and biscuits would have been wasted on the remarkable woman who had just departed.

Hector hoped he would have the opportunity to get to know her better before he departed this reality with Lucifer.

What a thing to think! Who would ever have considered that such a thing was possible? Yes, theologians generally taught that God and the Devil were real, but in his experience, none ever suggested that an actual physical interaction could happen with either one.

At that moment, Hector knew he was somehow special, and that shook him to his very core. He then began to hope that he would not be a disappointment to Lucifer.

Yes, *Lucifer.*

While she might insist on being called Lucinda or Luci, when it all came down to it, she was Lucifer, the acknowledged Lord of Hell, and he would do well never to forget that fact. He would need to remain on his guard, in the event she was merely playing some sort of game with him before she destroyed him.

Thinking about it, he wondered if he actually cared if he died or not, as he'd been not-quite-actively seeking it for the past decade. All the stupid things he'd done since Amelie's passing had possessed a credible and significant chance of ending him, but even knowing that, he'd participated in them, had perhaps even wanted Death to come for him.

And then he thought some more and realized that he would not miss this opportunity for anything, deciding he should live at least a little while longer.

## Six

Despite their previous conversation about calling, the only notification Hector had that it was almost time for the journey was when Sean, the chauffeur who had taken him to the restaurant and then back home again, rang his bell. As before, the young man was smartly attired in a fitted black suit, matching waistcoat, white oxford shirt, and a blood-red silk kerchief peeking out over the top of his breast pocket.

Knowing the "young man" was actually a member of the "Fair Folk" was a bit disconcerting, but Hector determined to keep his mouth shut about what he might or might not know. He was certain the reading he had done on the subject of Luchorpáns was rife with inaccuracies.

"My Lady has instructed me to bring you to the residence, Dr. Rhoades," Sean told him politely. "Please get your things together, and we will be on our way."

"Please come in, Sean, while I close up, then," Hector told the young man. He stepped back and stood against the door to ease his guest's entrance.

"No, thank you, sir," Sean replied. "I'll wait for you outside."

"If you're certain," Hector said, feeling a bit hurt, but keeping that fact to himself. He had been taught from his earliest memories to be a considerate host, and though this "Sean" might be nominally some sort of servant, he had never been a fan of the whole upstairs/downstairs way of things that his parents had known. "It may be fifteen or twenty minutes before I'm out the door."

"That's fine, sir. I'll be waiting for you there. My Lady has let me know that you will be traveling light. Otherwise, I would offer to bring any bags to the car."

Going back into the house, it took Hector only fifteen minutes or so to write a note to his housekeeper with final instructions on closing up the flat. Then he made a call to his attorney to let him know he was leaving town a bit earlier than expected, grabbed up one or two afterthoughts, and then snatched up his bag. There was a visual once-over of the front room, and then he headed out the door.

Sean had the limousine parked right in front of the building in the loading zone. A parking enforcement officer seemed to be deciding whether to stick his nose in things. How would the Luchorpán handle it if such a thing happened?

Pausing on the front stoop, he thought a moment, then pulled his keys out of his pocket, put them on the side table inside the front door, then turned the inside lock on the door and then closed it behind him. There was a finality to the *click* of the lock that was a trifle unnerving, but he affected to ignore it in front of the waiting chauffeur.

There was no reason he could think of that he might need those keys for his journey, and in the event something fatal happened while he was gone, he would not be in any condition to give much of a shit about anyone getting in.

"It's a bit of a trip to our destination, Professor," Sean said as he slid back into the driver's seat, latched his seatbelt, and started the massive limousine. "There are refreshments available in the console next to you. Please feel free to indulge."

"Speaking of indulging," Hector said, pulling a tin from his bag, "I've brought some biscuits along with me. Would you care to have a few?"

"Biscuits? Really?"

"Oh," Hector suddenly realized why there might be some confusion. "Shortbread cookies. I'm used to calling them biscuits, as I wasn't raised here in the States."

"I never would have guessed that," Sean replied, mirth in his tone. Hector knew Sean was trying to be funny, as he did not have anything like an American accent, any more than the Luchorpán did. "Sure, I'll have a couple."

Hector held the tin through the open interior window and waited while the driver picked a few tasty morsels for himself. Then he sat back to enjoy the ride.

"So, it's a substantial drive, then? I hadn't really thought about that," he admitted. "How long will the drive be, do you think?"

"From here? Maybe an hour and a half, depending upon the traffic," was the answer. "If I was somewhere I could do even a little magic, I might be able to shorten it up, but my Lady has forbidden my doing anything that ostentatious."

"Magic?" Yes! The Luchorpán had opened the door to questions! "What kind of magic?"

"Oh, come now, I know you had some sort of discussion with my Lady the first day. You at least have an inkling of what I am, Professor," the creature chided him. "I know I don't look fully human, even when I'm using a glamour."

"A glamour?"

"Illusion to make me seem human and which usually keeps you lot from giving me much of a second look," the Luchorpán explained. "I have a feeling you're not quite as susceptible to it as most of your kind, Professor Rhoades."

"Please, call me Hector, since you're not one of my students," he replied automatically. Unless he was dealing with people in an academic setting, he really preferred to be addressed by his chosen first name. "Yes, she said what you were, and I've done a bit of reading on the subject, but I suspect most of it is wrong. If you're of a mind, I'd enjoy learning the truth about Luchorpáns. I believe it's better to take the time to learn the truth of things than to simply assume."

The "young man" laughed, and he glanced in the rear-view mirror, his eyes dancing with mirth.

"Then you're the first human who does, Hector," he chuckled. "But then, if you were not that sort of person, you wouldn't be doing what you are about to do with my Lady. And I thank you for not referring to me by that bastardization of my people's name."

"I try to get things right as close to the first time as I'm able."

The Luchorpán laughed again. Hector found the sound delightful and wondered if perhaps that was part of the creature's residual magic. What little he had read about all of the Fair Folk suggested such a thing might be a survival tool, if what he had read was to be believed.

"You're wondering about me, aren't you, Hector?"

"Well, yes, but I don't want to offend you, Sean."

"You can ask me whatever you like, Hector," the demon replied. "If my Lady trusts you, I can do no less."

"You know what she is?"

"I could feel her presence before she even knew I was in the area, Hector."

"Oh? What does she feel like to you?"

"Unlike anything you could ever imagine. The sheer amount of power she exudes is intoxicating."

"And you trust her?"

"I have no reason not to trust her, Hector," Sean said. "She has kept her word for everything I asked of her when first we met."

"How long have you known her?"

"Five hundred years, I think, give or take a decade or two," the Luchorpán said, after thinking about it a moment. "We met in Ireland while she was pestering the Priests there."

This time it was Hector's turn to laugh.

"I imagine she had fun doing that to them, too."

"You have no idea," Sean agreed. "And then she rescued me from a Priest who would have destroyed me as some sort of demon-spawn."

"So, you owe her, then."

"No, actually I don't," Sean replied, surprise in his tone. "At least as far as she is concerned. I offered to perform a task for her to even up the Ledger and she declined. Told me she didn't think what the Priest had been planning to do was right and right then and there said she was sending me on my way."

"That must have been a surprise."

"You have no idea," Sean said. "She was the first Celestial I'd ever met. I had no clue what to expect. We Fair Folk generally avoid deities and the like when we are able, and I would have done the same when I sensed her approach if I had been able to do so."

"Well, I'm glad she was able to rescue you, Sean."

"Me, too, Hector," the Luchorpán agreed. "Me, too. Otherwise you'd have to find your own damned ride to my Lady's place."

"Screw you, Sean."

An upright middle finger from the driver's seat was Sean's reply, followed by laughter from them both.

The two ended up getting into a discussion about religion, politics, Celestials, the Fair Folk, and cilantro versus coriander. Hector discovered that the Luchorpán hated them both, which meant corned beef and cabbage was never on the menu. Hector, on the other hand, enjoyed them both, which helped when one was having either corned beef and cabbage or a tasty burrito.

As they traveled, Hector realized that he had not really thought about where the Devil might live while spending her time on the Earthly plane, and was slightly surprised when Sean finally pulled into the driveway of an otherwise unassuming ranch-style home in West Hollywood. Several varieties of roses filled the flowerbeds, which surrounded a small angel-topped fountain. The front curtains were drawn, a common theme in most neighborhoods.

Sean asked Hector to wait, got out of the front seat, and rather ceremoniously opened the door for the bemused human. As Hector emerged, the Luchorpán gave an ornate bow, grinning like a five-year-old boy as he raised his head.

"A pleasure to serve you again, Hector," he said, tugging at his forelock in the age-old way servants had been doing for countless centuries. Hector knew it was all in fun, but played the part of the honored guest, gave a mighty sniff, and moved up the walkway.

"Thanks for the great time and conversation, Sean," he said from the side of his mouth as he passed his giddy chauffeur. "You made the drive a lot better than it might have been."

"That's my job, Hector," the chauffeur replied. "All part of the service."

"It may be your job, but I think you went above and beyond and actually made it fun. I learned shit along the way, and I really appreciate that, Sean," Hector countered. "Tell you what, when I get back to terra firma, if I survive all of this, we'll go see the Lakers play a game."

"I'm holding you to that, buddy."

"Good."

Conversation was cut short as the front door opened.

As he got closer, Hector saw that the door opened into a small foyer, beyond which stood yet another dark wooden door, this one featuring a blood-red stained glass and iron center. It made for rather a gruesome impression upon first viewing, but knowing what little he did about the Devil, it seemed perfectly in character. It was likely designed to make visitors uncomfortable enough to decide to leave on their own.

Only a moment later, the inner door was opened and revealed something much larger and more ornate than the home's exterior suggested would be found within. Another servant welcomed him to Luci's home and took him to the suite of rooms that would be his quarters while he waited on their departure. As he suspected, the rooms beyond the unwelcoming foyer were warm, comfortable, and nearly beckoned him to come in for a visit.

It was a relatively long walk to his rooms. It was plain to see that the interior of the place was far larger than the exterior suggested, reminding him of a television show he had loved since he was a child growing up. He smiled as he realized he wwould be going on his own journey in a similar position as some in that show.

Once he arrived in his rooms, he was pleased to see they included a spacious bedroom, an equally large sitting room, and a full bathroom with the kind of bathtub so many people wanted but rarely received. It was more than long enough to accommodate him laying down, if that was his desire when bathing, and was high enough that the water would come to just above his chest were he to sit up inside it.

A small part of his mind suggested that it would also make for a perfect drowning pool, but he drove that thought away, trusting that he was safe here as the Devil's personal guest.

Before departing, the servant, a livery-clad, dark-haired young man, had relayed Luci's welcome, asked him if there was anything special he might require and then informed him that dinner would be served in the dining room at five o'clock. When Hector asked where that room could be found, the servant told Hector that he would arrive at ten minutes to five to escort him there.

With that, the servant excused himself and Hector set about exploring his temporary quarters. They could easily rival the accommodations at a high-end hotel.

"This place seems to be far larger on the inside than it would appear from outside," he said aloud. "For some reason, I don't think I'm at all surprised by this."

"Talking to yourself, Professor?"

Hector spun around to see Remy standing just outside the doorway, a silver tray in her hands. She bestowed one of her rare smiles on him and he waved her in.

"Well, hello, my friend," he said to the majordomo, inviting her to sit. "I know you're not into eating and drinking, but I'll do the eating and the drinking and we can chat."

"You know, Professor, if you like, I can always have the interior redone in blue," she told him.

"That's the outside, not the inside, and I'm sure you know that."

"Of course I do, Professor, but I had to be sure of you."

"Indeed you did," Hector smiled back at Remy. "I hope I'm not keeping you from anything."

"I suppose I have a few minutes to indulge you," she replied. "I've brought some Pu-Ehr and some cucumber sandwiches for you to enjoy."

"You've won my heart, Remy!"

"Oh, I'll bet you say that to all the girls."

"Only to you, my dear. Only to you."

## Seven

The two days he had spent before their journey's onset had been invaluable as a preparation tool. Remy, being the hyper-efficient individual that she was, had been careful to provide as much information as she thought might be useful for the neophyte traveler.

During that time, Hector discovered that the undead majordomo had a sense of humor so dry it could wick moisture from desert sand. He also discovered that he very much enjoyed spending time with her. He sincerely hoped that feeling was reciprocated, but then with her personality being what it was, Hector would never know how she truly felt unless she told him.

He came to look forward to their occasional periods of time spent doing something together. Remy was a font of information, sharing bits of history that remained unwritten, but witnessed by the woman who shared them with him. Hector found it fascinating to learn about things that affected the regular people in the societies Remy and Luci had encountered over their time together, rather than the stories of how the gentry lived their own lives. In his opinion, those stories had been done to death.

He also learned more about the truth of who the Devil was and was not, through the eyes of one who had once been mortal and knew her better than anyone else but her celestial family. Lucifer did not bother to tempt mortals into committing evil acts. She punished those who chose evil actions on their own. That kept her busy enough as it was, even though she was not the one, usually, who bestowed whatever punishments were dealt to the souls who were directed to her domain.

In between those times, Remy gave him at least some idea of what he could expect to encounter and see during his time abroad with her Lady, and in a very private moment alone, asked him to keep an eye on the Devil in her absence. He made what promises he was able that he would do just that.

"How do we get there?"

"You might not like this very much, but it's the only way," Luci told him. "Your bag is secure, correct?"

"It is," he assured her. "Thank you for the gift, by the way. I'm sorry I didn't say something about it earlier, I've been so distracted with preparations. I'm ready to go whenever you are."

"I'm glad you like the bag. I imagined your old bag's sheer weight could become overwhelming if you had to carry it far at all, so I procured a suitable alternative for you to use in its place."

"How does it stay so light," he asked. "I know it has all of my things in it, but you'd think it was empty."

"It's designed to store things in the space between molecules. It's sort of a benevolent black hole, I suppose you might say. It swallows things up, but keeps them handy in the event you want to have them back again," Luci replied. "I'm not certain of the exact details, I'm just pleased that such a thing exists. It's something to do with quantum physics; the real quantum physics, not the ones that Earth's learned scientists have so far uncovered. My technical, um, people, in Hell could probably explain it to you, if you wished."

"However it works, I am grateful for your thoughtfulness."

"It's not thoughtfulness, my dear Hector. It's self-interest, and with that said, you may wish to stand back," she advised him. "It might be a bit of a surprise for you."

Rhoades did as he was bid and prepared himself as best he could for the promised surprise, but he still stumbled backward when it arrived. It was only due to excellent reflexes that he caught himself before smacking the back of his head against the red brick wall that stood tall behind him.

Between one breath and the next, a pair of massive, shining white-feathered wings seemed to sprout from Luci's back. The Professor's mouth dropped open as he stared at them in wonder.

As Luci dropped the torn ruin of her silk blouse to the ground, it dawned upon Hector that her entire torso was covered in impossibly bright, white feathers, gleaming so brightly that he was practically unable to make any sense of her form at all. He could, however, catch a better view of her if he did not look directly at her, in much the same way you can discern the galaxy Andromeda on a dark night if you don't stare directly at it.

"Well, I'll be damned. You look an awful lot like the Harpies of Greek mythology. Did you know that, M'Lady?"

"It's Luci, as I clearly recall telling you. And yes, I did know that. I recall quite clearly what Virgil said, of the 'vision' he had seen, of one of my lesser helpers. 'Bird-bodied, girl-faced things they are; abominable their droppings, their hands are talons, their faces haggard with hunger insatiable.' You will find multiple references to me and my—staff—that are similar, though largely inaccurate. It's difficult for minds with no experience of something they cannot imagine describing some things, even when they come face-to-face with them, as you have."

"So, the stories of angels being winged creatures—"

"Yes, there is a common thread running through most of the descriptions.  How much is based on eyewitness evidence and how much is plagiarism, I will never know.  Having said that, there are things you will see that will likely remind you of other things you have read, in the Classical literature, and, I must admit, in such dubious sources as The Fortean Times and even The National Enquirer.  There is a kernel of truth in many of the stories, though by no means all."

"That is true of many historical writings, Luci. Even books such as the Judeo-Christian Bible are the product of Chinese whispers, mistranslations, and flat-out embellishment; for the sake of it, I have observed. I imagine the descriptions of Hell are colored by the cultural expectations of those whom you have allowed a glimpse of the place?"

"Quite so, Hector.  Now, we must be going. Step a little closer, I need to protect you for a while.  We'll be passing through a rather dangerous place, where the basic physical laws of the universe break down a bit."

"One more moment, if I may?"  Hector did step closer, but he reached out toward her shoulder, his fingers spread in preparation for stroking the feathers there.

"What did you expect? Giant bat wings? I'm an angel, remember, Professor," Luci said with some asperity. "They're part of the package."

His eyes looked a little glazed, as though he was dazzled, and Luci waved her hand in front of his eyes to break his shock. He blinked. Good.

"You really want to touch them, don't you?"

Hector looked a bit guilty as he nodded. Luci could just make out tears brimming atop his lower lids.

"Very well, you may, but don't take too much time at it. We're on a schedule, after all."

"They're lovely," he breathed as he reached out a tentative finger to stroke the edge of one wing, his touch gentle and light when he did. A single tear escaped the natural dam of his left eyelid. "Absolutely amazing!"

"I've had them a long time, so I don't necessarily see them in quite the same light as you," Luci snorted. "Thank you for reminding me—hey!"

The Professor had come closer and was carefully spreading the feathers apart to see how they were anchored. At her exclamation, he came back to himself and stepped back, blushing furiously. Jostled by the sudden movement, another tear fell, this time cascading down his right cheek.

"I'm sorry," he apologized, using the back of his hand to rub the wet, salty evidence of his awe from his face. "I forgot myself."

"It's okay, Professor," she replied kindly. "I should remember that this is an especially unique experience for you."

"It is!"

"Want to take another look?"

"Ah—no. I think I'm good. For now."

Luci pretended she did not hear the last bit.

"I had no idea. Where do your wings go when you're not—wearing them? I mean, they're huge, yet there was no indication of them—"

"Yes, I know. They're there, and they're not there, simultaneously. They're matter and not matter. It's a physics thing. I could explain it to you, but as I alluded earlier, your idea of the physics of the universe is stuck in the models that were developed in the mid-1920s, and that doesn't really do the universe or its maker justice. The entire design is a lot subtler than any of you realize. Even your understanding of quantum physics is short of the mark. It's more like entanglement theory, but no strings attached."

"Theology is my strong suit, not mathematics, so I'll leave it all to you," Hector told her. "So, how will this work out?"

"You haven't really thought this through at all, have you?" Luci said. "It's not like climbing into some sort of vehicle and sallying forth. There are barriers established between the planes to prevent unwanted intrusions."

"That makes perfect sense," Rhoades agreed. "Otherwise, the question of your existence would have been answered long ago."

"Indeed, sir," she told him. "And now, it's time to get moving. Whatever else I might be capable of doing, the slowing or stopping of time is not one of my gifts."

She stepped forward and easily picked him up before he could offer any protest, unlikely as that might have been. She wrapped her huge wings around him, protectively, enfolding him securely against her chest like a parent comforting a child.

"This is the only way it's going to work," she said. "You're going to have to relax. It will make this much easier on both of us."

"You've got to be kidding me," he muttered, his voice muffled against the thick feathers that covered her breast and upper torso. "I can truthfully say that this is something I never considered being in the realm of possibilities for me."

"Well, that's no longer the case, so loosen up, and we can be on our way."

Luci could feel it as he forced himself to relax in her grasp. She was glad he seemed to have this much self-control.

"Now, hold on. We're taking off!"

She bent her knees and then leaped into the night sky as her wings made a mighty downstroke. The human in her arms took a sharp intake of breath.

Luci laughed.

"You'll be fine, Professor," she assured him. "I haven't dropped anyone yet—that I did not intend to drop, that is."

"No problem," he said, his voice tight and controlled. "I trust you!"

"I can't say I've heard that very often from a human," Luci laughed. "Now, you might want to close your eyes because you might get nauseous otherwise, with what's about to come up."

Hearing this, Hector screwed his eyes shut and focused on the sound of Luci's wings as they periodically moved in the still night air. He found it oddly comforting. It sounded something like a great bird at close proximity.

Wherever it was that they were flying, there was periodic turbulence, and he was glad Luci had advised him to close his eyes. While he still became a bit sick at his stomach, keeping his eyes shut helped to minimize the level of discomfort he might otherwise have experienced. He realized they were flying forwards and upward but they also seemed to be slipping sideways, as well. He was unsure whether it was quick, or taking a long time. At some unknown point, he dozed off.

Some untold time later, he woke as he became aware of what sounded like wailing some distance away.

An impending sense of dread threatened to overcome him, but he took comfort in knowing Luci would keep him safe from whatever might threaten.

A shudder of mirth moved through him as he realized who and what he was trusting, at the same time being certain he was right to do so. His theology professor would have been horrified.

"Are you okay, Professor," Luci's voice came to him, concern in her tone. "Are you going to be all right?"

"I'm fine," he reassured her. "I just realized I'm quite literally in the hands of the one person I can trust the most."

Luci turned that around in her head a bit before responding.

"I'm not sure I have ever heard something like that said regarding me," was her stunned reply. "Whatever gave you that idea?"

"It's just a feeling I have," Rhoades said. "I know that I can trust you completely."

"I'd suggest you were insane, but I promised you I would do what I could to keep you safe, and I stick to my word."

"As I said."

"Well, then, perhaps we have both gone around the bend," she said with a snort. Shared laughter ensued.

They flew on in silence for what seemed like a long while, and when he could no longer keep from saying anything about it, he asked what the odd noises were that he had heard for so long.

"That's the sound of damned souls," Luci replied, her voice curt. "It carries a long way."

"Damned souls?"

"Does it surprise you? Despite my being an amiable sort, I still have my permanent job," she said.

"Actions do have consequences, even if those consequences aren't an immediate sort of thing. As you might imagine, those who arrive there generally aren't terribly happy to find themselves there."

"I would imagine not," Rhoades agreed. "They would have thought, I believe, that Hell wasn't actually a thing."

"Oh, you would be surprised how many 'clergy' of one sort or another end up with a room in my domain," she said, her voice dark. "They generally argue their presence using vain reasons to excuse their bad actions."

"I'm going to assume that all denominations are represented there," the Professor opined. "What about atheists? Do they automatically go there?"

"An intelligent question, Professor! I'm impressed," Luci exulted. "Just because one is a non-believer or even agnostic, that doesn't mean they are set on a track to Hell. If they are decent folks who don't do evil, they have every chance of going to Heaven when they finally fall over."

"I can imagine they end up a bit surprised."

"I can verify that, yes," she said with a soft chuckle that was almost blown away by the sound of the wind through which they continued to move. "But once they're there, they appreciate that they didn't end up with me as their eternal host."

More quiet flight, then…

"How much longer will we be traveling? I didn't realize you would have to actually take time to move between one place and another."

"We'll be there in a few of your minutes," she said. "Normally, no, it would take almost no time at all, but with you being mortal, I had to be careful to keep you healthy. Remy doesn't have those kinds of issues to take into consideration.  In my reality, the entire trip is over almost instantly.  For your corporeal body to survive the jump between universes, I need to make the sideways slip a lot more slowly than normal. I would really rather not lose you, like luggage on a budget airline, if I can help it."

"I'm sorry, then that I made things more difficult for you, my Lady."

"Just call me Luci, Hector," the Devil said with a loud sigh. "At least, when we're in private. After a trip like this, keeping things formal seems a bit overdrawn."

"Yes, M—Luci," he corrected himself mid-sentence.

"You'll get the hang of it, Hector," she chuckled. "We'll be landing in a few moments, so brace yourself. I'll get you to your quarters where you can rest for a little bit."

"Thank you, Luci. I appreciate that."

# Eight

They were greeted by a contingent of demons who seemed to have been apprised of Lucifer's arrival sometime before their landing. There was no fanfare, the reception being quiet but respectful. Lots of bowing and scraping, which Luci accepted serenely as her due.

The demons all seemed to move about in a constant haze of self-colored smoke that boiled and flowed around them. Hector caught glimpses of limbs as the creatures moved, but it was difficult to get a clear look at what was concealed by what he imagined was sentient vapor.

She introduced the lone living human to those assembled and advised them that he was there under her protection and that those who thought to 'play' with him were risking their very existence in Hell. Hector got the impression there were other, less desirable "levels" to which they could be moved, and wondered for a moment just how much Dante Alighieri had seen, assuming he had been a visitor, and not just a creative writer. She seemed to reference some previous human visitor, but as Rhoades had no details and would not unless Luci offered them to him, he resolved to leave it alone.

A pair of goblets and a covered pitcher rested on what appeared to be a silver tray, held by a squat lumpy creature with far too many legs and sharp-looking jagged teeth. It seemed a bit odd to see a smoke-enveloped arm supporting a tray, but it was clearly something very normal in the Devil's ken, and so Hector decided to keep his mouth shut about it.

"Thank you, Jonny," Luci said, pouring a thick, dark fluid from the pitcher into both goblets. She handed one to Rhoades before taking the other for herself and raising it in salute. "Enjoy!"

Sniffing first at the contents, he recognized the aroma, smiled, and took a careful sip.

A sweet burst of coffee, chocolate, and bourbon exploded across his tongue as the thick stout danced across his parched taste buds. A second, deeper swallow followed that discovery and was accompanied by an enormous grin.

"This is amazing! Where did you get it?"

"I've got a couple demons learning how to make the stuff," she explained. "I import the ingredients, and then they work their own magic on them."

"They're doing an excellent job at it."

"When the whole craft beer craze started, I got into it, so Jonny here and his assistant, Kevin, have been refining their skills ever since then. I wish I could grow the hops and grains and all that here, but they are specific to your Earth."

"My Earth? Don't tell me that my Earth is the only one with beer!"

A nod. A touch of sadness in otherwise inscrutable eyes.

"Indeed, that is the case, though not the only one with coffee, as it happens. The quality of the beer may also be an Earth yeast thing, I think." she elaborated. "Whilst other realities may have fermented beverages, only yours has the ingredients available that makes something like this tasty treat possible. Be happy that Jonny and Kevin here have the gift of turning it from potential breakfast cereal into something wonderful."

A queer look came over his face, and then Hector burst out laughing.

"What's so damned funny?"

"I was just thinking about a bumper sticker I once saw at a pub."

"A bumper sticker. Really. Don't leave me hanging, Hector!"

"It said 'Save the Earth! It's the only planet with beer!'"

At that point, Luci joined the giddy human in laughter.

"Yes, you're right. I get why things are so funny," she choked out.

"Jonny and Kevin? Those don't sound like very—uh—demonic names to me," Hector asked once he got his laughter under control.

"Their given names are different, of course, but as a reward for their continued expertise, I allowed them to pick new ones. Thus, Jonny here, and Kevin, who, I believe, is currently tending the next batch."

"Pleased to meet you, Jonny," Rhoades told the grinning fiend politely. "This is truly excellent!"

The creature gave him a low bow, which surprised him. Then it spoke, which was even more surprising.

"Thank you, my Lord," it said in an unexpectedly high-pitched voice. "We call this one 'Pirate's Booty.'"

"I think any self-respecting pirate would be pleased," Rhoades told Jonny with approval, giving it a firm, friendly blow to the shoulder. "I look forward to trying more."

The thing beamed happily and ducked its head. Hector imagined it must be a unique experience to have a human, dead, or otherwise, be friendly toward it, rather than terrified. He decided that he would much rather have a positive relationship with the creatures than an antagonistic one.

Luci watched the interaction between the human and the demon closely and was pleased that the human did not react in a negative way to something that was so far beyond his normal encounters. It seemed that Hector Rhoades was far more flexible than his predecessors had ever been.

Luci continued to be surprised that the human seemed to accept all these new experiences with ease and no appearance of distress. She wondered if there would come the point where that equanimity disappeared, and she would have to deal with the fallout. In every previous interaction that had proved to be the case, but she held a sincere hope that this Hector human would be someone different.

The last fellow—what was his name—Tristan, that was it—had gone completely mad before Luci had been able to return him to the Earthly plane. She'd had to render him unconscious to fly him back, he had become so paranoid of everyone and everything around him.

It had taken all of two weeks. How long would Rhoades last, compared to that current record?

It was probably fortunate that no one believed his ravings when he was installed in his local funny farm for an extended stay. Wings? Demons? Dragons?

Poppycock!

After a few years of medication and therapy, he had been declared 'cured' and was released back into the world. Psychiatrists had declared him to no longer be a danger to society and able to care for himself.

He had played their game so well, they never saw the deceit he had practiced. No one realized his intent before or after his release. Not until it was too late, anyway.

When Luci found his partially charred corpse later, she had Remy dispose of it and decided it was best not to involve the authorities. They would have made too much trouble.

After that final, fatal act, Tristan had made his final trip to Hell and would remain there for eternity as he was tortured for his attempt to blow up the entire building. He had not paid attention to the fact that he would have been unable to destroy Lucifer. Earthly fire would not so much as scorch her skin.

This time, however, he would never go mad and lose touch with what he saw and experienced during his personal eternity. That was one of the most terrible unspoken torments of Hell.

Luci's unspoken hope was that she would never need to do anything similar to her current traveling companion. She was becoming somewhat fond of him, and the thought of his losing his mind disturbed her more than it should have.

# Nine

Luci excused herself to take care of something important, but not before instructing another demon to show Rhoades to his quarters. She took a moment to watch the two of them wander away, the incurious demon glancing over its shoulder occasionally to ensure its charge still followed. Confident that the Professor was in good hands, she went about her own tasks.

The demon had been introduced to Hector with a name that sounded more like a growl than anything else. After several attempts to pronounce it, he had given up, despite having learned at least nine languages including Arabic, Pashto, Dari, and Urdu, during his time in Iraq and Afghanistan. That he had been unable to get things right distressed him, as Hector had always taken it as a point of pride that he could pronounce even the most unpronounceable names.

"I'm terribly sorry. Would it be acceptable for me to address you as Trevor," he asked, embarrassment written all over his face. The demon, unused to such expressions, did not recognize what he was seeing. "It's the name of someone I knew back on Earth."

The Earthbound Trevor had been a valet of his acquaintance, and it seemed an appropriate nickname to bestow upon the misshapen creature, considering its current function.

The creature, something that appeared to have been crafted out of night terrors, had been assigned as Rhoades' servant and demon-Friday of sorts, while the human was in Hell, shrugged disinterestedly, and began to trudge away. Mindful that he had no idea where he was going, Rhoades hastened to follow along.

"Thank you for helping me out," he said to the demon as they walked along. "I'm sure I would have had a terrible time finding my quarters on my own."

The demon glanced over a lumpy gray shoulder. For the first time, it seemed at least mildly interested in its unexpected charge.

"Rrrrrrrhoads?" Rhoades was startled to hear his name rendered as a near growl. The demon seemed to be asking a question.

"Yes, Dr. Rhoades," he agreed. "I hope we can get along while I'm here, Trevor. I'm sorry I can't say your name properly. My mouth, throat, and tongue don't seem to be built for it."

"Ssss'okay, Rrrrrrhoades," the thing replied. "'Trrrevvvorrr' isss finnnne."

"What do you do when you're not squiring guests around the infernal plane?" Rhoades asked as he caught up to walk alongside the affable monster out of his most horrific nightmares.

The thing chuckled.

"Sssssquiring. Funnnnnny."

"Excuse me?"

"I torture. Ssssquiring issss difff'rent," it told him, the sibilants in its words drawn out as it spoke. Rhoades was surprised that it somehow managed to avoid biting the forked tongue that in reptilian fashion, frequently flicked out to taste the air. "Change of paccce. Nice."

"You normally torture souls? Do you enjoy your work?"

"Issss boring," was the reply. "Doing ssssame thing all time. Better to have conversssation, yessss?"

"In most cases, yes, certainly!" Rhoades agreed. "Did someone else take over for you while you're helping me out?"

"Issss not important," Trevor told him. "Other demon will alwayssss ssssstep in. Sssssouls always need attention."

"Well, as long as I'm not getting you into trouble," he told the creature. "I don't want to be a bother."

"You diff'rent," it said as they continued to walk. "No ssssscreaming. No crying. No try run away. Make you interessssting. No bother at all."

Rhoades was glad he was not an inconvenience. He had nothing against Hell's staff, and in his experience, knew it was much better to have a friendly relationship with co-workers than something more adversarial. Becoming friendly with Trevor would not be a bad thing in the least.

"How long have you been working in Hell?"

"Don't know time, but long time," the demon told him. "Had ssssame sssssoul thoussssand yearssss, I think."

"A thousand? That's incredible!"

"Issss job ssssecurity, yesss?"

Rhoades nodded and then began to laugh. Trevor joined in, its own laughter sounding remarkably like a tipper truck full of gravel being poured onto a pile of empty tin cans. Rhoades would have considered it terrifying if he did not know its source.

"I imagine that wasn't your first soul, Trevor," he suggested. "I'm guessing you've had other souls before that?"

"No. Wassss midden ssssshoveler for fffiffffteen thoussssand yearssss before that," the demon admitted.

"My Massster come, ssssay enough shit sssshoveled. Time for new thingssss. She give me ssssoul for work, instead."

"That must have been a nice change of pace for you."

"Is all job," Trevor replied. "Whether sssshovel sssshit or torment ssssoulsss. Good to be useful, yessss?"

"I can certainly agree with you about that, my friend."

"Friend?" the demon appeared to be perplexed. "I friend to Rrrrrrhoads?"

"I can't see why not, Trevor. Is that a problem?"

"No problem at all, Rrrrrhoads! Issss all good!" Trevor enthused. "Take good care of you!"

Rhoades was not quite sure how anything with such a hideous and misshapen face could successfully display joy, but damn his eyes if he was not seeing that right now as the thing capered happily. Was the concept of friendship so rare that it would cause such enthusiasm?

When they arrived at the suite of rooms that would be his quarters, Hector was shocked to see some sort of organic surveillance device hanging from the wall above the doorway.

It looked like a naked brain, sporting one-hundred or so unshielded eyes, all swiveling independently in chameleon-like fashion and presumably reporting in real-time to some sort of central control demon. A fat droplet of viscous, pink liquid fell to the floor beneath it.

Trevor reached down, swiped the goo off the floor with a many-jointed finger and wiped it on one of the forks of his tongue. The demon closed his eyes in pleasure as he appeared to savor the experience. Hector felt his gorge rise in protest at the sight.

Trevor took out a key, unlocked the ornate lock, and then opened the door, stepping back to allow his charge to enter. Hector shivered involuntarily, stepped beneath the grisly security system, through the doorway, and then looked askance at Trevor.

Trevor looked back at him blankly and said "N'glargronth. They neverrr ssssssleep. Everrrr."

Hector shivered again but fought to regain control of himself before panic could overcome him. His innate good manners helped him to do so.

"Well, come on in and have a seat, Trevor," he told the monster. "Take a load off for a few minutes."

The demon did not need to be asked twice, but still seemed just the tiniest bit nervous when he sat down in one of the wooden chairs at the table. Perhaps it was the fact that he sat almost on the very edge of the seat as though anticipating being called to his feet once more.

What was it like to be a demon in Hell, when your overlord told you that you had to guide and protect something that you would normally torment? This Trevor had told him he was just another job, but there had to be some sort of prestige attached to Lucifer herself, pulling you off your long-time labor and giving you something so unique to do.

Exploring the suite of rooms, Hector found a front room where he could potentially entertain if there was anyone worthy of that; a royally appointed bedroom; a closet packed to the seams with clothing of all sorts, and another room that would serve very well as an office space where he could write things down in as uninterrupted a manner as possible.

The walls and the ceilings were all unrelenting black stone, but tapestries and pictures lined the walls, giving them the color they would not otherwise possess.

Hector wondered if these were normal decorations for the quarters, or if they had been added to the room as a consideration of his origins. He supposed that if the opportunity to ask about it occurred, he might take advantage of it, but until and unless that happened, he would not push it.

It occurred to him that all the clothing would fit him perfectly. He wondered how something like that would even be possible but then realized that at least in her own domain, for Lucifer, anything was possible.

A small kitchen was in the corner of the front room, with a wood stove, rather than anything more modern as a cooking surface. Hector wondered how he would get the foods he might like to cook and eat.

"Say, Trevor, this kitchen is wonderful and all that, but how do I get food for it?"

"Not your worry," was the reply. "Tell Trevor what need, and I get for you. You hungry now?"

A tell-tale gurgle from his stomach announced that that was indeed the case.

"'Sssscuse for little bit," Trevor told him. "I be back ssssoon with foods. Go have lie-down in bedroom. I get you when food isss here."

Almost hearing the featherbed calling to him, Hector nodded and left the demon to do whatever it was he had to do while he got some much-needed sleep, noting a well-appointed bathroom leading off from the privacy of the bedroom. Hector assumed there would surely be hot water available, given his location.

# Ten

Luci heaved an enormous sigh as the demon led the Professor away to the rooms that would serve as his quarters during their stay in Hell, or however long he'd be able to tolerate its insanity. She could only hope he was made of stronger stuff than the last human who had come along for the ride. The demon had been given direct orders to protect the human from any and all harm and had been made to swear an oath to that effect.

She made her way to her own quarters, not too far from where she had landed. Opening the door, she saw they were the same as they had been when she left them. Not even the tiniest bit of dust could be seen on the furnishings. Her infernal cleaning crew was top notch, after all.

She removed the stinking clothing she wore and climbed into the steaming bathtub that had already been run for her arrival. Water at a temperature that would have been fatal to a mere mortal cleansed the reek of extended proximity to humanity from her unscarred flesh. Vigorous scrubbing to the point of pain left that flesh tingling and eager for more, but knowing there were other things she must address, she decided against that indulgence.

Washing of her thick dark hair commenced, with Luci finger-combing the thick white conditioner through her hair to remove the tangles even she, the Lord of Hell, could not avoid. Yes, she could choose to cut her tresses and avoid the unwanted tangles, but her vanity did not allow her to ever seriously consider the possibility. Besides, she would have to do it here, in eternal Hell, rather than on Earth, where some twerp would surely obtain a strand of her hair and make an ass of themselves over it. Doing it in Hell would, on the other hand, signal that change was possible...something undesirable in a place where changeless eternity was an integral part of its horrors.

Climbing out of the water after a twenty-minute soak, she toweled off, drying her hair with a little bit of the power she possessed, and then clothed herself in a black silk men's suit. A blood-red blouse stood out against the jacket, matching breast pocket kerchief bringing it all together. Black leather flat-soled shoes completed the ensemble. She left her hair loose, hanging full and wavy along the sides of her head and down her back to the hem of her suit jacket.

Going to her desk, she pulled a small cellophane bag from her pocket, opened it, and poured the contents into the cut-crystal bowl that rested within arm's reach. Pursing her lips, she picked up one of the shiny chocolate malted milk balls and popped it into her mouth, delighting in the rich flavor of one of her few guilty pleasures.

"Excuse me, my Lady, but there are some matters that need your immediate attention," said a voice from the doorway. Irritation coloring her expression, Luci turned to face the demon who rode herd on things in Hell while she was away.

"You would think that in a thousand years, you would have learned to knock before interrupting me," she snapped.

Then she sighed. She had remonstrated her secretary many times before about this and expected she would do it again and again. Her own sort of Hell, perhaps.

"Hello there, Jarzuur," she replied. "What is so very important that I can't get a breath in before I have to deal with it?"

"If I had any other option, my Lady, I would have taken it," Jarzuur apologized. She could tell that he meant what he said, but she was still annoyed at the interruption. "There are some demons who are defying your orders, and I am sure you would not want that to continue."

Luci let loose a string of multilingual profanity that made even the normally stoic demon flinch. The Devil might appear to be a dainty little thing, but that helpless appearance was pure deception, and the demon Jarzuur knew that quite well. His direct service to her had already covered several millennia, and he understood her patience only extended so far before she would decide that she had had enough and acted, rarely in a way that did not involve destruction and violent disincorporation.

"Can someone, anyone, explain to me why some around here appear to forget who runs this circus?" she demanded. "Do they have some sort of irrational death wish? Are they really that incredibly stupid? Are they incapable of learning from the mistakes of others?"

"I couldn't say," the demon replied deferentially, prepared to leap out of the way in the event his Master responded more physically. She had in the past, and it was a wise demon who avoided getting in Lucifer's way when that happened. "I have done all within my own power to keep things running as you decree in your most recent absence."

He remembered but did not mention aloud the previous demon who had held his position. While Jarzuur was generally on Lucifer's nice list, rather than the naughty one, he preferred to avoid bringing up unpleasant memories.

Ag'draxoth had not ended well at all. It had been a few millennia ago, but in Hell, time did not really matter, now did it?

"Who has started the bullshit this time?"

"Almun, my Lady Lucifer," Jarzuur said. "He has drawn near a half-dozen other demons to his side."

"Who?" Her voice contained the promise of destruction.

"Dorgen, Bugmoth, Ig'drun, Ongromuth, and Dralran, my Lady."

"I'm not surprised to hear that Ig'drun and Dralran have been pulled into this nonsense, but the other three? I thought they had more sense than that. However did he manage that?"

"Previous oaths, I believe."

"Has it been that long since I reminded everyone here that oaths to anyone but Me are forbidden and invalid," she demanded, her voice becoming a dreadful roar more monster than humanoid. "Call an Audience and make certain that those six attend. Do not give them any suspicion that I am aware of what they have been up to, Jarzuur. None."

"Of course, my Lady," was the demon's prompt reply. Maybe she would not find out about his own relatively minor misdeeds that had occurred during her absence. "As you say."

"Good."

"What reason shall I give for the Audience?"

"It needs no explanation," she told him harshly. Then she reconsidered. By their nature, demons tended to be stubborn bastards at the best of times. "Bring in the most egregiously stubborn soul of the day. Be certain to also send the summons to any of the other demons who might consider the same sort of disloyalty. I believe it is time for a reminder of how things are around here—and what happens when you forget that one important thing."

She knew. Oh, by the soul-crushingly dark infernal depths, she knew!

"Hope has no place here, Jarzuur. Never forget that."

If his body had contained blood instead of the thick ichor that oozed, like chilled molasses, through whatever passed for his "veins" the demon would have flushed in terror. Jarzuur babbled agreement and left the chamber to complete his errands. He knew he was getting the single, oblique warning, and knew better than to push things. Having seen so very many previous examples of Her Ladyship's wrath, he saw it for the gift it was and held it tight.

"Brerthramoz, bring the Professor here," Luci said into thin air once she was alone, knowing her words would be heard and obeyed wherever she might be. Then she remembered an especially important consideration.

"Gently," she added, popping another malted milk ball into her mouth, and savoring it. No sense in the demon taking her initial words in a literal sense, oath, or no oath. The creatures could be disturbingly single-minded at times. "There isn't a rush."

There had been a time when that one soul…but no, now was not the time to remember that bit of unfortunate unpleasantness. At least she had remembered before it happened again.

An hour spent at her ledgers looking through various reports, setting things to her calendar for discussion with appropriate parties, and munching through a disturbing number of milk balls, and it was nearly time for the Audience she had called. It was not as though the demons did not know what would happen to them if they rebelled.

While a demon did not end easily, they could indeed be ended, especially when their Master willed it. The only question was how terrible that ending could be made, and that was something determined by the heinous nature of the offense that caused them to be ended.

Her previous second had tried to do favors for the other demons who came as close to being "friends" as possible when one is a demon, a "not-enemy," using his station to smooth things for them. When Luci discovered his duplicitous ways, she had responded accordingly, with his death being a protracted and quite painful thing, indeed. The demon's screams had echoed in the corridors of Hell long after the demon himself had passed into the silence of the Void.

She smiled as she recalled the look on Jarzuur's face, and wondered what mischief he had been about in her absence.

It did not take much to get her minions to reveal themselves.

A glance.

A smile.

A slight tilt of the head.

Some felt guilty enough that their confessions came bubbling out like the lava that seethed through the Earth like a geothermal circulatory system. Others, like Jarzuur, tried to hold it in while they tried to figure out what it was, exactly, that she knew.

She hoped she would not have to make an example of him, as she rather liked the stuffy old thing.

Perhaps her plans for the mutineers would have their intended effect, and he would stop doing whatever it was that he had been.

"What have you been doing, Jarzuur? Please don't disappoint me. You know exactly what happened to your predecessor," and then she laughed.

She was still laughing when there came a knock at her door.

"Come!"

The Professor's demonic escort opened the door and then stood aside for his charge to enter. The human entered the chamber and faced Luci.

"I'm sorry for the time it took for me to get here," he apologized. "I felt a need to scrub the long journey from my skin and get changed into something more presentable. I hope I haven't overdressed."

"Oh, not at all, Hector! In fact, it's perfect," she assured him. "Once we enter the audience chamber, move to my left, just slightly behind my left shoulder. I am assuming from your history that standing for perhaps long periods is not going to be an issue?"

"Not at all, Lucifer," he reassured her. He decided that since Trevor was present, he would keep things relatively formal. "I can stand immobile for several hours when necessary. Palace guard duty is hell on Earth...' he tailed off, quietly.

"That's good to know," Luci replied with a smile. "How is Brerthramoz treating you? Is he meeting your needs?"

"Trevor? He's been perfect. He's particularly good at anticipating my needs."

"Trevor?"

"I had a difficult time figuring out how to pronounce it when he told me his name," Hector apologized. "I hope you don't mind that I gave him a nickname."

"My dear Hector, by naming him, you have nearly made him yours," Luci told him with a touch of asperity. That was then softened with a slight smile. "Enjoy your demon."

"My demon?"

"Well, he remains mine, but for all intents and purposes, he is now yours."

From the corner of his eye, Hector watched as the demon in question absorbed all he was hearing. It was difficult not to laugh at the expression of what could only be called "joy," evidenced by the near-jig the creature danced, the tentacles on his head performing their own little hula-like writhing and wriggling. Even the ever-present demonic smoke seemed to exhibit a cheerful aspect, if that was possible.

Luci and Hector shared a look, both smiling at the happiness the demon exhibited.

"You've given him a gift, Hector," she told the human, her voice soft, almost tender. "Do your best not to disappoint him, and he'll be yours forever, however long that might be."

Hector nodded his understanding, noted the implicit warning, and filed it away for later. He had not missed, however, that it appeared he essentially owned a demon, and was not quite certain how he felt about that. Did it amount to slavery, or was it something else? His own, personal demon. He decided to think about that bit of information when he had the time.

"Yes, ma'am," he replied.

And Lucifer began laughing all over again.

Trevor wandered over and pulling out a small bundle from somewhere on his person, handing it over to

Hector. Luci noticed a certain level of deference a demon did not normally display being shown to the human the demon served.

"Lunnnnch," the demon intoned with a bow to Hector, then turned to face Luci. "My Lady?"

"Thank you, but no, Trevor," she seemed to be testing the name. "I've eaten already. Please, Professor, don't stand on ceremony. I'm sure you're famished!"

Not needing to be told twice, Hector unwrapped the fancy cloth napkin, smiled with delight at what he found inside, and then happily tucked in.

Luci sat back and watched the human eat his meal, deriving pleasure from the sight. It had been somewhere near eight hours since he had last eaten, and that could not have been easy on him. Humans, it seemed, were able to go long stretches without eating, but in her experience, some tended to become a bit churlish when their stomachs were empty.

She could wait for him to finish his meal, such as it was. As Hector devoured the savory edible treasure chest, Luci gazed at the demon who had been renamed Trevor and wondered anew about her companion.

# Eleven

As instructed, and with his appetite sated for the time being, Rhoades took his position to the left of and slightly behind where Lucifer sat on her throne. He imagined that was where Remy normally stood during these visits to Hell, and he wondered if she enjoyed the opportunity for a vacation from such a duty. As she seemed devoted to her Master, he decided it was unlikely and quietly blessed her for her willingness to step aside, for now, at least.

Looking down, he saw a few yellowish crumbs from his brunch on the lapel of the black silk suit coat he wore and brushed them away, a smile blossoming on his face at the memory of from whence they had come. When he had returned from wherever it was that he procured the ingredients, Trevor had produced a surprisingly tasty Cornish pasty and realizing how ravenous he was, he had devoured the thing. Who knew something that looked like a sack of gray whatever-the-hell-it-was could not only cook but cook well?

It was not long before a small procession of damned souls was ushered into the room, kept in line physically and temperamentally by the twin rows of armored demons that flanked them. No two demons were exactly alike, he saw. Numbers of eyes, arms, legs, skin tone, height—all differed.

In looking at the line-up before them, Rhoades wondered why they would have been there in the first place. What would require the opportunity for an audience with the King of Hell?

"What have we here," Luci asked the room at large. Her tone was dangerous, and Hector watched as several demons shifted uncomfortably where they stood. The Lord of Hell might appear to be a slight, weak human female, but it was clear her demons knew she was far more than she appeared to be. "Why am I here wasting my time when I could be doing something else?"

A demon dragged the first soul forward, throwing him to the ground a few feet from where Luci reclined. The damned soul stared up at her, confusion on his face, with his hands covering his naked genitals, as he was obviously ashamed that he was so exposed. The damned did not deserve the gift of clothing when their souls were being laid bare for all to see.

"Who—who are you? You're not the Devil!" the man's bluster was almost enough to make Luci smile, but that was not the correct tack to take in situations such as this. "I won't talk to some evil, damned whore!"

The silence that greeted that statement should have alerted the damned soul to his mistake, but he was too full of himself to take heed. Hector watched as demons waited for their Lord and Master to respond. He was glad he was not the idiot who groveled before Luci. So very glad.

"An evil, damned whore? Really? What makes you so certain I'm not the Devil," she asked him, her voice deceptively calm. Hector marveled at her apparent restraint. "What are you basing your thoughts on?"

"The Devil is a man! The Bible says so! Women are simply helpers!"

The response was, to say the least, enlightening. Even the demons in the room moved back a step as it became apparent that their Master had had enough of human stubbornness and was about to take steps to deal with that intransigent attitude.

Luci stood, growing in stature by at least double her original human height, eyes flashing with anger, her skin flushing a deep blood-red and a set of curved ebony horns erupting from the top of her skull, sliding easily through the silken waves of her dark hair. She glared down at him, her eyes no longer appearing human. Instead, they were almond-shaped pits riven with fire.

"I believe you are incorrect," she roared down at the defiant soul whose expression changed from self-importance to terror. If he could have pissed himself, Luci was certain the soul would have done so at that point. She looked up at the room in general.

"Perhaps I've been away so long that there are those who have forgotten who rules here? Are any of you really that foolish?"

There was no answer, only a tangible sense of terror from everyone in the flame-lit chamber. Who would dare to backchat the Devil when she was in such a mood? It would have to be a fool, it was clear.

Only a very stupid entity, and it seemed as though there were none present at that moment in time.

Even the idiot who groveled on the stone tiles before Lucifer kept his mouth shut. Perhaps he thought the monster before him might forget he was even there if he made himself into a small enough ball on the highly polished black flagstones. It was all Hector could do to keep from laughing.

"No one has yet told me why this waste of a soul is in my presence. Does someone care to inform me, or should I just try guessing?" Her anger and disdain could be felt by everyone there. "Anyone?"

"My Lady," the heavily deformed and scarred demon who had brought the soul forward said with a deep bow, "this soul arrived here this morning, in company with several others, immediately following an aircraft crash, and doesn't seem to accept its fate. I realize you would not normally wish to deal with such an issue, but I could not resist the opportunity for such an education."

"And why should that matter to me, Berrenoth," she asked the demon, her voice flat and unfriendly. "Put it in its cell, chain it to the wall, and leave it there. It's not as though it has any choice in the matter. Its actions made certain of that. What did you do in life, mortal?"

The groveling wreck on the floor stared up at Luci, mouth working, but only a croaking sound emerging. The Devil sighed and went down onto her haunches, lifting the man's chin with the claw of her right index finger. It was a delicate motion, nothing rough. Nevertheless, it was still terrifying, in its own way.

"What did you do in life?" she repeated, her voice harsh. By some hellish twist, blood began to ooze from where Luci's claw had penetrated the skin of the former pastor's jaw. The Devil sniffed at her claw and then slowly and deliberately licked the dark red blood from it. The sounds of retching came from the figure on the flagstones.

Luci's eyes became fiery slits as she redirected her attention back to the soul. She put out a taloned hand, closed it around his bloodied chin, and wrenched his head back up to face her.

"Make me wait, and your punishment will be far worse than the one you already deserve," she told him. "I am your Master now, and you will obey Me!"

"I saved hundreds of souls, perhaps thousands of the souls of the faithful, from eternal torment in Hell. I performed the works of Almighty God during my time on Earth so that I might enter His Kingdom."

"For the last time, you sniveling shitbag, what did you do in life?" she thundered so loudly it made the air shimmer. From the corner of her eye, Luci saw Almun and his cronies attempt to leave. A squad of heavily armored demons cut them off from their escape. Her nostrils flared, and her lips twitched, her expression one of fury.

From the look on his face, it was clear that the demon knew his attempt at mutiny was over. Luci gave a toothy smile at the thought, and the former pastor screamed in terror when he saw the predatory grin appear, believing it applied to him. The jagged teeth and fangs that crowded the Devil's mouth might have contributed to the former pastor's reaction.

"I was the pastor of my own church," he choked out, a weak and painful-looking attempt at an ingratiating smile on his face. "I did good works. I brought people to understand God's Will. I brought them to the light. All that I did for the glory of God! I shouldn't be here!"

"Well, you ended up here for a reason," Luci told him, her words surprisingly clear, considering what her mouth now contained. "The karmic scale doesn't make those kinds of mistakes. How did you live while you ran that megachurch of yours? Did you live a simple life, or did you live in luxury?"

"I lived in luxury, as the good Lord would have wanted me to, to show that I was in His good graces!"

"Let me guess, the aircraft that crashed was one that you had obtained with money fleeced from your parishioners? It was a gift to yourself to stroke your ego and make you seem more important to the sheep in your flock? Am I right?"

"Fleeced? Certainly not! Those tithes were given with generosity and love! The jet was only a small one, so

I could move more quickly between my congregations across the world. It belonged to the church."

Luci's lip curled in disgust. Sophistry!

"Did anyone but you, your family, and your private staff ever ride in the aircraft?"

"No, Ma'am, it was not their right to do so. Only those who had made more than a million dollars in donations to the church were permitted aboard the plane as a guest of mine."

Luci stood once more, a frown on her terrible face. It was obvious to all present that this was exactly the wrong answer. Hector could almost feel the Throne room's other occupants' attempts to not run in the other direction, away from the Devil's wrath.

"So, you're telling me that you used the donations you were given by the faithful to make your life better? This 'Prosperity Gospel' garbage is one of the most selfish things humanity has dreamed up in recent centuries. That's a kind of evil that will make you end up here."

"I only did as I was taught!" There was a note of desperation in his argument. "The good Lord wanted this for me,"

"Trust me, that's not at all true," she replied. "I am at least passing familiar with what my Parent wants, and that's not it."

"But that's how I was taught," he wailed. It was a familiar refrain used by everyone from Torquemada to Nazi war criminals. *I was only following orders.*

"That's no excuse, and you know that," Luci told the man in an unfriendly tone. "Your explanation is empty. No substance to it. Otherwise, you would not be here. For your information, once your plane crashed, information was released on how truly corrupt your

107

organization was. There will be little to no mourning at your passing. Indeed, there will likely be many cries of 'I hope he burns in Hell'."

The man began crying, begging Luci to relent and send him on to some imagined heavenly reward. Certainly, a fool of the first order.

"Not happening, bub. Berrenoth, see to it that he is flayed and hung upside down in an Ant Room. Make it a painful one." she said and waved him away to the three-armed demon, whose name was, it seemed, Berrenoth, who began to drag him away, but her attention was abruptly taken by something else. "What is going on over there?"

Her voice was a deadly growl, echoing her anger at the unwelcome interruption. All who stood in her line of sight moved away quickly, so she could see what it was that so offended her.

A soft muttering could be heard from one corner of the room, and Rhoades' attention was drawn to what appeared to be a white-robed individual speaking to one of the guardian demons, gesturing urgently at Luci. The demon held its spear-point only the barest fraction of an inch from the front of the robed figure.

"Lucifer, I'm glad to see you're back again!" she called out, waving at the Devil with one well-manicured hand, like one of those vapid celebrities who were famous for being famous. For some reason, Rhoades felt offended at the gesture, but would not have been able to say why had he been asked.

"Kushiel, what are you doing here? You know I'll be busy for at least the next few weeks getting caught up," Luci said, shifting back to her human form and speaking in a much calmer voice, but an edge of malice still colored her tone. "What in blazes do you want that cannot wait those few weeks?"

"I wouldn't be here if it was not absolutely necessary, Lucifer. You know that." To Hector, it sounded as though the newcomer was trying to dominate the conversation, and even though he had not known her all that long, he knew Luci would not permit something like that to continue. He also knew that he did not like the interloper at first sight, but kept his face schooled to a neutral expression, as there was no sense in antagonizing anyone. This was obviously a royal court, of some sort, and it was usually best to avoid antagonizing the head of any court, royal or otherwise.

At Luci's nod, the demon let Kushiel pass by, but followed along close behind as that person made her way to the throne. Rhoades assumed the new visitor was an angel, based upon the name she called it by. Despite that, it appeared celestials did not have carte blanche to walk in whenever they pleased.

Rhoades took a long look at what was only the second angel he had ever seen. There were differences beyond just clothing choices.

Unlike Luci, this one sported a head of thick, wavy, long red-blonde hair, an almost boyish chest, and was slender nearly to the point of looking underweight. He wondered if she had always looked like that or if it was something she had done to herself. Could angels gain or lose weight? A question that religious scholars had likely never even once considered until this very moment, but then, for most everyone else, angels were something believed in, rather than experienced. He realized that Thomas Aquinas had not been here, or he would have known that several angels can actually be in the same place at the same time. However, he would have to enquire later of Luci just how many could dance on the head of a pin. Maybe after she had calmed down a little?

Hector knew that if he dwelled upon these thoughts for too long, it might drive him mad, or even madder, if one considered that volunteering to accompany the Devil showed a distinct lack of sanity to begin with. He wondered if he should ask Luci about it, but decided this was something he should keep to himself, at least for the time being, anyway.

"I need to speak with you privately, Lucifer," Kushiel told Luci, looking around at the occupants of the densely packed chamber. She did not look at all pleased. "It's important!"

Luci gave a deep sigh and gestured at the other occupants of the room to leave. Almost all of them filed out without a word. The soul who had challenged her authority was not given the opportunity to leave in his own time and was instead dragged from the room by one ear, gibbering and pleading for mercy that would not be forthcoming.

It was easy to see that Berrenoth was going to take out his own anger on the condemned soul, but Rhoades saw nothing wrong with that in this case. He had never had any use for the "prosperity gospel" types, either. It all seemed to be some sort of "get rich quick" grift from off the backs of gullible people looking for whatever answers they could get from someone who claimed to possess them.

Almun and his cronies were also taken from the chamber, but they would be receiving a visit from the Devil as soon as she could find the time. She determined that time would be sooner, rather than later. It was high time she called a stern and very public halt to demonic mutineering. It would not last, but perhaps it would slow things down just a tick.

Remembering her current aspect, Luci returned completely to her less threatening appearance. For now, anyway, there was no need to intimidate her sister. There would always be time enough for that later on.

After the door was closed, Kushiel looked pointedly at Rhoades. Her expression was not pleasant. Rhoades pegged her as someone who was used to getting what she wanted.

"This is private business, Lucifer," she told the Devil, her expression hard. "That one needs to leave, too."

"No, he—"

The angel called Kushiel leaned forward just the tiniest bit as she stared into the Professor's eyes and then jerked back as though she had been physically shocked. It was all Hector could do to keep from cracking a smile. The angel's expression was hilarious.

"It's alive!" she cried out, stunned, her voice going up two octaves and pointing at Hector, as though there was anyone else who might have fit that bill in the room. "How is a living human here? Why is it here?"

*It?*

Hector felt a little irritated at being referred to as though he was a thing, rather than an intelligent being, but knew better than to express that emotion to the angel. Having seen what Luci could do, he had an idea of what this Kushiel might be able to accomplish, should the mood take her.

"He is here under my protection Kushiel," was the reply. "You will not lay so much as a feather-tip on any part of him."

Hector felt it was kind of the Devil to remind her sister that he was no mere object. He also noted that Luci did not identify him by name, which he found interesting. "He's under oath to keep anything he hears to himself. He has been made aware of the consequences of breaking that oath."

Oath? What oath? Rhoades thought but wisely kept his mouth shut. He wondered why Luci would have said such a thing to her sister, but knew better than to ask for an explanation. One would come if the Devil felt so moved to do so.

Kushiel looked uncomfortable, but then gave a shrug of feigned resignation. Luci was not fooled. Her sister was as transparent as a glass noodle in a bowl of clear broth. With that thought, Hector experienced momentary regret that he had not indulged in a bowl of phở before leaving on his journey, in case it was his last.

He wondered if Trevor might be able to assay Vietnamese cooking and resolved to find out.

That was, if he was not obliterated in the next few minutes by the newcomer.

"Your house, your rules, I suppose," the angel said. Although her words suggested acceptance, her physical attitude said something else entirely. "That doesn't mean I have to like it, though."

She directed another glare at the lone human in the room.

"So, what's so damned important that you felt it was appropriate to interrupt me on my first day back?"

"Sariel is causing trouble in the outer planes again," Kushiel explained. "Our Parent isn't happy."

"Shocking," Luci replied, her voice flat. "But then, when *isn't* she causing trouble somewhere?"

"It's got out of hand, Lucifer! You need to do something to stop her."

"I? No. If They're so upset about things, They can deal with her, Kushiel. I don't know why this should involve me."

"You know exactly why, Lucifer. She's never really paid attention to anyone but you," the angel said, her expression a bit desperate. "You need to pull her back into line!"

"I'm not the one who needs to address that, Kushiel," Lucifer told her with some asperity. "I'm not her Parent, after all. I've got my hands full enough with what They put on my plate a literal eternity ago!"

"But— "

"They figure that since They put me in this position, I'm the one to punish her bad behavior, but that's just pushing over Their responsibility onto someone else so They can pretend to be the 'Good Guy' here. I'm not playing into that nonsense." While Luci's physical form might have appeared human, her eyes once again flared, the dancing flames from her eye sockets licking at her brows, but leaving her skin and eyebrows unburnt.

Hector watched as the angel called Kushiel visibly flinched and Luci's mouth curved in a wicked smile. That smile verged on being bloodthirsty.

"They're not going to be happy about— "

"Do I look like I give anything like a tiny shit about how They are going to feel about this? I really don't. They can shove those angelic rainbows up Their celestial ass, as far as I'm concerned!"

The angel called Kushiel gasped and looked more than a little shocked, one hand raised to cover her mouth. She glanced at Hector, and an angry glint came into her eyes. She could not retaliate against her sibling, but a human—now that was something else again.

"So, mortal, do you see what you've fallen in with? Are you sure you want to carry on with whatever nefarious bargain you've made with Lucifer here? Is it worth whatever prize you haggled for? Was your soul worth the cost? Is it worth the wrath of your god?" As close as the angel stood to him, Hector saw that she had inhuman-appearing golden eyes, much like those of a hawk. More information filed away in his mind for a later time.

Luci was surprised to note that the human did not so much as flinch. In fact, he stood up just the tiniest bit straighter and then made the barest suggestion of a bow of respect with only his head. In the realm of respect, it was barely there but did exist.

"I've made no 'nefarious bargain,' as you put it, ma'am. I'm here merely as an observer and traveling companion. There is no 'prize' as you put it, at the end of our association, and my soul remains my own. I will say, however, that while I am officially here as a neutral party, I can understand Lucifer's outlook in this situation," although he was not aware of it, his parents would have recognized the expression he now wore as the polite but mulish one he wore when he was being dressed down as a junior officer. "Bearding the lioness in her den really isn't a good idea."

"What would you know of anything like that," Kushiel snarled. Luci wondered if Rhoades would survive the encounter and prepared herself to do what she must to protect him from her sister's wrath.

"My life has taken me in many different directions, but one of those directions was a career in the military, where it was drummed into all of us who served that we must own both our successes and our errors in life. As for my 'god', as you put it, while I have the utmost respect for Them, as the Ultimate General in this situation, They must own and act upon it accordingly."

Kushiel rocked back on her heels, visibly stunned at the human's succinct and unflinching reply. Truth be told, Luci was a bit gobsmacked, herself. While she knew the human was no shrinking violet, not with what he had seen so far in their association, his open support of her in her opinion of who bore responsibility for what was a great surprise. His tone had been firm, but respectful, though his attitude was not what Luci would consider to be deferential. He deported himself as a military man would who addressed someone of equal rank, which was exactly what Kushiel needed, since she always appeared to seek situations where she would be able to respond in a punitive way.

In the privacy of her own mind, Luci hoped They would not think unkindly of this human. He had even seen her transformation to one of her other forms with no forewarning and had not so much as gasped in shock.

"He speaks the truth, Kushiel," Luci moved to intercept any outward demonstrations of her sister's anger. "You know full well that a mortal soul can't utter an untruth in my domain. The celestial magic of its construction forbids such a thing."

Kushiel began to sputter with rage, but Luci put up a hand to silence her.

"Go," she said. "Send this message along to our Parent: 'If You are so concerned about whatever it is that she is doing, then do Your job and intercede. I'm not going to do it for You'."

The other angel's eyes went even wider with shock and horror, her black pupils nearly filling their golden irises.

"I can't say that to our Parent! That is unheard of!"

"Then perhaps it is time that it should be, Kushiel. I've got my hands full with my duties here. These human creatures breed like rabbits, and this place is filling up with them at an exponential rate."

Then another thought came to her. It was an ugly one, and come to think of it, entirely something Kushiel might do in a situation such as this.

"You know, come to think on it," she said softly. "Perhaps our Parent sent you to fulfill this entire errand on your own, and you decided to hand it off to me, rather than do it yourself. Would that be closer to the truth?"

Kushiel's face went from an angry red to a stark white as she blanched. The cat, as it were, was out of the bag, and she fell back a step as though her sister's words were a physical blow. In the realm of the Celestials, words could have far more power than they did anywhere else.

"Get out, Kushiel," Luci told the other angel, her face a study in tightly controlled anger. "It's time to get your hands dirty, I suppose. If They are paying attention, and you had better hope They are not, They aren't going to be happy with you at all for pulling this shit."

"Lucifer, you wouldn't—"the tone of desperation and fear in the other angel's voice was tangible.

"No, Kushiel, I'll do you the single favor of not passing this along," Luci assured her. "But if you ever try this crap again, I won't be so understanding. Now go away, and don't come back here unless you are specifically invited—and never forget that you owe me and that one day, whenever that might be, I'll call this favor in."

Without another word, the now frightened angel turned and left the room, closing it carefully behind her as she did. Luci turned in her seat to face Rhoades.

"Hector, what you have just seen is to be kept between us," she told him, her face stern. "Am I understood?"

"Of course, my Lady," he replied politely, with a deeper bow than he had given the recently departed Kushiel. "None of it is my business, after all."

The Devil gave the human a long look, one eyebrow raised. Then she shook her head and sighed deeply.

"Kushiel doesn't like to dirty her own hands and doesn't like to be perceived as being the bad guy in any situation. This was simply her way of trying to keep that perception in others' minds," she explained. "She doesn't realize that we've been on to her game for almost as long as we've existed."

"You said something to her about mortal souls not being able to tell lies in Hell," Hector said. "I didn't know that was a thing."

"Well, unless you were going to try to tell a lie, you'd never had known that was the case, correct?" She asked him. "Were you intending to tell any lies?"

The Professor's expression was thoughtful.

"I can't say I was planning to tell a lie, but what if a situation was such that a lie needed to be told to prevent a worse situation?"

"No way to avoid it, sorry to say. They set it up that way when They built the place. You'll just have to try to avoid doing it in the first place."

"I make it a point not to lie, Luci," he replied. "I've got enough filth on my soul already without adding to it."

"Let's not get into that nonsense, Professor," Luci admonished him. "You've lived your life as you saw fit under whatever circumstances prevailed at a given moment. Once you cross the veil, karma will direct your soul in the correct direction."

"You can't tell where I'm headed?" Surprise colored Hector's face.

"That's not my bailiwick, actually. I just keep things going as smoothly as possible once a doomed soul arrives," she replied. "I might be able to predict where someone will end up based upon immediate information, but as for simply looking at someone and knowing, I'm as in the dark as almost anyone else. There are a lot of people who try to do deals with me towards their end. I no longer try to explain to them that it's pointless. I do, however, have an impressive collection of fine art and plunder as a result of people assuming I'm lying when I tell them I can't help. Who am I to disabuse them? They're already on the slippery slope, anyway."

"Almost?"

"Well, there is—" Luci replied, pointing upward. The light of understanding dawned on the mortal's face.

"Ah, yes. *Them*."

"You're learning fast, Hector."

"I try, anyway," he said with a smile. "To answer your previous question, no, I was not planning on lying to you about anything. I've had to practice deception in the past, and while it was necessary, I never actually liked doing it."

"Then you won't have any problems here, I would think."

"I suppose it makes sense, doesn't it," Hector decided, after a moment's thought.

"Yes, well, it does cut through the bullshit in a big hurry, Hector," she said, laughing, and after a moment, the Professor joined in.

<h1 style="text-align:center">Twelve</h1>

In the aftermath of the unexpected angelic interruption, Luci did not seem inclined to continue the audience in her throne room. Hector felt he could understand her lack of enthusiasm to do so. He sensed her underlying current of anger and was quite glad that none of it was directed at him.

Instead, they went to her quarters and shared a small lunch. Rather than anything elaborate, the meal consisted of simple sliced meat sandwiches served on halved, sesame seed topped rolls, eschewing more modern styled slices of bread, all washed down with a bottle of rich red wine.

Hector wondered where the meat came from, but then decided he really did not want to know after all. It did not taste bad, so he had no reason to complain. He felt confident the Devil would not serve him anything he could not eat.

Lunch was a quiet affair, with neither feeling the need to fill up the silence with conversation. It seemed as though Luci had a lot on her mind anyway, and the human knew already that if she wanted to talk, she would. He imagined a lot of her silence had to do with her recent encounter with her sister. He knew from personal experience that families were not always an easy thing to deal with.

The silence gave Hector a chance to think about what he had experienced in his travels with the Devil. So far, it had been nothing like he might have imagined before it began. He was eager to learn more about his benefactor but preferred that knowledge appear in a more organic form. If he were honest with himself, this was even more of an exciting and enlightening adventure than he would ever have thought possible.

"It seems I have to deal with an attempted coup," Luci broke the silence. Hector paused in his eating, sipped a bit of wine to help wash down the food in his mouth, and gave her his full attention. "I really wish I didn't have to deal with this sort of garbage so often. I've got other things I must address."

"I didn't think it was possible for that to happen here," he said. "I'm assuming it's demons, rather than souls. Am I correct?"

"You are exactly right, Hector. I received word of their duplicity shortly after we arrived, and I had them 'invited' to the audience. I had planned to make more of a public example of them, but then my pain in the arse sister made her entrance, and everything else sort of went by the wayside."

"What will you do with them? I'm assuming that you're not going to let them get away with anything."

"You can bet your life that I'm not going to let then get away with what they were planning, but now I'm going to have to decide what I'm going to do," Luci explained. "For now, I've had them taken to the lower levels, and they are contained until I can figure it out. Whatever I decide, it will still be as public as possible. It seems that every so often, some of my demons forget their place."

"How often do you have to deal with such things?"

"Maybe once every few hundred years. Some demons appear to have shorter memories than others, so I make public examples of them."

"Aren't you worried that you might eventually run out of demons?"

Luci laughed.

"I can always make more," she told him. "I will never 'run out of demons.'"

"You can create demons? I thought only God created—"

Luci made a face.

"It's not the same thing. I'm not my Parent. 'Creation' isn't in my job description. Demons are condensed from the sins and vileness of the souls who come to be punished here in Hell," she explained.

"So, you have control over that? It doesn't happen spontaneously?"

"Heavens, no!" she exclaimed. "That would be chaos, and I cannot abide that. When more demons are required, I do what I must to fill that need."

"You make that sound unpleasant."

"It is. In the extreme," Luci told him. "I'd really prefer not to discuss it further if you don't mind."

"You said that some of the conspirators were to be made examples of? What does that mean, exactly?" Hector asked, taking the hint, and moving back to the previous topic.

"The ringleaders are destroyed completely," Luci said, her voice cold. "I cannot afford to allow them to continue to exist. There is too much chance of their followers getting bright ideas and making things even worse."

"Something tells me that you've learned that lesson the hard way," Hector surmised, his voice bleak. Luci appeared surprised at the man's intuition.

"A few millennia ago, I made the mistake of allowing the instigators to continue to exist," she explained. "Some of their followers took it into their heads to attempt a rescue, and by the time it was over, several hundred demons met their end."

"You destroyed them all," Hector asked, incredulous.

"I destroyed about seventy demons when the carnage finally came to its end. Those seventy demons slaughtered any demons they came across who knew their position and maintained their loyalty." She said. "I had to make a special trip out here to put my foot down on their throats. Demons may not have souls but, like any living creature, they are still driven by a survival instinct, like nearly any other being. Most heed that instinct and don't act out."

"If you were away, how did you find out about it? Can demons just wander away from Hell at any time?"

"Great Deity, no! They're metaphysically stuck here in Hell, but that doesn't mean they don't try to escape it, unless I specifically permit them to do so," Luci elaborated. "My Parent let me know what was afoot, but beyond that, They left me to my own devices."

"What about the stories I've heard about demonic possession?"

"That's a hoax, Hector," she replied. "People who were suspected of being possessed were either insane to one degree or another, or they would not conform to their own societal norms, which will usually get you a diagnosis of insanity from the nasty control freaks who imagine themselves the final moral arbiters of any society. Again, even freed by my permission, they would need additional permission to possess a living creature, and that's not something I permit."

Hector spent some time absorbing what he had been told and picked at the food on his plate. The pasty Trevor had made for him had been filling, but he did not want to offend his benefactress by declining the luncheon she shared with him.

Also, he was not at all certain when he would have the opportunity to have a full meal again, and had long ago learned to take advantage of such things whenever possible.

"You said you destroyed them," Hector finally ventured. "What did you do, exactly?"

"I incinerated them," Luci replied simply. "Whilst normal fire won't do much more than give them a mild hotfoot, the fire I can produce myself will burn them to less than ash."

"Less than ash?"

"There won't be so much as soot left behind."

Hector shuddered at the terrifying thought.

"The ringleader and his second face destruction. It is my hope that his cohorts will see the error of their ways and repent."

"Repent?" Hector choked on the sip of wine he was swallowing at that moment. Luci gave him a look.

"Come now, Hector," she chided him. "I'm their deity, after all. I don't demand their worship, and honestly, I wouldn't want it, but I demand that they are completely obedient to me. I'll keep an eye on the other three demons who followed, with the hope they see the error of their ways, but if they continue with this silliness, they will meet the same fate as those ringleaders."

"So, you demand obeisance, but not worship? Got it." Hector's face was impassive, hard to read.

Luci looked at him, her face neutral and her mind racing. There was definitely more to this fellow than she had at first imagined.

# Thirteen

Luci called it a day and sent Hector off to his quarters while she did whatever it was she needed to before she retired for the day.

He had wondered if he would be included in her visit to her new prisoners, but that did not appear to be in the cards, and he found himself being escorted "home" by the attentive Trevor.

"I am yourrrssss," the demon hissed happily, glancing back at the human. "My Lady has ssssaid sssso."

"I suppose that's the case, Trevor," Hector responded as he cut sideways to get out of the way of another gigantic demon that lumbered down the aisle towards them, seemingly oblivious to his presence. "Does that bother you at all?"

"No, it does not," Trevor replied. "Thisss meansss I will not have anotherrr job asssignment."

"I don't want you to think of yourself as my slave, Trevor," Hector blurted out. "You're not a slave!"

"Without a Massster, demonsssss fade away, Hector," Trevor replied, his face bearing as close to a serious expression as Hector had yet seen on the demon's face. "Issss good to be yours."

"If you say so, Trevor," Hector allowed. "But I'm not sure how much I like the idea."

The demon made a face and then chortled, a deep, disturbing laugh that sent shivers down the human's spine. If this was a demonstration of a demonic sense of humor, it disturbed Hector to his very bones.

"Funny human, Hector. More fun to laugh with you than hurting damned sssouls," Trevor continued through his laughter. "Good feeling inssside for me. I care for you. Keep you sssafe. No worriesss for you."

They walked on for a bit before Hector spoke again.

"Can you get hold of a pack of playing cards, Trevor?"

Once they returned to their quarters, Trevor had trundled off in search of the requested pack of cards, eventually returning with a pack so old that it had probably been antiques on an antebellum Mississippi riverboat.

After a double count verified that the ancient deck was complete, Hector proceeded to instruct the demon in various card games, from games of chance to those that required more thought to succeed.

The demon proved to be an excellent student, and in no time at all, was playing Gin like an old hand. Hector had decided that learning games that improved the mind might amuse the demon less frighteningly and determined to see that idea through.

"You know other games, too, Hector?"
"So, you're enjoying yourself, Trevor?"
"Oh, yes, much!"
"Pass the crisps over, will you please?"
"I get more. Bowl almost empty now."
"Do I want to know where you're getting them?"
"You sssure you want to know?"
"Uhhh—likely not, Trevor. Thanks for pointing that out."
"I be right back, Hector."

Too many bowls of Crisps of Mysterious Origin and several games of cards later, Hector was forced to call a halt to continued rounds just so he could get some sleep.

"You sssleep now?" the demon wanted to know. "I get you anything to help?"

"I'll be fine, Trevor, thank you for asking," Hector replied. "What will you do while I sleep? Do you sleep?"

The demon appeared shocked at his question.

"I not sssleep while you sssleep! Guard you, Keep you sssafe!"

"Surely things aren't that dire here, Trevor," Hector countered. "I *am* Lucifer's guest, after all."

"Oh, no, Hector! Other demonsssss use you as lev'rage against my Lady, they get you alone. Not let that happen," the demon said, his tone serious.

"Would some of them maybe be your friends, Trevor?"

The demon looked shocked, at least from what Hector had learned of the creature's expressions in the short time since their acquaintance began.

"No! Hector isss only friend of me," was his reply. "Demons not have friends, only not-quite-enemies. Demons all look for best chance for rank."

"Even you?" Hector asked cautiously.

"No need for more rank, Hector," Trevor said, his face settling into something approaching smugness.

"And why would that be, Trevor?"

"I be yours, not just assssignment, and you be only live human with demon. No way be more special than that, yesss?"

Hector was forced to agree with the happy demon, said his goodnights, and retreated into his bedroom, where he found his covers had been turned down and an iron bedwarmer with an exceptionally long handle rested atop the hearth of the bedroom's glowing fireplace. Then he remembered something.

"Trevor?"

"Yessss?"

"Help yourself to the deck if you want to play Solitaire while I'm asleep."

"Really? Not just play with you?"

"Really, Trevor," Hector assured him. "Have fun!"

## Fourteen

"Did you deal with your—uh—the demon mutineers, then?" Hector asked Luci over breakfast. Trevor had offered to make them both a veritable banquet, but he had politely declined the demon's largesse. He needed to remain in fighting trim, not balloon up into something grotesque.

"I will be doing that later this morning, Hector,' she replied after swallowing the bite of buttered toast with what appeared to be strawberry jam. From what he had seen so far, the Devil ate a light breakfast of tea and toast, rather than breaking her fast with something more substantial, but then, as she had already said, she did not *need* to eat. "I would like you to come along when I do."

"Of course, Luci," he agreed. "Whatever you need, if I'm able, I'm your man."

"So noble," she chuckled and then sipped at her tea. "Whatever will I do with you?"

"Did you and Trevor have a decent evening then? I heard he came looking for a pack of cards."

Hector imagined that little went on in Hell that Lucifer did not know about almost as soon as it occurred. He nodded.

"I wasn't tired when I went back to my rooms, so I decided that if Trevor was interested, I'd teach him at least a few card games."

"Really?" Luci asked, intrigued. "And how did that work out?"

"He's really quite good at them," Hector replied. "I taught him a few versions of Poker, Gin, War, Solitaire, Blackjack, and one or two more."

"I'm impressed! Did he show a particular favorite?"

"He skunked me twice in Gin, so that's probably his favorite," Hector said. "At first, I had to make him understand that it was okay to defeat me, but once I managed that, he was more than a suitable opponent."

"Gin is fun," Trevor piped up from across the room. "Makes head all fizzy."

Luci laughed, then Hector as well, when the inadvertent pun penetrated their thoughts.

"Come here, Trevor," Luci told the demon, her voice stern. The demon hastened to obey, coming to stand next to her, eyes downcast. She reached out a hand and touched the creature's warty shoulder. Trevor gave a sudden gasp, and Hector watched as he tensed up. He imagined that physical punishments were the norm in Hell, rather than the exception. Demons would require that type of firm hand, after all.

"Relax, Trevor," she told the demon, her voice kind. "You're fine. It sounds as though you are taking good care of our esteemed Professor here. I'm pleased that I chose his caretaker so wisely."

Trevor raised his eyes to look into Luci's, an expression of hope plain to see in them.

"My Lady isss happy with what I do?"

"Beyond measure, Trevor," she replied. "Keep up the good work. Now, would you please go and collect the Professor's warmest jacket for him?"

Once the ecstatic demon was gone on his errand, Luci's expression changed from its affable one to one that was far more serious. Hector braced for the worst.

"You've done more with him than I had anticipated, Hector," she told him with no preamble. "Previous visitors have barely tolerated their escorts if they tolerated them at all. You are probably the first to treat a demon as an individual."

"He *is* an individual, isn't he?"

"Yes, he is, but in this case, you've let him know that he is."

"Is that a bad thing?"

"Not necessarily, but it will bear watching."

"He told me that demons don't have friends, is that true?"

"What brought that up?"

"He told me that I was his only friend."

Lucifer put down her teacup, brow beetling as she considered his words.

"He's right. Demons don't have friends. I wasn't even sure they understood the concept. I wonder how Trevor has grasped it?"

"He told me that demons have what he called 'not quite enemies,'" Hector worked to remember the exact phrase the demon had used. Luci nodded.

"I'd say that describes a demon's normal relationship with other creatures. They're always working to improve their position over one another, and friendships don't rate when your existence is all about what level of power one can achieve over one's fellows is involved."

"Trevor said something to the effect that his somewhat unique position put him outside that particular competition," Hector said.

"Oh, shit," Luci breathed as she realized something. She stood.

"Brerthramoz— oh yes—Trevor, come here *now*!"

There was a sodden-sounding *pop*, and the demon appeared before them both.

Hector gasped.

Even allowing for the wild permutations a demon's form might take, Trevor did not look at all well.

The demon wailed in pain, one eye swollen shut, and the hilts of at least four blades protruded from various points on his fleshy body.

Some of his tentacles had been torn away from his scalp, leaving oozing green demon ichor in their wake. Hector immediately went to the creature, and without thinking about what he was doing, wrapped his arms around him, trying to will the demon back to health.

"I'm so sorry, Trevor! I didn't mean for this to happen to you!" Hector exclaimed, using his sleeve to wipe away the ichor that streamed into the demon's single good remaining eye.

"Stand aside, Professor," Luci was beside them, one hand raised. Her eyes were once again flame. The demon wailed in terror as it beheld her terrible visage.

"Don't end him!" Hector pleaded, placing himself between the pathetically whimpering demon and the Lord of Hell. "It's not his fault!"

Luci's eyes returned to their human-appearing state as she dropped to her haunches and stared at the man. She shook her head and sighed.

"Hector, did you really think I would hurt him?"

"I don't know *what* happens when a demon is injured, Lucifer," he replied, his eyes looking a bit wild. "He shouldn't suffer because of his current assignment."

"Relax, Hector," she told him, gently removing the demon from the human's embrace, then moving Hector to one side, out of her way.

The Professor watched as the Devil placed both hands on the demon and shut her eyes. A red glow began to emanate from her body, which then began to shift and contort as the glow grew in strength. It was not long before Hector had to look away, but not before he *saw*.

Yes, it was terrible, all right, and he hoped he would never, ever see it again.

*Nothing* should have that many tentacles and eyeballs and *teeth*, and he was not sure if there hadn't been extra heads before he averted his eyes and shut them tight. How had Myra not run screaming when she saw—*that?*

It was all he could do not to do that himself, even while continuing to remind himself that this was, perhaps, the Devil's true form. This reminder that the Luci he knew was a mere mask shook his certainty, but he also kept tight hold of the knowledge that Lucifer had not yet done anything to truly make him suspect her of ill intent towards him.

Several minutes later, there was a soft susurration and a sigh of relief.

"It's okay, Hector," Luci's voice came to him. "You can look again. Unless you've decided it's been all too much, and you want to return to your home."

Hector opened his eyes again and turned around to see Luci, back in her human form once more, a companionable arm around the now-healed demon's "shoulders." From what he could see, there was no evidence that the creature had ever been injured.

"No, I'm not leaving, Luci," he told her, his expression hard. "I'd really like to know who did that to him, though."

"Are you sure about that, Professor?"

He noted the form of address she used for him and chose not to comment on it.

"Yes to both, my Lady," he replied. *Two* could play at the title game. "If he's *my* demon, as you put it, it's *my* responsibility to make sure he's out of bounds with the other demons."

"And how do you think you can make that happen?"

"Will you allow me to do what I need to do, My Lady?"

"It's Luci, Hector," she remonstrated him. Hector smiled at the small victory. "Yes, I will."

"Thank you, Luci."

"Okay, then," she said, rising once more, and extending a hand to help Hector to his feet. "How may I help?"

"I want their names and where I can find them, as well as reliable backup when I go to collect them."

"You're quite serious, aren't you?"

"Serious as a heart attack, Lucifer."

# Fifteen

The first demon was taken quite by surprise.

The fiend appeared to believe that he was immune to any sort of punishment for behaving as any demon might under similar circumstances, but the addition of a human, with human morals, to the Hellscape, turned the status quo on its figurative ear.

"Brabnigran?" Said a harsh voice behind him. Turning, the three-armed demon saw the human standing there, flanked by a pair of muscle-bound throne-room sentries. Brabnigran's bilious yellow eyes shot wild glances from the human to the largest of the two demons. "You're coming with me."

"You look for new guard? Old guard, not any good!"

Why did the demon think that bluster was going to change things? There was no chance the creature did not know his actions would bring about severe consequences.

"You're a cocky little shit, aren't you, Brabnigran," the human replied. "He's fine as he is. You, on the other hand, have some questions to answer."

The demon openly scoffed at Hector's words.

"You no boss to tell Brabnigran what to do."

This close to Hector's face, he could see that the fiend's many teeth appeared to be jagged, not because they were designed that way, but because they had been broken at some time or another in its existence.

"Our Lord Lucifer say Brabnigran come along nice or we bring you along—not so nice," growled the sentry to Hector's left. The human was glad that threat was not being aimed in his own direction. "Brabnigran no have choice. Come now."

"No! Brabnigran do job here! All you go ssscrew off!" The demon turned to leave, bravado making him more than a little foolish.

The subsequent bloodcurdling scream Brabnigran uttered shortly became a squeak, then a grunt, and finally, muffled sounds of extreme discomfort.

"We go now," the sentry who had spoken before announced and turned to leave. "Get other demon later. More fun for me when they try to run. Not like they get far."

"Glad I can brighten your day, Gilrubin," Hector replied. "Am I saying your name right?"

"Gilrabin," the sentry corrected, with an accent on the second syllable. He bestowed a toothy grin on the human. "Is okay. Nice that you ask."

Hector glanced up at the demon who hung captive in Gilrabin's grasp.

"Can't he choke to death with you holding him like that?"

"No, demons not die unless my Lady will it," Gilrabin explained. "Can be hurt bad, be made unconscious, but not die."

"What if the demon is cut up?"

"Head stay alive," the demon continued. She glanced at her captive and shook him, hard. "Demon skull too hard to break. Even for me."

Hector felt his stomach lurch at what the demon was describing. This was cruelty of a sort he had never considered.

"Well, let's get him to the dungeon or whatever, and then we can go find the other asshole who beat the shit out of Trevor."

"Sound good, My Lord."

"Please call me Hector, Gilrabin."

"Hec-tor? You sure?"

"Yes, please," he replied with a smile. "If we're going to be doing things like this, we might as well be on a first name basis, right?"

"As you say, Hector."

"He actually ignored the fact that Gilrabin told him I had ordered him to come before me? My creatures tend to remember that I not only brought them to be but that I can destroy them with a thought. I wonder why Brabnigran seems to have chosen to ignore that fact?"

"He didn't seem to care," Hector told Luci a short while later. "Brabnigran doesn't appear to be the crunchiest taco shell in the box."

"I'll have to remember that one," the Devil chuckled, then grew serious once more. "I know you want to play with him yourself, but this is something far more serious."

"I know, and I don't like it much, but I know you will want to make an example of him," Hector replied with a sigh of resignation. "A very public one."

"At least Gilrabin was there to hear what he said," she mused. "I'll have her testify to that fact before sentence is given."

Hector did a double-take.

"*Her?*"

"Yes. Her. I thought you knew."

"Ah, no, I had no idea. It didn't come up in conversation, but thank you for correcting my first impression," the human replied. "She's built like fourteen brick shithouses piled atop one another—plus the old

Roman Colosseum—just like the cherry on top of the multiverse's most muscular sundae."

"And she doesn't even have to exercise," Luci quipped, grinning. "I coalesced her that way when she came to be. Most times, I coalesce them for a specific task. In her case, I was building an army."

"What in the world did you need an army for?"

"Keeping the rest of my demons in line. The best design needed to be that brick shithouse. Bulk, muscles, maneuverability, and more than average intelligence."

"Gilrabin told me that demons' skulls are too hard for anyone to break them and actually destroy them," Hector asked, remembering what the demon had told him earlier. "Is that true?"

"Yes, it is," she replied. "I wanted to be sure that they couldn't be killed without my doing it for them."

"Why would that be?"

"Well, just consider that if this had not been the case, Trevor might not have survived the beating he received."

There was nothing Hector could say to that. He had another thought.

"Then what task was Trevor coalesced for?"

"Shit shoveling, actually. He was good at his job, and honestly, I liked him enough that when a vacancy came up in a direct attention situation, I thought of him."

"He said something about that to me before," Hector said. "How did the vacancy come up?"

"Remember how I've told you that I periodically have to end a demon or two?"

"Ah," Hector nodded. "Understood. It sounded to me as though Trevor really liked the promotion."

"Wouldn't you, if you'd spent several millennia shoveling shit?"

"You make an excellent point, Luci."

The Devil rewarded him with a smile and the barest nod of acknowledgment.

"Most even marginally-intelligent creatures tend to want to stay as far away from feces as they possibly can. Demons are no exception to that desire."

"Where would shit even come from?" Hector wanted to know. "Who uses the head in Hell?"

"You'd be surprised, and just as you humans work to keep such things contained, someone needs to do that sort of dirty work here, too. Unfortunately, some of Hell's denizens don't behave in a civilized manner, so a clean-up crew needs to follow along to pick up after the circus goes through town."

"I didn't think demons ate, so they wouldn't—" he broke off.

"I've no idea what makes it happen, but yes, they do create a veritable mountain of end product, Hector," she replied with a grimace of distaste. "So, shit shoveling is a necessary position to fill here in Hell."

Hector thought about the monstrous demon who had passed he and Trevor earlier and was horrified to consider the sheer amount of waste material that creature would likely produce over a single day. Just the thought caused him to feel a bit of nausea.

"I believe this is one of those things about Hell that I'll set aside, at least for now. I don't really even want to think about it," Hector decided. "If you don't mind, that is."

"If that's what you want, Hector," she replied. "This isn't something that you have to worry about. But it's just one of the many minutiae that *I* must pay attention to, at least to one degree or another. Such is the lot of the Lord of Hell, I suppose."

"I'm glad I don't have a job like that," Hector told her.

"There are plenty of people out there who essentially have that job, although it is normally referred to as 'janitorial services' by the politer folks out there."

"I had not considered that fact. It's true. Someone has to be the one who makes sure the necessities of life continue to be completed smoothly and invisibly."

"It's been true since the dawn of civilization, really," Luci told him. "Someone had to clean the shit out of the caves when someone didn't make it to the midden heap in time."

"So, I would guess that someone else took Trevor's job, then."

"No, as I recall, I made another demon double up on the job. He's not quite as on the ball as our Trevor, so he seems content with the job he was assigned."

"I suppose that makes it okay, then, I suppose," Hector suggested. "I'd hate to see someone be assigned that as a punishment."

Luci laughed. It was her deep, full-throated expression of ineffable joy.

"As a matter of fact, Driathlen has a subordinate."

"A subordinate?"

"Yes," Luci replied. "A certain short, dark-haired, wanna-be Aryan, actually."

The description evaded Hector for only a few seconds, and then he, too, began to laugh.

"Really? Him?"

"He absolutely loathes it, actually," Luci said. "He was seriously under the impression that he was on the fast-track to Heaven, and so when he arrived here, he insisted that he was owed—*owed*, mind you—a shining, giant, pristine palace in Heaven. It was my distinct pleasure to disabuse him of that notion."

"In Hell, souls are usually tortured in a way that is related to whatever it was that got them sent here, but his insane insistence of a misdirection dictated that he receives special attention."

"So, he's been doing that for almost eighty years now?"

"Oh, much longer than that! Hell's time runs differently for damned souls. Much differently. He perceives time as being far longer than you do. For him, it's been at least a thousand years, and he's feeling every nanosecond of that eternity. It makes his torment that much sweeter for me."

"You enjoy it?"

"For some, yes, I take delight in it!" She admitted. "Others, not so much. But for the special ones like Torquemada, the Borgia popes, Idi Amin, Saddam Hussein, bin Laden—damned souls such as theirs receive extra attention from me. Their sins were not small, not by a long shot, so their respective punishments reflect that."

"What do you do with a soul like Hussein's?"

"Well, one of these days, I'll take you by his Hell and let you watch for a bit—if you think you can handle it," Luci told him. "I must warn you, however, that it is not pretty, although I find a kind of beautiful justice in it."

Hector thought about the atrocities that Hussein and his subordinates had inflicted upon the people of Iraq and wondered what punishment would be enough to be something truly terrible for the man. Just thinking about it made his nausea rise, so he did his best to pull his thoughts from the subject.

Luci noticed his reaction and decided a distraction was in order. She handed him a clean napkin.

"Here, Hector, wipe your face. We're going to have company soon, and I don't need you to embarrass me in the process."

## Sixteen

Two weeks had passed since the attack, and although Trevor had been physically healed, he was still very much emotionally damaged. Hector did what he could to bolster the demon's self-esteem, but there seemed to be some sort of post-traumatic stress syndrome that colored everything the demon did. Trevor's formerly unassumingly amusing assertive self appeared to be out of commission, at least for the time being.

While Trevor was still ever-attentive to Hector's needs, he was visibly nervous about walking out in the open. More than once, Hector had inserted himself between the stricken demon and himself.

Hector found it heartbreaking, and then, strangely, sad, because he was feeling sympathy for a demon—but that demon was his friend, and that was what mattered most to him. You did not abandon a friend, especially when they were going through dark times.

"I'm worried about him," Hector told the Devil when he finally could hold it in no longer. "He needs help I'm not qualified to give him."

"Hector, there is no one in Hell other than you who has any chance of helping him," Luci said, her voice bleak. "If you cannot help him, I will need to find you another bodyguard."

"But I don't want another bodyguard! I want Trevor!"

"Then you need to do what you can to help him, Hector."

"But— "

"You have no choice, Professor. I can only allow this to continue for so long before I *must* intercede. I know you have developed a special relationship with this demon, but he must earn his keep," she continued. "If he can't step up when push comes to shove, he is useless as your bodyguard. There is no other choice."

"How am I supposed to help him? I have no clue what I need to do," Hector protested. "I'm a soldier, not a psychologist."

Luci stared at the human, amazed that this human, of all the humans she had taken with her on this journey over countless millennia, was so much more than the sum of his parts. She had brought Professor Hector Rhoades along as an amusing toy, but her wannabe toy had developed a distinct personality that continued to surprise her.

"As a soldier, you've had to help your comrades in arms during tough times, Hector. Perhaps you can draw upon that experience to help Trevor," Luci counseled him. "Continue to be his friend. If you can get him to talk, do that. It may sound stupid, but talk therapy really can be helpful."

Luci found herself surprised that she was interested in the mental health of a demon. In the past, she had made a practice of destroying such unfortunates, and she would have done the same with Trevor, but the human had developed a relationship of sorts with this demon. She had learned enough about humans in her exceptionally long existence to know that you never knew what they might become emotionally involved in and that destroying those involvements could cause unforeseen complications. Lucifer had experienced enough complications with the humans of her acquaintance over the millennia to want to avoid doing it again if it was not absolutely necessary.

"Promise me you won't do anything bad to him, Luci," Hector plead with her. She noted how childlike his plea seemed. "He doesn't deserve it."

"Hector, I can give you some time with him, but I can't give you forever," she replied, steeling herself against the emotions the human's helpless attitude conveyed. "So, don't dawdle, Hector."

"How long do I have?"

"I can't give you a hard and fast deadline, Hector, but you need to at least make some sort of a breakthrough soon," Luci told him. "And now, get out of my office. I have some things to take care of, and you don't need to be here for them."

"See you for dinner," Hector asked. "Trevor said he's making something special. I have no idea what he considers special, but I thought you might want to join me. You can call me the equivalent of an ambulance, if that becomes necessary."

"Well, if he does poison you, I'm sure it would not have been deliberate, Hector. Of course I'll join you," Luci replied, wondering where the demon could have found recipes, and then wondered if whatever-it-was it would be edible. The Professor seemed healthy enough, so that was a good sign. "What time?"

"As near as I can tell time here, since my watch doesn't work down here, when whatever that unholy shrilling sound happens."

"Ah, yes. Then. I'll see you then."

"What *is* that nasty sound all about?"

"It doesn't translate well, Hector," Luci replied. "Just know that you probably want to be locked indoors whenever it happens."

"You're joking."

"No, not this time. Anyhow, get ye gone. I've work to get done."

After Hector left, and Luci locked the door behind him, she went to one of the walls of her office and tapped a certain sequence of knocks, at which time the wall spun about, revealing a very long, wall-sized floor-to-ceiling bookshelf, stuffed full of scrolls, handwritten manuscripts, and more. Book collectors and literary historians might have offered their very souls to Lucifer in exchange for even a glance at the words contained within that shelf, but they would never have that opportunity. There were volumes contained in that bookshelf that should never again be revealed to human eyes, as they were almost too terrible even for angelic ones.

The fabled Mad Arab's dreaded tome had a place on that shelf, and although there was no truth to the stories behind it, once a book becomes well-known enough, it develops its own sort of power, a power that could be dangerous in the wrong hands. Whilst this one would not summon demons or other fantastical creatures, it could drive mortal minds to insanity. That was the reason why Luci had taken it from its author in the first place. He had begun to believe the gist of the words he had written inside the thing.

"I should probably destroy it entirely," she said aloud. "It won't make the memory of the thing disappear, but at least it would no longer be available to fall into the wrong hands."

As she said this, she pulled it down from its place on the vast shelf and beheld its gruesome cover, wrapped in a sheet of black-dyed leather that had come from no dumb animal. Just looking at it made her shudder. Why anyone would think such a thing was appropriate was beyond her ken.

The Nazis, who had skinned humans for their unique tattoos, had a special place here as well. As their punishment, they were forced to endure "live" skinning of their own flesh from their bones with no respite. Such was eternity that there was no blessed unconsciousness or madness into which one might fall to gain relief from the unending torment. Punishment was punishment. The continuing hatred the more civilized inhabitants of Earth kept for the monsters, even after several decades, made certain of that.

Putting the cursed book back on its shelf, Luci was reminded that she needed to check on some of her inmates. Mengele, for example, needed a slight change to his torture regime. The bastard had always been a bit of a masochist, although that was something he had kept from his superiors in the Party.

For Mengele, change-ups in his torture routine kept things from becoming barely tolerable, as he would have no idea what might be coming up next. He was one of those for whom Lucifer devised especially horrific tortures.

As far as she was concerned, *nothing* was too extreme, where was that sadistic Nazi was concerned.

She thought again of destroying the tome, now safely back with its fellows on the shelf, and realized that hateful though the thing might be, she considered it a sin to destroy thoughts and ideas, so she could not give in to her earlier thoughts. Those who had burned the Library at Alexandria also spent their eternities in her attentive custody.

Moving to another part of the vast bookshelf, she chose a specific book, taking it from its shelf and then going over to the overstuffed black leather couch that occupied one corner of her office, a tulip glass full of a thick, dark stout waiting for her on the coffee table in front of it. Jonny and Kevin had sent some over to her for her consideration, and knowing how well they brewed beer, she had no doubt it would be at least as good as their previous offerings. A careful first sip proved her right.

Shedding her shoes, she curled up on the couch, opened the book, and began to read, enjoying the words the author had thoughtfully transferred from his brain to the page. Writing was something Luci wished she was gifted in, but it was not her forte, so she relied upon others to do it. This was an author she had read and even reread many times over the years, and through discreet channels, made certain that the publisher kept supporting him.

It was not deep reading by any stretch of the imagination but instead was escapist fluff. The hero of this piece was barely three-dimensional, but Luci enjoyed the fact that the character appeared to learn and grow from one book to the next, instead of being a cardboard cutout sort of main character. Yes, his character had remarkably similar adventures from one book to the next, but that character growth enabled him to approach these similar situations in different ways.

Whenever she could, she tried to take out at least an hour a day to read, uninterrupted. When she was still Earthside, Remy kept her from being interrupted and took that duty to her undead heart. Luci knew that more than one unwise individual had, at times, been violently dissuaded from doing so.

It was difficult for Luci to set the slim volume aside once the appointed hour was up, but she somehow managed to do so. That it was during a pivotal scene didn't help, but she knew she had more actual work-related duties to accomplish before her day was completed.

Once the book had been returned to its place on the bookshelf once again turned away from sight, Luci called to her assistant, who would come immediately, no matter where he might be at any given time.

## Seventeen

Trevor had outdone himself for the evening meal.

A roast beast of some sort, done to a perfect medium-rare state accompanied by potatoes, carrots, onions, green beans, and other, not-so-familiar tasty treats were served up. Hector could tell that the demon was pleased with himself, and it made him happy to see the demon something other than afraid of his own shadow.

"This is wonderful, Trevor," he enthused once he had had at least a bite of everything on the table. "I don't know how you did it, but I'm very pleased with all of it!"

"Isss good?"

"More than you could possibly know," Hector reassured him. "Where did you find the recipe for this?"

"Damned soul was chef. Learned from him," the demon explained. "Had to cheat foods for some stuff. We not have here."

Luci swallowed down the bite she had been chewing and then washed it down with a long drink of the same stout she had been drinking earlier in the day.

"This is really quite good, Trevor," she agreed. "You have a gift I had no idea you possessed. I'm glad we've had the chance to discover it."

The demon visibly preened under the compliments he was receiving, and that pleased Hector. Perhaps this would help his standing with the Devil and help to prevent his destruction.

"Thank you for chance to cook, My Lady," the demon enunciated very carefully. Luci shot a look at Hector, but the human gave an almost imperceptible shrug. "Always wanted to try, but not have chance until now."

"You're welcome, Trevor," Luci replied after a moment's thought. "Who was this soul you learned from?"

"French chef," the demon supplied. "Helped Nazis. War criminal."

"How did *you* come to talk to him? You had a different soul you were in charge of," Luci asked him, eyes hard.

"Would sometimes watch Verenema torture him," Trevor explained with no display of guilt. "Mine not always need close watching."

"How did recipes come up?"

"I ask him what he do when alive. He tell a lot. Verenema mad at first, but decided it okay me come in to ask."

"Why were you interested in recipes, of all things?"

"I hear dead humans talk about food they like. Food they miss. So, wanted to know what were."

"You don't *eat*, Trevor," Luci asked the demon, very confused. "Why should any of that interest you?"

The demon gave her an untranslatable look.

"Just because *can't* not mean not still int'restin'."

"You have me there, Trevor," Luci admitted with a sardonic expression. "Whatever your reasons, I'm glad you were so curious. You can cook for me anytime."

"Got go check dessert," the demon announced. "Stupid thing like falling in if not careful."

"Sounds like a soufflé of some sort," Luci noted as Trevor trundled away into the kitchen. "I wonder what it is."

"He seems to be a bundle of surprises, Luci," Hector said. She noticed the light, hopeful tone in his voice and smiled.

"Fine, take all the time you need to put him as close to back on track as he was before the attack," she allowed. "It would be incredibly stupid to destroy such a font of culinary creativity."

"So, did you get all your stuff done today?"

"Most of it, yes," Luci replied. "Still lots to see to before we head out again."

"I imagine so."

"You've been patient with me while I've been doing my thing. What have you been up to while I've been occupied elsewhere?"

"I've been doing some exploring. While Trevor's been recovering his bearings, Gilrabin has been watching over me."

"Gilrabin? Are you serious? Big? Blue? Fangs the size of chopsticks?"

"Yes, *that* Gilrabin."

"Color me stunned."

"How did you manage to talk her into it?"

"She wanted to learn how to play cards, too."

"Cards? Seriously? Dare I ask what her favorite game seems to be so far?"

"Hearts."

Once again, Luci wondered what she had brought down with her into Hell. Professor Hector Rhoades was much more than he appeared to be.

"Are you trying to subvert my demons, Hector," she asked him with some asperity. "Taking over Hell through the cunning use of playing cards?"

"That wasn't my intent, Luci," he replied, eyes wide. "They do seem to like playing cards, though, don't they?"

"It might be a way to keep them out of trouble, anyway," Luci said, her expression thoughtful. "I'll have to have a talk with Trevor and Gilrabin when I have a free moment."

"So, in your wanderings around Hell, what have you discovered, Hector?"

"The demons here are ruled by fear rather than loyalty. That's not always a good thing. It may be part of what leads some of them to try to rebel."

"They should have learned from my own failure at rebellion," Luci snapped.

"Youngsters rarely learn from the examples of their elders," Hector pointed out. "If they did, we'd have far fewer regrets later in life."

"These aren't children, Hector," Luci said, making a face. "They're demons."

"Yes, I know that, but for all intents and purposes, they are *your* children, Luci. You're just a much stricter parent than any others I've seen."

"My Parent annihilated the vast majority of your species with a flood, Hector, I've never even gone that far in disciplining my demons."

"Not my point, Luci, but I know you know that I'm right."

"And what do I do with this revelation you've announced?"

"That's up to you," he replied. "It's food for thought, though, I believe."

At that moment, showing exaggerated care, Trevor came back with two crème brûlée dishes containing what indeed appeared to be a soufflé erupting from each one. He tenderly placed them in front of his dinner guests and stood back to wait for their opinions.

"What is this," Luci wanted to know.

"Chocolate ssssouffle," was the prompt answer.

A shared glance later, spoons were applied to the twin desserts, then transported to taste buds, not knowing what to expect. The rich explosion that burst over those unsuspecting taste buds would have brought each of them to their knees if they were not already sitting.

"This is absolutely amazing, Trevor!" Hector exclaimed. "I don't think I've ever tasted anything this good before."

"I must agree that I have rarely tasted anything quite this good, Trevor," Luci said. "My congratulations on building this wonderful meal!"

"Have you tried it, Trevor," Hector wanted to know. "Chefs normally do things like that."

The demon appeared to be scandalized at the thought.

"Eat food is yours? Not do that!"

"How in the world did you get the spicing correct for everything, then? That's one of the reasons chefs taste what they're creating."

The demon shrugged his reply. Hector made a decision.

He scooped up a small bit of his own dessert and held it out to Trevor, who visibly recoiled.

"No!"

"Yes, Trevor," Hector disagreed. "Try it. I think you'll like it."

With a fearful glance at Luci, who pretended complete disinterest, Trevor took the spoonful of soufflé. After glancing at both Luci and Hector, the demon placed the spoon in his mouth.

His eyes widened to cartoonish proportions as the tiny sample melted over his tongue. The biggest grin Hector had ever seen spread across the demon's rather elastic face.

"Is *good!*" Trevor said excitement foremost in his tone as he almost reverently handed the spoon back to Hector. "Is *very* good!"

"And now you've introduced eating to my demons, Hector," Luci grumped after Trevor left to get a clean dessert spoon for his human friend. "What will *that* do to Hell now?"

"They say that the way to a man's heart is through his stomach."

"The way to a man's heart is through his second and third ribs, Hector."

"You know what I mean, Luci," Hector replied with a soft chuckle. "Perhaps it's a similar situation with recalcitrant demons."

"You'll pardon me if I choose not to investigate that possibility, Professor," she said. "I don't need to also worry about keeping enough supplies around to feed a legion of demons, so you keep this to yourself. Make sure you tell Trevor the same thing. He doesn't need to make himself any more of a target than he is already."

"Point taken, boss."

"Oh, go screw yourself!"

Hector could not have controlled the laughter that erupted from him if he had tried.

# Eighteen

"I thought I'd take you on a tour of the place, as I'm caught up for the morning," Luci said the following day. "How's Trevor this morning?"

"I think he may be pumping that chef for more recipe information," Hector replied. "He appears to be intent upon learning every possible recipe that exists."

"He's in for a big surprise then," Luci noted. "The sheer number of recipes that exist would provide for meals for the next several thousand years, even if he were to make six of them a day during that time."

The demon in question wandered up with a package artfully wrapped in what appeared to be pale blue muslin.

"Lunch, Hector," he told the human as he handed it over, glancing at Luci as he did. "Enough for both."

"Thank you, Trevor," Hector replied with a smile, tucking the package into his miraculous bag. "What is it?"

"Is surprise."

"Oh, aren't you just the big old bundle of surprises," Hector said with a mock scowl.

Demonic laughter followed them out the door.

"I don't believe I've ever heard a demon laugh simply for real humor, Hector. I must thank you for that."

"My pleasure, Luci."


"Where are we headed?"

"You had expressed some curiosity about how damned souls are tortured in Hell, so I thought we could start there."

"Oh?"

"Have you changed your mind then?"

"No, I guess I haven't. I'm a theology student, so I suppose I should learn more about what I thought I believed."

"Thought?"

"Well, you know perfectly well that you've managed to set just about everything I thought was true on its spiritual ear," Hector explained. "It's probably better to find out what the truth really is, right?"

"Exactly, my friend," Luci replied, clapping him on the shoulder in a companionable fashion. "You may want to grab your jacket. Some of the places we'll be visiting might be a mite chilly for a living mortal being such as yourself."

"That can vary?"

"It all depends upon the particular Hell for the damned soul, Hector."

"For example, someone who loves the warmth and sunshine might end up in a frozen Hell, if it pertains to their torture. I try to make things as personal as possible, so their torment is as on point as possible."

"So, what happens with Nazis?"

"Well, we have one in this chamber, so come on in and watch."

"Won't we be a distraction?"

"Not at all. Unless I will the prisoner to see us, we will remain invisible to them. That just makes things easier on me and on whoever is overseeing the particular prisoner."

That was the first time Hector had heard Lucifer refer to a damned soul as a "prisoner," but when it came right down to it, that is exactly what they were in the scheme of things. Then that made him think of something else.

"It is taught in some religions that a soul is only tortured for a while and then they can move on to a level above Hell, but below Heaven. Is that true?"

"Not really, no," Luci replied. "Torture is eternal, at least in my time here. Your average damned soul has a difficult time accepting and owning up to bad deeds in their time on the temporal plane. That's simply the way it works."

"So then, someone like Caligula or Hitler would likely have no chance of getting out of here. If someone is insane, will that excuse them for bad actions in life? Sort of like 'innocent by reason of insanity'?"

"There is no hair-splitting allowed for such things here. Caligula was batshit crazy, but that doesn't excuse him for what he did in his lifetime, even if he *did* love his horse to distraction. Hitler was a frightening bastard with delusions of godhood. That he believed he was doing something his god would approve of doesn't absolve him of his sins. He is responsible for the torture and murder of millions of innocent souls. He'll be here forever. Plus, once they cross the Veil and move into the Void, they come back to full sanity. There is no insanity to buffer whatever punishment they might receive."

"What about souls you tempt into doing bad things?"

At this, Luci's eyes turned to flame as she glared at Hector.

"I do *not* do such things. Humans are badly enough behaved on their own without encouraging them to do evil acts. I punish evildoers, and I already have *far* too many to oversee without increasing those numbers."

"My apologies, Luci," Hector said earnestly. "I'm just trying to understand how such things work."

The Devil's eyes returned to "normal," and she gave Hector a hard look.

"I'm sorry if I took your questions badly, Hector, but I'm really quite tired of being accused of encouraging bad action in others. As I said, my hands are full enough without making my life even more difficult."

"Some religions claim that you want to grab as many souls as you can in some battle with the Divine."

A string of profanity that came from languages both still alive and those long-dead flowed from the Devil's mouth, some of them Hector knew. He winced at some of the choice phrasings Luci used as her words seemed to char the air around them. Hector was privately pleased to know that none of that invective was in any way aimed at him.

"Once again, I have enough on my plate without being an avaricious asshole," she replied once she had calmed down enough to begin speaking calmly once more. "In point of fact, I would love nothing more than to have this entire place emptied and thus be able to live my life with far less responsibility than I have been tasked with for so many millennia."

"Where would humans have gotten the idea that you wanted to corrupt souls?"

"I really have no idea. I get along just fine with my Parent, even though we only see one another once every few millennia. The misinformation is more than a little annoying."

"I'm not trying to piss you off, Luci, I swear that to you," Hector told her, genuinely contrite. "I'm just trying to understand things, even if I can't share any of what I've learned with the world I come from."

"Well, for now, keep your mouth shut and simply observe," and she stopped outside an otherwise nondescript door. "I know he can't hear you, but for now, listening is better than opening your mouth."

Then she opened the door wide, and they both stepped inside.

It was several minutes before Hector could get his head around what he was seeing, and even though he knew the torture was for good reasons, it still made him sick to his stomach.

The Nazi was a skeletally-skinny kid with bleach-blond hair, dark eyebrows, and a sneer on what might have been a handsome face had the evil in his soul not marred his appearance.

He was dressed in rags, and a patch denoting a Star of David was affixed to the front of the distressed uniform shirt he wore. Around him stood numerous other inmates who wore patches indicating they were Jewish, gay, Romani, or whatnot, but the focus seemed to be on the Nazi.

What appeared to be a concentration camp guard threw the door open and began barking orders in a language Hector did not understand. At a certain point, the guard pointed at the Nazi and drew his pistol. The imprisoned Nazi abruptly lost his self-important attitude and began to plead as he tried to tear the patch from his shirt. Hector noted that the fabric showed an amazing level of sturdiness, as it never even parted its stitching.

The pleading became even more desperate, and Hector could imagine he was able to understand what was being said. It gave him a warm feeling inside, too. No punishment was too terrible for a deathcamp Nazi, as far as he was concerned.

At a certain point, the guard, if that was what he was, grabbed the protesting damned soul by the scruff of his shirt and dragged him out into the open area in front of the barracks. The inmates who had been there, watching, slowly filed out behind the guard and his intended victim.

Once they were in the open, the guard aimed carefully and shot the Nazi in the knee, which exploded into a bloody mess from the impact. Unable to stand on the ruined leg, the Nazi fell to his remaining knee, screaming in agony. The guard smiled at him, a vile, cruel expression suffusing his face.

Upon looking more closely, Hector realized he was looking at the Nazi himself, but not as he was now, starving and at the mercy of cruel overlords. This was the monster, this one fattened on the goods and mortal terror of those who he now tortured and murdered on a mere whim.

"He's endured this since he died?"

"Yes."

"How long ago did he die?"

"He was killed during the liberation of the concentration camp in which he abused and murdered innocent human beings. Hundreds of them personally. Thousands peripherally. A right sadistic bastard, as I'm sure you have noticed in your short time here."

"I couldn't nor would I argue in his favor, now."

"Temporally, he's been here not much time at all, but in the time sink that Hell can be, it's been an eternity for Herr Nazi here. Do you think he's suffered enough?"

Hector did not even have to take a moment to think about it. His opinion of the putative "Master Race" had been burned into his own soul as a child when first he heard of their terrible deeds.

"There isn't enough time in all of eternity for that bastard to even approach atoning for his monstrous actions."

"Are you sure?"

"Without question, Luci."

"Very well," the Devil replied. "Let's move on, then. Good work, Abrenath!"

The fat Nazi glanced up at Lucifer and gave a toothy grin, then went back to giving his attention to the groveling wreck on the ground before him.

"Good to meet you, Abrenath!" Hector said, his voice soft, but he knew the demon would still be able to hear him. The demon looked a bit startled at the acknowledgement but then gave a curt nod after a quick glance at Luci, as though seeking permission to respond.

They visited sinners, both minor and major. There did not seem to be anything like a set arrangement to the quarters, but Luci appeared to know every resident soul and the crimes for which they were now receiving their punishments. With each one, Luci told Hector why they were now being tormented and then asked if they continued to deserve their punishment. With each one, he gave an assertive "yes."

Hector followed along, noting each damned soul as they went. Some seemed to be straight out of Central Casting, while others looked "normal" and "harmless," requiring some level of explanation from the Devil as to why they were there. Men and women. Old and young. No one, it appeared, was immune from a potential eternal residence in Hell. In some cases, it was hard to watch a younger person be subjected to torture, but the sentences seemed appropriate under the circumstances.

Perhaps an hour and a half of normal time later, they entered a chamber that opened into an outdoor scene. A bridge was overhead, and there was a partially submerged vehicle in the water that Hector was stunned to realize they were standing on top of. It was just one reminder that he was not in the real world but instead occupied an elaborately staged reality.

He could see that the water had filled the vehicle's interior already and that two figures were inside. One occupant was still strapped into her seatbelt. The other appeared to be fighting to free herself from the water-filled vehicle's cabin before she drowned.

Pale, slender fists beat at the glass, their already-ineffectual blows becoming weaker and weaker as oxygen-starved lungs ran out of fresh air to fuel them.

After ducking down to see who was inside the vehicle, with a started exclamation, Hector staggered back and then moved away, his breakfast abruptly splashing down into the faux water. He blindly made his way to the chamber door and left the room.

When Luci emerged a moment later, she found Hector dry-heaving outside, on his knees, one hand out and pressed against the wall. He looked up at the Devil, fury on his face.

"You *know* who that was, don't you, you asshole?"

"Of course I do, Hector," she replied, her voice calm. "I thought you should see her."

"I wasn't there when it happened, why would you think I'd want to see that happen," he demanded. "Just imagining it has been difficult enough!"

"Don't you want to see her punished?"

"She can rot here forever for all I care! My wife, on the other hand—I just can't—" and another round of dry heaving began.

Luci put out a hand to touch Hector's shoulder, but he flinched away from her touch.

"I'm sorry this has brought back such terrible memories, Hector," she said, her voice soft. "But, I think you needed to see it since I know you were away when it happened."

"I didn't need to see *that*!"

"You did, Hector," Luci insisted. "I know that you've been trying to die for a long time now, but you're not the sort to commit suicide, so you're trying to find other ways to die. Did you think you might die here with me?"

"It's none of your business, Lucifer," Hector muttered just loud enough for her to hear him, his voice thick with grief.

"Technically, it is, Hector," she disagreed. "Your sister-in-law's actions brought her down here to my domain for special attention. I thought it a good opportunity for closure."

"I don't need this kind of closure!" he yelled. "I just want to go back to my quarters for now, please, Luci. Just leave me alone."

"Very well, then," she said a moment later. "I'll get Gilrabin out here to escort you back there. I don't want you wandering around without a guide. Who knows where you might end up."

"Just leave me alone, Lucifer," Hector grated out. "I need to be alone for now."

"I understand that Hector, but you still must follow my rules," Luci reminded him. "Gilrabin, come here now!"

With the now-familiar "pop," the gigantic demon appeared before them. She bowed low to her Master and then began to smile at Hector, but upon seeing his expression, the smile was wiped away as though it had never been there.

"Gilrabin, please escort the Professor back to his quarters," Luci instructed. "He is to be molested by no one while you travel there, and you have my permission to give anyone who might try an object lesson in why persisting would be a very bad idea."

"Yes, my Lady," Gilrabin ground out in her incredible baritone. "No one?"

"Ah, well, our Trevor is allowed to interact with the Professor, of course, as well as yourself."

Was that a sigh of relief from the enormous fiend? Luci was not quite sure but chose not to pursue that thought, at least for the time being, anyway.

Without another word, human and demon left, the demon being oddly solicitous of the human. Luci watched their progress from a distance and was a little surprised when, once they reached the Professor's quarters, he actually invited the demon in, closing and locking the door behind them.

# Nineteen

"Sorry you saw that," Gilrabin rumbled from her seat at the table. "Sure it was hard."

"Why would she even show me that?" Hector asked for the dozenth time. "She should have known better!"

"Boss know what she does," Trevor advised him, handing him a strong mixed drink. As many times as Hector had espoused the idea of simple Scotch, neat, the demon continued to insist that he broaden his horizons, whether he wanted to do so or not. "Hard to trust, I know, but good to trust her."

A careful sip of his drink revealed something that tasted like gin, but with something else that had a more flowery flavor, with crushed ice and a slight fizz that suggested something like soda water. The cucumber garnish, however, confused him. It was not like other drinks he had drunk in the past, but that was not to say that whatever it was was not tasty. He took another sip and decided his first impression had been the correct one. He'd happily drink another, should the opportunity arise.

"What is this drink, Trevor? I don't believe I've ever had one like it!"

"Learned from bartender. He bad man, so he face much punishment."

"It sounds as though you're figuring things out, anyway. That's good, right?"

"I'll take your word for it, Trevor."

The demon giggled in response. Then, a sobering thought came to Hector.

"Trevor, you know she was talking about ending you if you didn't get your shit together, right?"

"Is ugly thought, I know," Trevor replied philosophically. "What she say make sense, though. Demon got to have purpose. Earn way. No free lunch here."

Hector laughed.

"You picked that one up from me, I think. 'There ain't no such thing as a free lunch.'"

"That what I say, Hector, and is still true."

"You're oddly calm about the whole idea of being destroyed, Trevor."

"Not calm," the demon replied. "Just understand how Hell works. You learn that sometime, too. Is not bad thing."

"Do you have no sense of self-preservation?"

"I here for my Lady and you, Hector. Good to make friends," he said the last word with a tone of reverence. "Now Gilrabin is friend."

"Sorry you have bad time, Hector," Gilrabin growled from her seat as she shifted a stack of cards from one row to another. "Boss no try make you mad. Always reasons for what she do."

"I don't appreciate being her guinea pig, you know." Hector was a little surprised to hear the demon refer to the Devil as "boss," but said nothing about it. Perhaps it reflected some sort of special relationship between the two of which he was currently unaware.

"Not know 'guinea pig,' but can guess though," Gilrabin opined. "Boss like you. Order all over place no one bother you, or she get real mad. Maybe even purge, like she do before. Almost no one stupid 'nuff do that thing."

"I don't believe I've met any truly stupid demons yet," Hector suggested. "Why would there be stupid demons?"

"Why there be stupid humans?" Gilrabin wanted to know. "Stupid is same everywhere. No matter what place you from will always be stupids. So, smart demons and stupid demons."

"Do you know any stupid demons?"

"I know few. Not enemies with some."

"So, you don't have a problem being friends with a stupid demon?"

"Friends?"

"Someone you just like being with and having fun with them."

"That friends?" Gilrabin wanted to know. "That good word. Good 'scription. Thank you, Hector, for new word."

"My pleasure, Gilrabin."

"Hope be friend with Hector sometime," Gilrabin blurted. Hector paused and took the demon's massive paw in his comparatively tiny one.

"We're friends now, Gilrabin," he told her. "Don't ever forget that."

The demon sat back, her expression stunned.

"We friends?" There seemed to be something important in her question. "Is that easy?"

"Of course we are Gil! I hope you consider yourself to be my friend as well."

The demon's sky-blue hide flushed a deep cerulean. Hector realized that he had once again poked at the status quo in Hell and that he would most likely get a visit and commentary from Luci. He wondered if he would be colorful commentary or something more cut and dry. Who knew with the Devil?

Now, he really did not care what she thought.

"Gil? Is short for Gilrabin? I like! Hector first Not Enemy Friend," the demon ground out. "Good feeling inside to think about. You call me anytime, I be where you are as soon as able."

"That's kind of you, Gilrabin. I appreciate your kindness."

The big demon looked uncomfortable at his words. After only a moment's thought, Hector realized why.

"Oh, don't worry," he hastened to reassure her. "I'll be certain to tell everyone who asks that you're a right bastard."

"That good," she replied, an expression of relief overtaking her face. "Hard to keep order if others think you weak."

"Kindness isn't a weakness, Gilrabin, but I'll keep your secret."

"Gilrabin, you try choc'lat?" Trevor brought a platter to the table that appeared to hold about a dozen powdered sugar-dusted dark chocolate truffles, each about the size and general dimensions of a plump Bing cherry. The big demon looked down at the platter full of tasty treasures, curiosity on her broad, warty face.

"You call me Gil, Trevor," the demon said abruptly, looking up at the other demon in the room. "Is our friend thing, okay?"

"Is good, Gil!" Trevor burbled happily. "I do!"

"Go ahead and try one, Gil," Hector encouraged her, gesturing at the carefully arranged plate candies. "You might be pleasantly surprised at the taste."

Gilrabin chose a truffle and picked it up between her thumb and index finger, showing remarkable care with something so very delicate. She turned it around gently in her thick fingers, then brought it to her immense nostrils and took a deep sniff. A wide smile revealed a mouthful of very sharp teeth, and she placed the aromatic treat into her mouth, allowing it to rest on her long, pointed tongue.

Hector watched as bliss registered on the demon's face. She closed her mouth and allowed the chocolate to melt on her tongue. He made a quick suggestion to Trevor, who looked surprised, but then nodded and made a trip to the kitchen in the back. This time, he held a glass of ice-cold milk, which he put down in front of Gilrabin.

"Have a sip of that, Gil," he suggested.

"Sip?"

"Just put a small amount of it into your mouth and swallow it slowly. You might like how it tastes."

She picked the glass up and did as she was bid. Only something so non-human could have smiled that large without hurting itself. It seemed that yet another demon had discovered something new that she liked.

"This is eating and drinking?"

"Yes, it is, Gil," Hector replied. "I'd suggest you not share this gift with anyone else. It might have bad results."

The demon seemed to consider his words, then she nodded assertively.

"Demons get stupid sometimes," the demon volunteered. "No need encourage it."

"Wise thoughts, my friend," Hector told her. "No sense in asking for trouble."

Gilrabin erupted in laughter, which transformed her appearance from threatening to something far better natured and even friendly.

"I been here long, long, long time now. Most demons here now not here when my Lady made me," she told the fascinated human. "Being good at job and obeying my Lady put me in better place than when I knew."

"What did you do before you became a Throne room guard?"

"Basic soldier when my Lady first came to Hell," Gilrabin replied. "Moved up ranks as far as could go."

"Lucifer told me that she made you when she was still working to get Hell into shape, but I'm still a little fuzzy on that. How does Hell even need soldiers? It's not as though a demon can even escape Hell, from what she has told me."

"You imagine Hell with chaos? Remember most demons not have friends, just not-enemies. All work for selves, not real helping. When jobs not done, bad for all. Must be order for Hell to work right," Trevor cut in. "Way lots demons in Hell, too easy things get crazy. Must have soldiers keep order."

"Go on," Hector said, interested to hear what the demon had to say. He was intrigued to hear the demon's understanding of what amounted to government.

"Soldiers always ready to remind other demons they must listen and obey. Not have many not enemies when you are soldier. Not-enemies sometimes think can be sneaky and get away with shit."

"I could see that happening in that case."

"Can be not-enem—no *friend* with you, Hector," she told him with another big smile. Snagging another truffle from the plate, she popped into her gaping maw. "Not even need choc'lat!"

All three began to laugh.

Lucifer, always aware of what transpired in Hell while she was resident, was quietly pleased. Hell needed some changes, and Professor Hector Rhoades would be the one to help that happen.

When she had first begun to seriously consider acceding to his request, it had been simply to have more opportunities for fun at his expense. That had changed, however, once she discovered that at heart, he was a very compassionate man.

If a human could get so upset about a demon's well-being, a creature that he had been taught all his life was something so terrible that should be avoided and shunned at any cost, was eye-opening. She had always thought humans to be entirely too unwavering in their beliefs, and Hector Rhoades had thrown that opinion into a chaotic whirlwind.

She wanted to see what he could do to shift things about in the glowing embers of Hell itself.

If he got over his current fury at her, that is. She might deserve his anger, but it was not anything that could be pussy-footed around. It would be interesting to see how he resolved his anger with her.

"Gil, eh? You're making friends all over the place, aren't you, Hector," she murmured. "I hope it's a good decision on your part."

## Twenty

"You talking to me again, Hector?"

The human looked up as Luci came over to sit next to him. He gave a deep sigh.

"You could have warned me, Luci," he said, his voice flat with distaste. "I did not need to see that."

"I thought you should, Hector," she replied. "As I said before, you never had the opportunity for closure."

"Seeing her drown is not my idea of closure," Hector snapped. "It rips me open all over again!"

"She isn't drowning, Hector. Her sister is!" Luci snapped right back. "I would think you'd want to see her sister being punished for what she did to your wife."

"Pernille can drown forever, Luci," Hector muttered. "She killed my Amelie."

"And she is, Hector," Luci assured him. "She is no longer intoxicated, but she sees her sister drown and is unable to do anything at all to help her. That is her punishment for the harm she has done."

"How long has it been for her? It's been a little over ten years for me."

"Thousands of years, Hector," Luci replied. "And she has relived that death a million times more than that."

An ugly smile crossed Hector's face.

"I suppose I can't ask for more than that, so it will have to do."

"You know they were both drunk that night, correct?"

"Yes, I do. Pernille should never have been driving. Someone should have called a cab for them."

"I suspect they were using the same poor judgment, so many other drunk humans do in such circumstances."

"That doesn't matter."

"Doesn't it?"

"She was alive long enough to see her sister die before she died herself. That is part of what creates her personal Hell. From what I can see, your wife was unconscious before she died, so she did not know she was drowning when it happened."

"It still doesn't matter," Hector insisted. "If she had gotten a ride home from someone sober, they might both still be alive now."

Luci decided that was the time to stop talking about it. There was no reason to aggravate the man any further than she had already.

This was the first time in her existence that she had brought a living soul face to face with a situation such as the one he had so recently seen, and it interested her to see his reaction. He likely would not appreciate finding out that he was, essentially, a lab rat, but knew it would be a bad idea to share that with him.

"Was there anything you wanted to do in Hell before we head out to our next destination?"

"I wanted to see how you coalesce new demons, but you said you didn't want to get into that."

"It puts me in a place where I'm not comfortable, Hector, but, since I put you through what I did the other day, I suppose I can coalesce one demon so you can see how it happens," she told him. "But you have to promise me you will watch. You will *not* turn away if you don't like what you are seeing."

"I promise, Luci."

"Very well, then," she said. "Go to your quarters and dress light. The chamber we must use is very warm, even hot, and you want to be as comfortable as you are able if you are going to stand in there for any length of time."

"Yes, ma'am," he replied. "Where shall I meet you?"

"I'll be at your door in the next half hour. Be ready."

It was a long walk to their destination. The last half mile or so required them to walk down a torchlit corridor.

They spoke little as they walked, beyond Luci advising Hector of what he should and should not do during what would transpire. The Devil implied the process could be involved and exhausting. She had already intimated as much in their original conversation before she said she did not want to speak about it any further.

When they arrived, the chamber itself was bound shut with iron, wood, and what appeared to be pieces of rune-inscribed paper that had been stuck to the door itself.

"Seals," Luci explained, her voice terse. "No one is allowed in here without my express permission, but knowing how demons are, I'm not stupid enough to give them the chance to sneak in on their own."

"That makes sense," Hector replied and stood back as Luci undid all the closures on the massive door before she opened it. The grinding sound it made as he swung open somehow managed to sound more than a little threatening, like something out of a horror film.

The interior glowed orange and red, but when he walked inside, he saw it had nothing to do with fire.

There was a pool of sorts in the chamber that one might believe was filled with molten lava, until one looked more closely.

This was no pool of melted stone and metal, this was some sort of ethereal substance that glowed with a weird light of its own. Hector was both pulled toward and repelled by it in equal measure.

"You feel it, don't you," the Devil asked as she shed her clothing, leaving herself entirely naked. Hector noted that what flesh he saw was entirely unmarked by scars or other imperfections. She was as perfect as an angel, which she was.

"Yes, I do feel it, and honestly, all it makes me want to do is to run, screaming, as far away from it as I possibly can."

"That proves that you are, when it all comes down to it, a good man, Hector Rhoades. This pool calls to its own and wants them to enter its substance, but that never ends well."

"What do you mean?"

"If you were to try to enter this pool, your body would disappear, and your soul, or what was left of it, would become part of Hell itself. I'm sure that's nothing you want to experience, am I correct?"

"More than a little, Lucifer."

"Bright boy," she murmured. "Now, stand back and watch, and as I said before, do not look away. You wanted to see how this works, well, you must take the bad with the good."

With that, Hector did as he was told and watched most carefully.

At first, Luci was the Devil he knew, but over several minutes, her body began to shift and change, and he found himself looking at the horrific-looking creature he had caught a glimpse of as she healed Trevor.

Multiple heads, eyes, so very many teeth, and features too terrible to describe met his relatively innocent eyes. Only his promise to her kept him from looking away.

As he watched, she dipped her hands into that pool of sin and then began to shape something. Fascinated, he watched as she pushed and pulled at it, concentration prominent on whatever it was that passed as her "face" in this form.

Whatever it was, this demon was small.

As Hector watched, he saw Luci give it four legs, what appeared to be a tail, then finishing the form with a crudely shaped head.

What seemed to be something like sweat poured from her form, and the thing she was coalescing seemed to soak up the moisture that emerged from her form.

Some untold time later, she put the new demon down and then sat back. Between one instant and the next, she was back in her human form, and at that point, Hector could see how exhausted she really was.

"What may I do for you to help, Luci?"

She looked at him. Was that gratitude on her face?

"This creature needs to finish forming, but it can do that without my help."

Hector looked at it. It seemed more of an animal shape that something he would associate as being a demon.

"What is it?"

"Nothing meaningful. It's yours. Take it to your quarters, and it can hunt and kill any vermin that might invade while you're not paying attention. Oh, and it needs a name. I'll let you give it that."

She reached over and picked up the thing. Burning blue-white eyes stared back at her with a combination of curiosity and dread.

"You belong to this person here," she gestured at Hector. "You will protect this person at all times, even if it means you give your life doing so. Do you understand me?"

The creature made a noise Hector assumed was an affirmation. Luci looked pleased and then put it down on the ground. Over the next few minutes, the cloud of smoke that Hector had become accustomed to seeing with all demons began to take form. Shortly thereafter, its legs and tail were obscured, only appearing occasionally in glimpses as the smoke moved.

Small it may have been, but with its glowing blue-white eyes being its most prominent feature, it looked terrifying.

"I don't need—"

"Hector, you wanted to see, and now you have. I have no other place to put a demon, so this one is yours. I'm not sure, but you might even be able to take it away from Hell when the time comes for you to head home," she said. "I'm not going to make any promises about that, though."

"Why would I even want to take something back with me from Hell?"

"I don't know. Humans do stupid things, sometimes, for the things they care about."

"Who said I care about this thing?"

"Hector, I've known you long enough to know that there is no telling what you will end up taking a shine to. Just bring it home, give it a name, and don't worry about it after that."

Hector agreed, upon which time Luci got herself dressed again, and they left the chamber. He waited while she locked things up again, and then they made their way back down the long corridor and then the winding pathways they had taken before they finally, some sixty minutes or so later, returned to Hector's quarters.

"You could always get to know each other better, I suppose," Luci suggested, her exhaustion now even more evident as Hector looked at her. She seemed to divine his concern. "I'll be fine after a bit of rest."

"I thought you weren't subject to being like this," Hector said.

"For mortal concerns, that is true, but with something like coalescing a demon, I must exert control over the substance I'm working," she explained. "You should have seen how bad it was when I had to repopulate Hell after the last purge."

Hector shuddered at the thought.

"Now you go get some rest, yourself, Hector. Take this little demon with you and give it a job."

"It? This one doesn't have a gender?"

"Not until you give it one. You'll have to name it, as well, since it's yours. Naming it seals the deal," Luci said. "I'll call on you once I've regenerated a bit."

Luci waited until Hector had gone inside and shut the door behind him, gesturing for Gilrabin to stay outside a moment.

"Yes, my Lady?"

"I see that you and the Professor are getting along like a house afire."

"Hector is friend," the demon admitted with a sheepish expression. "Is bad?"

"No, not at all, Gilrabin! I'm glad you've become his friend," she reassured him with a warm smile. "You having fun learning to play cards?"

"Oh, yes!" the demon said with a pleased grin.

"Have a favorite game yet?

"Hearts."

"What do you like about it?"

"Have to think ahead about what do next," Gilrabin explained. "Is good for thinking other ways."

"So, you use card games to make you a better soldier?"

"Yes. Strategy."

"I'll have to keep that in mind, Gilrabin. Have you considered teaching some of the other Throne room guards how to play?"

The demon cocked her head to one side, as though thinking about the idea for the very first time. A few moments later, she nodded.

"Is good idea, my Lady," she growled. "Will talk to other guards and see what say."

"Keep me posted, Gilrabin. I'll want to know how they respond."

The demon straightened and saluted.

"Oh, and Gilrabin?"

"Yes, my Lady?"

"I'm glad you've become so close with Hector and Trevor," Luci said. "It's always good to have friends."

"Is true, my Lady. Friends good."

"Anyhow, Gilrabin, I won't keep you. I'm sure you're eager to get back to your cards."

"Thank you, my Lady."

Luci turned and began to walk away and then stopped and turned back.

"Hector and I will be leaving in the next few days for the next leg of our journey," she said. "I will be holding an audience in the Throne room before then to wrap up some necessary business before that."

"Yes, my Lady."

"Make sure that the mutineers are present," she told the demon. "Caged, gagged, and bound. There is no reason to let them think they're going to get away with anything."

"As you say, my Lady."

With that, Luci turned away once more and strode off to her own quarters.

When she arrived at her quarters, Luci was stunned to discover a feast laid out for her. Some sort of roasted meat, vegetables, fruits, desserts, and more. The scent of it all was maddening, and it was all she could do to lock the door behind her before she descended upon it, ravenous.

Yes, Trevor had outdone himself. If not for Hector's initial bravery, she might never have known this was even possible.

# Twenty-One

"I had no idea it would take so much out of her," Hector said to Gilrabin as he sat in the overstuffed armchair in his quarters. His new demon was perched on the back of the chair, surveying its surroundings. "Have you been with her when she's done that before?"

"My Lady not want other demons in chamber," Gilrabin noted. "I know she vul'ner'bul after making new demons, so not good to have sneaky demons around her when do."

"You'd never think of doing something bad to her when she's that weak, right?" Hector asked, and reached up to tickle the end of the little demon's tail. Turning around, it nuzzled at the back of his hand.

Gilrabin appeared shocked at the human's suggestion of potential disloyalty. Hector hoped he had not undertaken too great a risk with the direction of the conversation.

"I loyal to my Lady, Hector! She need, I die for her," her face took on an angry expression. "No question. Just do!"

"Easy, Gil, I thought I should ask," Hector replied, putting a hand on the demon's arm. "Wouldn't you ask someone else that sort of question?"

"Not like question, Hector," Gilrabin muttered darkly. Her face threatened mayhem without having to speak a single word. He began to understand one of the reasons she was so successful in the work she did for Luci. He would never, ever, want to get on this demon's bad side.

"What does she normally do once she's created demons?"

"She recharge, guess you call it. Not sure how. My Lady not share that. She stay private."

"How long does that take?"

Gilrabin shrugged.

"Depend how many demon. How much she fight to make. How fast. Many thing help decide."

"Did you want to learn another card game or play a hand of cards?"

"No," she replied. "Want stand guard at my Lady's chambers. Watch for danger."

"Did she ask you to do that?"

"No, but is important."

"Why would you do something you hadn't been asked to do?"

"Think about it and decide My Lady is friend and boss. She maybe not think that way, but is way of things. She need someone watch her back."

"Want some company?"

"You no need do that."

"Well, it never hurts to have someone watch your back, too, Gil."

The demon considered his words, then grinned.

"Is good idea! Bring cards and maybe foods. Make party of it!"

"Sounds like an excellent plan. Trevor!"


Trevor packed up a substantial quantity of food to take with them, after which the human and three demons returned to the outside of the Devil's quarters, where they sat down in the black dust and nibbled tasty snacks while playing Hearts. Hector was reminded of his younger days when he and his compatriots would stand in a long line for extended periods where they would need to find ways to entertain themselves and one another. It appeared that humans were not the only creatures out there who required that sort of entertainment to maintain some sort of focus.

"You okay, Hector," Trevor wanted to know. "You do bad at cards today. You never thisss bad."

"I'm sorry, Trevor," Hector replied. "I'm preoccupied, I suppose. It's making it difficult for me to play cards. Why don't you and Gil here play a few hands together, and I'll try to get my mood to improve. Does that work for you?"

"You want talk, Hector?" Gil asked him, what he had come to recognize as concern on her now less-alien-seeming face. "Sometimes talk helps."

"Not sure you'd understand it, Gil, but I appreciate the offer."

"Try, Hector," she insisted, putting a massive hand on his shoulder, not ungently. "I not understand, I tell you, and maybe you explain more."

"Lucifer took me to the chamber where the person who was responsible for killing my wife is being punished. She didn't warn me beforehand, so it surprised me," he explained. "I hate that woman, and I always will."

"Hate not good, Hector," Trevor piped up. "Hate bring people here. You not want end up here when you die, right?"

"Well, no, not really, I suppose," Hector admitted. "I don't think we'd be spending our time eating and playing cards."

"You right, Hector," Gilrabin agreed. "I have good idea you not like it."

"I think I'm allowed to hate her, Gil," Hector continued after several minutes' consideration. "I looked at the autopsy report. She had at least three times the legal limit of alcohol in her body when she died. She should have known better."

"Never have alcohol, so not know much 'bout it," Gil admitted. "Other than got many souls here die 'cause of it. Will say hate not good thing. You be careful with it."

"You've never had alcohol? Have you, Trevor?" Hector asked, ignoring the comment about holding on to his hatred.

"No, Hector," the demon replied.

"I'll have to introduce you to it, but if I do, you promise me you don't drink too much. No reason for you to be drunk," he told the demons.

"Not think get drunk, Hector," Gil answered. "Demon bodies different from human."

"Something to check out, anyway," Hector suggested. "It would be an interesting experiment."

"I go get?" Trevor asked.

"Not now, Trevor," Hector replied. "We'll check that out another day."

"Okay, I think—" and the door to Luci's residence opened, revealing the Lord of Hell, dressed in a robe, and looking a bit cranky.

"So, are you idiots going to just stay sitting out here, gabbing, or are you going to come in? You're keeping me awake, so you might as well."

The demons and the human sheepishly rose and filed in as the Devil stood to the side, one eyebrow raised, her lips pursed.

"My Lady, I—" Gilrabin began.

"You're not in trouble, Gilrabin," Luci advised the contrite-appearing demon. "I'll chew Hector out about it when I'm good and ready. I blame *him*."

Once everyone was inside, Luci closed the door and bolted it shut once more. She gestured to the living-room-like nook.

"Go. Sit. Trevor, you might as well put that food you brought on the coffee table. No sense in letting it go to waste," she directed them. "Now that we have four of us might as well teach everyone how to play Bridge. You *do* know how to play Bridge, right, Hector?"

"I do," he replied. "Glad to have the opportunity to play it again. It's been a long time since last I did. Do you know how to play, or is that a stupid question?"

Not even gracing him with an answer, Luci pulled a fresh deck from a drawer, unwrapped it, and handed it over to Hector, who pulled the jokers out and then shuffled the deck thoroughly.

"Okay, then, the game is Bridge," he advised the demons. "Sit back a little, and I'll teach you all how to play."

## Twenty-Two

Once the game had been explained well enough that the demons understood how to play, Luci partnered with Trevor, while Gilrabin partnered with Hector. In the end, Luci and Trevor won, but everyone remained in good spirits throughout.

The conversation had run the gamut from the minutiae of the daily life of a demon to religious studies, to what it was like living for literal eons and knowing one would likely exist for many more eons. Hector absorbed as much of the conversation as he could for later inclusion in the daily journal he kept. He found it all fascinating. Gilrabin's stories alone were something that could easily have been turned into a fantasy adventure.

After saying their goodbyes to Lucifer, Gil accompanied Hector and Trevor back to their own quarters. Knowing that Gil lived in a barracks, he offered to let her stay the night at his place, but she politely declined.

"Is okay, Hector," she told him. "Is good to spend time with you, but also good to remember where I from. I maybe come by later 'morrow to play more cards?"

"Of course, Gilrabin! Come by anytime! My door is always open to you!"

"Really?"

"Of course, really, Gil," he told her and patted her on her lower arm, which was as high as he could reach, she was so very tall. "I'll see you tomorrow, then."

"Wait, Gil," Trevor rumbled from inside the front room. He scampered off and returned a moment later with a small wrapped package. He handed it over to her. "You like this, I think."

The little demon ducked back into his and Hector's shared quarters and then out of sight.

"He good little guy," Gil said to Hector as Trevor disappeared. "Glad I spend time with him—and you. Good get to know others."

"Indeed," Hector agreed and then gave an enormous yawn. "Well, if you won't be staying, I'm heading in and going to bed. It's been a very long day, and I need to rest up. Lucifer said that we've got another busy day ahead of us."

"Audience in Throne room tomorrow morning," Gilrabin supplied. "Gotta finish up with bad demons and send on way."

"Send on their way?"

"Destroy. End. Kill. However want to say it," Gil replied, matter-of-factly. "In end, all means gone forever."

"Does that always happen with demons who rebel?"

"Most times," Gil replied. "Not let demons get away with things, or they think they can do any time again."

"Does that bother you at all?"

"I not do stupid things, so nothing be bothered about. Nothing to worry about if you do what supposed to do, right?"

"I think you have that exactly right, Gilrabin."

"You smart human, Hector. Don't expect see you here when you die."

"There are some things I've done in my life that I'm not proud of, Gil. Who knows, I may yet end up here."

"Hope not. You get sleep, and I see you in morning. My Lady put on good show for everyone, even you."

Hector smiled at the thought.

"That will be something to see, then. Goodnight, Gil."

"Night, Hector. Bye!"

Going inside and shutting the door behind him, Hector noted that Trevor had set up a glass of something, probably alcoholic, on the coffee table, some sort of glazed treat on a ceramic plate beside it. Taking the hint, Hector sat and gave the two offerings proper and respectful consideration.

The drink proved to be some sort of tasty bourbon, while the treat turned out to be baklava, of which Hector was quite fond, but which he only very rarely partook.

"Hey, Trevor! Where did you go?"

The demon emerged from wherever it was he had been and wandered on up to Hector.

"You need sssomething, Hector?"

"No, just wondered where you were hiding," Hector replied. "Why don't you get yourself a drink and your own piece of baklava, and sit with me?"

"You sure, Hector?" the demon asked, face mirroring his surprise.

"If I wasn't sure, I wouldn't have suggested it, Trevor."

"Okay! Be right back!"

Only a little more than a minute later, Trevor returned with his own helping of baklava and then went and poured himself his own shot of bourbon before going to sit in the chair opposite, but facing Hector.

"When you have your first sip of the bourbon, Trevor, do it carefully. The taste can sometimes be a bit strong, especially when you're not expecting it."

He looked down at the contents of the glass and took a deep sniff. Trevor sat back in his chair, then took a very tiny sip of the alcohol. His eyes widened in surprised, and then he gave a pleased smile.

"Now, when you're ready, have that first little sip. Let it rest on your tongue for a moment, then allow it to slowly creep down your throat," the human advised with his own happy smile.

Doing as Hector suggested, took a very tiny sip of the alcohol.

"Good," he breathed, once the first taste had been swallowed.

"Glad you like it," Hector replied. All

"All alcohol taste like this?"

"No, different kinds of alcohol have different kinds of flavors, just like different recipes taste different, depending upon the ingredients you use."

"So, beer taste like beer, bourbon taste like bourbon kind of ssstuff?"

"Not quite," Hector told him. "Every type tastes just a little bit different than the others. Remind me to ask about getting a couple different kinds of beer from Jonny and Kevin when we have the opportunity, won't you?"

"Will do, Hector," Trevor replied and took another careful sip after taking his first bite of the baklava. Another huge smile. "Flavors all go together and make different one!"

"Exactly, Trevor. That's sort of what happens when you make different kinds of alcohol, too. Maybe they'll let you watch how they do things in the brewery sometime."

"Would be good!" Trevor enthused. "Hope my Lady let me."

"I suspect she would have no problem allowing you to do just that, my friend."

The demon preened at the last word and crinkled his eyes in good humor.

"You good friend, Hector," the demon said after a few minutes of quiet sipping and nibbling. "Glad I meet you."

"The same, Trevor," the human replied. "I look forward to spending more time with you."

"You want more baklava, Hector," Trevor asked as he tossed back his last bite of the honey and nut-laden treat. "Got a whole tray in kitchen."

"I'm fine, Trevor," the human replied with a contented smile. "Why don't you take some of them to Gil, and she can share them if she likes."

"Good idea, Hector!" Trevor enthused. "I wrap some up for her and give tomorrow when see."

"Excellent idea, my friend," Hector agreed. "And with that, I'm off to bed. Early morning ahead, I think."

A thought occurred to him.

"I never asked, Trevor, if you actually sleep?"

"I not really sleep, but rest and think. Good time to think about thingsss learned during time with othersss."

"I suppose that's better than just saying they are not thinking about anything," Hector noted. "Well, whatever you do, have a good night, and I will see you in the morning."

The demon rose, gathered up empty glasses and plates, and disappeared once more into the kitchen.

Hector toddled off in the general direction of his quarters, climbed into bed, and was asleep before he realized he was actually that tired. His was not a restful sleep, however.

His dreams were tormented by memories of what he had seen in his sister-in-law's personal Hell. Making it worse was that in these nightmares, he was trapped inside the vehicle with the two women and was completely unable to save his wife no matter how he fought against his seatbelt. No matter how he tried to wake himself up, he was unable to do so on his own.

Hector had had a long period of something like this nightmare for a long time after his wife passed away, but with this new tearing open of his barely healed emotional wound, this new horror was even worse. He tried to scream, but no sound would emerge from a throat that already felt raw from over a decade of endless howling.

"Hector? Is okay, Hector?"

The concerned voice of Trevor roused Hector from what felt like the thousandth rerun of his wife's death. Opening his eyes, he was treated to the close-up sight of the demon leaning in close to his face.

"You okay, Hector?"

"Mm-fine," he mumbled. "Bad dreams."

"Bad dreams? You scream lots. Afraid you wake up my Lady, so I come wake you," the demon explained. "Scream loud, Hector. Way loud."

"How long have I been asleep?"

"Not know, but you go to bed maybe twenty minutes ago."

"Twenty minutes? That felt like a thousand years, Trevor," Hector protested, shocked that such a short amount of time had transpired.

"I hear dreams like time in Hell," Trevor said. "Time not same like real world."

"Who told you that?"

"I ask new dead soul once, when hear about dreams."

"Demons don't dream?"

"Demons no sleep, so no dreams, but still wonder what they like."

"Makes sense, I suppose."

"You want something help you sleep?"

"I don't really want to start dreaming again if I can help it."

"Got something help you sleep, no dreams. Promise."

"How do you know it will work in a living human?"

"Other couple humans who came use it and sleep fine," Trevor explained.

"Why were they using it? Do you recall?"

"Got scary thoughts in heads, and My Lady decide they safer sleeping."

"Ah. Oh. Probably not a good idea then, Trevor, but thank you."

"Why not?"

"It sounds as though that stuff knocks you out completely," Hector said. "I'd rather avoid that sort of thing if I'm able."

"If say so, Hector," Trevor said, regret plain in his voice. "You change mind, just say."

"I appreciate that Trevor, very much," he patted the demon on the shoulder. "Hey, you up to playing a hand or two of cards before I'm ready to try sleeping again?"

"Sound good! I go get bed tray, and you play in bed."

"Seriously?"

"Sure! Why not?"

The demon went off and then returned with what appeared to be an antique, ornately carved wooden bed tray. Laying atop it was the deck of cards he had originally brought to Hector's quarters, another couple squares of baklava, a sliced orange, and what smelled like hot peppermint tea brewing in a lovely Victorian-era ceramic teapot.

"You'd make a lovely homemaker, Trevor," Hector noted with a smile.

"What is 'homemaker,' Hector?"

"It's someone who makes people feel comfortable in their home by making sure that people want for nothing. They even manage to anticipate what others might want."

"Demon homemaker? Sound silly, Hector," the demon replied shyly.

"Doesn't matter what you are, Trevor," Hector said kindly, picking up the cards and gently shuffling them. "Not everyone makes a good homemaker, but I think you would be one of those rare people. So, you ready to play?"

"What play?"

"What do you want to play?"

"Gin?"

"Not going to let me sleep, are you?"

"Oh no, Hector! You sleep you need to sleep. I sorry!"

Hector realized something and decided to say something about it.

"Trevor, I've noticed that your 's' sounds are getting better. Why is that?"

"I work hard to sound more like you and my Lady," the demon explained. "Is little hard, but concentrate, and I do."

"It's quite the difference, Trevor," Hector replied. "Keep up the great work!"

They played a full game of Gin, this time, Hector managed to just about skunk his eager demonic opponent. It made him smile to see how thrilled the creature was to play the game. He had considered introducing the concept of gambling to the card games he taught them, but then decided something like that might lead to negative outcomes, and kept the thought to himself. Demons had enough issues without adding more to their own ledgers.

Once Hector felt he was becoming tired again, he sent Trevor on his way and lay back in his bed, staring at the obsidian ceiling. He was amazed the room could be as bright as it could, considering the sheer amount of black that was present. Of course, the furniture, assorted nicknacks, and wall hangings did provide some color and even some reflective surfaces that helped considerably.

This time, when he dropped off to sleep, his sleep was, in fact, dreamless. As a result, he slept through until morning, only rousing as the tantalizing scents of fresh hot coffee and something breakfasty made their way past his slumber and into whatever part of the human body connects directly to the stomach.

"Hector, sorry wake you, but my Lady say be at Throne room in next hour and half. Wake you now, plenty time for eat and shower, right?"

Grumbling a little, Hector voiced reluctant agreement and hauled himself out of bed. Feeling a little cold, he grabbed a light blanket from the back of the chair Trevor had occupied the night before and wrapped it around his shoulders before heading into the front room, where he knew breakfast would be waiting. The demon looked up from his breakfast preparations and took in the site of the afghan-clad human.

"You cold, Hector? I bring up fire little bit," he offered, moving toward the vast fireplace. "Sit down and have coffee. Warm up insides anyway, right?"

Nodding agreement, he did as he had been bid. Sips of invigorating coffee were interspersed with bites of what appeared to be a generous mushroom and cheese omelet with an enormous pile of sliced tomatoes on the side. By the time he started his third cup of coffee, he was almost human enough to engage in conversation with the politely waiting demon.

One would think he'd dealt with caffeine-deprived humans in the past, but Hector did not raise the subject. He simply appreciated the fact that Trevor never allowed his cup to become empty or anything near tepid.

"Thank you, Trevor," Hector finally said, once he had nearly finished his omelet. "I really needed this today."

"Thought you eat good 'cause don't know when you have lunch today," the demon replied. "My Lady not say plans past audience today."

"Could I prevail upon you for something I might be able to snack on and not be too obvious about it?"

"I have snacks in your bag, Hector," Trevor replied, an expression of proud accomplishment on his face. An icy chill ran through Hector as he absorbed the demon's words.

Hector sat bolt upright, and the demon flinched. The human fought to regain his composure.

"You were in my bag, Trevor?" He finally managed when he had grabbed hold of his temper. "I don't like to have other people in my bag."

Despite his attempt to remain as non-threatening as possible, he saw sheer panic enter the demon's eyes and instantly felt remorse. As far as he was able to tell, the demon did not have a single sneaky bone in his body if he had bones at all, and he should not be jumping to conclusions.

"Trevor, it's okay," he said and put a hand on the demon's shoulder. The tension he could feel there would have torn a mortal apart. "Just please ask me next time, before you get into it."

"Sssso ssssorry," the demon said, his voice tight, but still filled with fear. "Go tell my Lady you need ssssomeone elssse."

"No, Trevor, you don't need to do that! You're fine. You just didn't know, but now you do!" It frightened Hector a little that the demon seemed to have lost control of his s's once again. He liked the creature, and it almost hurt to see him terrified, especially of *him*. That was not how he wanted their friendship to be—and then it dawned on him.

"Do you think we're not friends anymore, Trevor?"

The demon did not say a word. He simply stared straight ahead, as though waiting for some ball to drop.

"Trevor, you and I are still friends," Hector reassured him, giving him a gentle squeeze. "Friends can forgive one another. Forgiveness is a good thing. I think it makes us all much better people."

And there it was. He thought of the demons as people, not monsters.

"Forgive?" Trevor whispered, but Hector could hear the hope in his voice. "Is okay? We friends?"

"Of course we're still friends, Trevor! You were and still are my first friend here in Hell. You'd have to work awfully hard for that to change," he surprised himself when he leaned forward and bestowed a one-armed hug on the demon. "I promise you, I'm not mad now."

The demon slipped an arm around Hector's waist and gave a quick one-armed hug of his own before slipping free to start cleaning up.

"You go shower now. Clothes be on your bed when you out."

"Special clothes today?"

"My Lady say things must be perfect. Not sure what means, but my Lady know what is, so I do."

Hector, knowing it would be a long day, and wanting to appear his best if he was going to once again stand at Luci's shoulder, scrubbed himself almost pink and shampooed his dark curly hair twice, scratching hard at his scalp to loosen up anything that might linger there. A bottle of some sort of cologne had been placed on the bathroom counter while he was showering, but he took it as an unspoken order that he use it. He could not imagine Luci would be steering him wrong with anything, so he did not question it.

When he emerged into the bedroom, wrapped in a generous Turkish bath sheet, he saw the day's clothing on the bed. Only his innate manners kept him from opining out loud about what he found there.

No shirt or pants were waiting there. Instead, there was what could only be called a robe, black, and velvety. He knew, even more, picking it up that it would only emphasize how pale his skin had become over the past few months. Hector wondered if there was a specific reason why Luci would want him in a robe but decided he'd let her share that information if and when she was ready to do so.

"Black velvet?"

"Is serious audience today, Hector," the demon explained. "Must look official. Black is official."

"I suppose you can't get quite more formal than that, my friend," Hector murmured. Out of the corner of his eye, he saw the demon brighten a bit at the word "friend." That was good. "Who will be there?"

"My Lady, you, Throne room guards, condemned, witnesses."

"Witnesses? What witnesses?"

"There will be some who just need to see," Trevor replied, his voice subdued.

"What's the matter, Trevor?"

"Some will still refuse to learn, no matter what they see," he said. "Those will die in time."

"That seems a shame."

"Most demons only look out for self. Not care about others. I thinking that not good thing."

"Excellent observation, Trevor."

The demon giggled, an odd sound coming from a creature that appeared incapable of such a thing.

"Different look for you, Hector," the demon observed as the human pulled the black velvet robe over his head and then arranged it to fall gracefully down his body, where its hem touched the floor. Whatever tailor had been responsible for its creation had an amazing sense of sizing.

"How did the tailor get my measurements?"

"No need tailor. Special thing in Hell."

"So, sort of one size fits all, but not quite?"

"Not sure what you mean, Hector, but sounds about right, maybe. Clothes change for you."

"So, you're saying that if I was a fat man, it would still fit me, with room to spare?"

The demon looked around.

"No other room, but yes, still fit fatter Hector."

"Fatter?"

Unaware of his unintentional insult, the demon just nodded, a pleased smile on his lumpy face. He enjoyed being able to surprise the human.

"So that's how the clothes Lucifer has given me all seem to fit just right?"

Another nod.

"You get skinny or fat, clothes always fit good."

"That would put clothing manufacturers out of business in a hurry, where I come from," Hector replied with a soft chuckle. "Not sure if that's necessarily a bad thing, now that I think about it."

"Must go now, Hector. Audience start soon and need talk with my Lady first for instructions."

"Then let's get moving, my friend," Hector responded. "No sense in making her wait, right?"

Lucifer wore her own black robe, although hers was silk, rather than velvet, with blood-red piping along the neckline and the bottoms of her sleeves. Her feet were concealed behind the voluminous skirt. Her hair had been immaculately dressed and was swept up in a tidy style that kept it out of her eyes but was still reminiscent of a crown. What appeared to be rubies were picked out in a regular pattern along its top line, increasing its similarity to a bejeweled crown. Without thinking about it, Hector dropped to one knee in a respectful acknowledgment of her status.

"Really, Professor? What brings on this sudden genuflection?"

"Today, you genuinely look the part of a monarch, and I was taught to pay respect to monarchs," Hector replied earnestly. "You deserve this show of respect."

"Well, color me surprised, Doctor Paul Ambrose Hector Montague Rhoades," she said with a coy smile. "Hopefully, this thought will inspire my subjects, as I have a serious and unpleasant chore to perform today."

"I understand."

"No, I don't think you do. Not in its entirely, anyway," she corrected him. "This is going to be terrible and ugly, but I still can't have you even showing discomfort in the least. Do you think you'll be able to do that?"

"Yes, my Lady."

"There you go again, Hector," she chided him. "Knock that off!"

"I'll go back to my normally disrespectful self once you stop looking like you're successfully outdoing Her Royal Highness Princess Diana in looking regal."

"Now that's someone I'm pleased never made it down here," Luci reflected, sadness in her eyes. "She was truly a good person. It's a shame her life was cut so short. There was so much more she could have accomplished by living."

"She really was an incredible lady. I wish I could have met her," Hector replied, his eyes just a little bit misty-looking.

"We could stop by Heaven at some point, and you could, if you like," Luci told him jovially. "It wouldn't really take any time at all."

"I didn't think you could enter Heaven," Hector told her.

"No, it's not that I *can't*, it's that I choose *not* to," the Devil replied. "At least for now. I haven't had anything come up that would entice me to do so. Unless, of course, you decide you'd like to visit there."

"Are you serious?"

"About that? Certainly."

"You never cease to surprise me, Lucifer."

"Good. I'd hate to disappoint you." She glanced at the delicate antique wristwatch that graced her slender wrist and then straightened to a regal stance. "It's showtime, kid. Let's get a move-on."

## Twenty-Three

The Throne room was crowded when they entered from the rear door. The crowd inside was not at all quiet. Numerous conversations were going on that seemed to range from one extreme to another, from what Hector was able to overhear.

"Almost like a Tower of Babel, but all in the same language, am I right?" Luci asked. Hector gave a snort. "I can zero in on particular conversations, but that's a perk of being who I am."

"Lucky you," the human muttered sourly. "It's all noise to me."

"Sometimes I think that might be preferable for me as well, Hector, but I don't have that luxury."

They waited for a few minutes until Hector could feel the tension building in the Throne room to the point that he felt as though he would have to fight to move through the air itself. The occupants of the Throne room knew that something was up, but they were not quite sure what that 'something' was. The resulting terror-infused aura that filled the room sent a shivering thrill up his spine.

Another few minutes and Luci gave a decisive nod to Hector. Taking his cue, he began his stately appearance around the back of the Throne and into the view of the nervous demons. In one corner, he saw several iron cages, each containing a single demon. From the looks on their faces, they appeared to have at least an inkling that things were not going to end well for them.

Good.

"All stand and welcome our Lady Lucifer, Dread and Terrible Lord of Hell!" Gilrabin thundered from her place before the Throne. The response was gratifying in the extreme. Even those demons who appeared to exist in a permanent slouch somehow managed to straighten up, if only a little.

Gilrabin clad in what Hector assumed was her best armor, stood near the Throne, intimidating just from her mere presence. No one got any closer to the gigantic, heavily armored demon than they absolutely had to. Maybe it was the spikes that lined nearly every exposed area of the armor. He had no idea. Whatever the reason, it was the safest course of action, Hector thought as he watched the demon work without even wiggling a tentacled eyebrow.

Luci emerged from behind the throne slowly, an intricately carved ruby-topped ebony scepter clutched in her left hand. Hector could not recall it having been there when they were in the anteroom together.

The Devil's expression was thunderous, and Hector reminded himself again how grateful he was that her fury was not aimed at him.

With the certainty of royalty, Lucifer sat down, not even looking behind herself to be sure of her seat first. She and Gilrabin exchanged glances. The exchange could not be considered friendly, but at least the demon would know the unfriendliness was not aimed at her.

Hector suspected Gilrabin felt the same as he about that fact.

"Bring the accused forward," the demon exclaimed. The occupant of the first cage was brought forward, festooned with manacles and chains to prevent any chance of escape. If he had not known at least something of what had brought this to transpire, he might have felt at least some tiny bit of sympathy for the creature, but knowing the demon was an attempted mutineer, this was not possible.

The demon's terror was evident as it was brought forward to face its sovereign. It knew that what it had done was wrong, but it was clear to Hector that it had not considered its actions that far, and now it would suffer the consequences of those ill-considered actions.

"Dralran, what have you been doing in my absence? Why should I allow you to continue to exist?"

The demon began to blubber and scream as Lucifer stared him down, her lips twisted in disgust and scorn. No words were required to get the demon to confess every tiny offense he had committed, and then the larger sins were revealed, and loud protests emerged from at least some of the cages on the far side of the room.

"Almun said we could do it! He said it would be fine!" The demon shrieked in terror. "Please, my Lady, please!"

"Gereniak, bring Almun here," Lucifer directed, her voice flat and unfriendly. "Bring him here now."

Hector did not know that screams could be so very loud, but the demon called Dralran screamed at a level that actually hurt his human ears before his keeper was able to gag him into silence. Almun, shrieking and unsuccessfully attempting to deny the accusations, was literally dragged over to face the Lord of Hell. From what Hector could see, the demon had no intention of admitting even any small amount of responsibility for his actions. That only one Entity in Hell was able to lie made those intentions meaningless but no less desperate.

This would not end well for Almun, but it was clear he did not realize that yet.

"Almun, who am I?"

"You are my Lady Lucifer," the demon stammered. "The Celestial Rebel, Lord of Hell, and She Who Keeps the Fires Burning."

"Then why have you been acting against me, Almun?"

"I haven't, my Lady!" The demon protested. "I have been loyal!"

"Almun, I'm no fool," she replied. "Don't make the mistake of thinking I don't know what you've been up to in my absence. In your mind, you may have been loyal, but you have also been disobedient, and I cannot abide that."

"But, my Lady!"

"Don't try to pretend you are innocent, Almun. I, of all beings, know when you're working against me, it's time for you to end. In your mind, you may not have been acting against me, but you also know that your intentions were not pure. There was something in it for *you*, and that's not how Hell works."

"No! my Lady!"

"Yes, Almun, I'm tired of your continued misbehavior," and then she did not appear human any longer. It was not the horrible form she had possessed while healing Trevor or when she created a new demon, but it was bad enough to behold.

Claws. Fangs. Tentacles. Flames for eyes.

*Antacid for my stomach*, Hector thought, making a note for whenever the nightmare he now witnessed was over. He also made a note to never again eat breakfast before an audience if he knew something potentially disturbing was on the agenda.

The screams were bad enough before Luci destroyed the demon, but once she started, Hector realized how terrible it really was. She did not destroy the demon immediately. No, she dragged it out, almost like a form of torture, which, come to think of it, it was.

It was torture not only for the condemned but for all the demons who watched it happen. Forbidden to look away, they all watched as Almun was very slowly disintegrated from his feet all the way up to the top of his skull.

It appeared that demons were "alive" until the point they were completely destroyed. Almun, it seemed, felt it as every centimeter of his body was burned away by Lucifer.

Dralran, wild-eyed but still gagged into silence, fought against his chains, trying with all his might to escape Luci's wrath, but his demon caretaker held him fast. He knew his days were numbered and would do whatever he had to to survive even a little longer. For this demon, at least, Lucifer had made her point.

A third demon was called up, and it fought tooth and nail to escape its keeper. Luci watched with some interest until things seemed to be getting out of hand.

"Ig'drun," she commanded, her voice honey running down sandpaper. "Come here now."

The demon ceased its fight for survival and began walking toward his Mistress, every step appearing to be a battle all its own. His eyes were wide and terrified, but against the command of the Lord of Hell, there was nothing he could do.

As he watched it all transpire, Hector wondered why the demons had been chained and caged in the first place and then realized that maintaining that sense of helplessness and terror would help Luci to keep the other demons in line. It was all related to the ending of the first demon, Almun.

Once the demon was within four feet of where she sat, Ig'drun fell to his knees, babbling apologies and begging for forgiveness.

"Ig'drun, you've been given a chance to atone before," she said, her voice deceptively gentle. "It is clear that my mercy at that time meant nothing to you."

"My Lady, please!"

"There are no more my Lady's, Ig'drun," she told him. "I'm fresh out—and I'm out of patience with your insolence. Goodbye, Ig'drun."

To Hector, it seemed as though Luci took more time to destroy this demon. One by one, digits, then limbs were slowly burned away by the eldritch light that came from where Luci's eyes should have been. The resulting smoke left a stink of brimstone in the air, rather than charred flesh, and Hector reminded himself that these were not flesh and blood creatures, but things created out of the stuff of Sin, itself.

Once the second ending had taken place, Lucifer stood, her form returned to its human-seeming, but flames had replaced the eldritch light in her eyes.

"Know that I know what happens in my domain, and if and when you disobey me or try to go above yourself, I will step in and make an example of you," she thundered. "Do not test me. You do not want to know what will happen when you do."

She turned to leave, then stopped a moment, and then turned back.

"Those demons who were not ended because of their attempted mutiny will be the lowest of the low. You may not kill them, but neither may you give them succor. For a time, they will live their own Hells. They are rendered Invisible to the population of Hell until I deem them rehabilitated."

The remaining caged demons were released from their cages, and their chains removed. At that point, their respective guards turned their backs and walked away, to leave each mutineer to face the crowd present in the Throne room.

The first blow took a demon in the side, and he fell to the ground, shrieking in pain. The second took another demon in the knee, and he also collapsed, his damaged knee now bending in an entirely new direction that Hector was certain was not at all normal for the affected demon.

He felt a touch on his arm and looked up to see Luci was resting a hand on his forearm. She jerked her head toward the back of the Throne room.

"Time to leave, Hector," she told him, her voice soft. "Don't want to ruin their fun, now do we?"

"I thought you said they weren't to be killed," Hector said once they had left the Throne room and entered the chamber behind it that served as the Devil's official office space in Hell.

"They aren't. They may be beaten and damaged, but nothing fatal is allowed. They will have nowhere to go as of this point."

"How long will you make them wait before they're no longer invisible?"

"Oh, I'm sure it'll be at least a few thousand years before I can even consider the possibility of trusting them again. I've got the time, and so have they, providing they don't do anything stupid again between now and then."

"So, you do give mercy, then."

"Hector, I'm not a monster, no matter what the Bible may suggest, but I do have to maintain order here in Hell, and the only way to do that is to mete out punishment where necessary."

"Is that why you had them caged and in chains when at the end you showed that you could make them do anything you wanted, chains or not?"

"It's all a part of the show, Hector," she explained. "I have to remind them who the big boss is, as they periodically seem to forget who that is. It's all rather annoying and truly a time-waster for me. I have far better things to occupy my time than deal with that sort of garbage."

"Sounds like some time I spent while I was still in the Reserves," he suggested. "Every so often, you need to knock a few heads together to make an impression on the other skulls in the room."

Lucifer laughed.

"I may have to steal that description from you some time if you don't mind terribly."

"Feel free, Luci," he smiled. "Leadership can be a royal pain in the arse at times."

"No doubt, my friend," she said, grinning.

## Twenty-Four

The mood in Hell was subdued for the next few days. Every so often, Hector would at least hear something about what torments the would-be mutineers were being subjected to by their fellows. When another demon attempted to intercede in a beating, that demon was also beaten to within an inch of its existence before it was taken before Lucifer for her own punishment.

Hector was glad he had not been there when that judgment was rendered. It was bad enough knowing the thing would spend at least no small amount of time swimming in a pit of lava.

Demons, it seemed, were difficult to destroy completely unless one was the Lord of Hell.

Trevor, disturbed by everything that had transpired, kept as close to their shared quarters as he was able, only emerging when he could not avoid doing so. Hector was glad that Luci seemed to appreciate the demon's value as a chef, so he had little fear that the creature's existence was in danger.

"You okay, Trevor," Hector asked the little demon about three days after the chaotic audience. "You've been pretty quiet."

"Am fine," Trevor insisted as he polished the already shining table. He'd been finding all the busy work he could to avoid having to think about what had happened. "All good."

Since no one but Lucifer could lie in Hell, it seemed the demon was doing some serious hair-splitting to get away with coming very close to it. Of course, a demon would have to learn how to do such things to survive in the harsh society that was the Netherworld. It was a sad truth for a demonic existence, from what he could tell.

"Trevor, you can talk to me if you like," Hector told the demon. "Whatever you say will just be between you and me."

The demon looked up from his polishing, his eyes huge in his lumpy skull. If he was not imagining things, Hector would have sworn he could see a tear swimming in the damn of the demon's lower lid, just on the verge of spilling over.

Coming to a decision, Hector poured two drinks and sat on the couch, motioning the demon to come over. After a moment's hesitation, Trevor did as he was bid. He sat, then leaned forward to pick up his glass, toasting Hector before taking his first sip.

"Demons be stupid," he began. "Okay, some demons be stupid. Not all."

"I think that just about anyone can be stupid once in a while. Even smart people," Hector told the demon. "I've done some pretty stupid things in my life, Trevor. Don't think I haven't."

The demon sat against the back of the couch and appeared to be considering the human's words. As he turned his thoughts around in his head, he finished about half the bourbon in his glass. Finally, he took a deep breath—did demons need to breathe? —and then began to speak again.

"My Lady Lucifer is Lord of Hell. She rules here and has final say. Almun and others did bad things. Some died. Some did not die, but will still suffer," he said. He took another sip of his drink before he continued. "Is kind of torture, yes? But torture in real life, not in make-believe, like in personal Hells."

"Yes, Trevor, that's very true."

"My Lady has right to say punishment, as should be," the demon opined like some conservative elder statesman Earthside. Another sip. "But maybe not so long for punishment? Sometimes meaning of punishment lost when it go on long time."

"What about the demons who beat you so badly?"

"At first, want revenge. Mad 'bout hurting."

"At first?"

"Yes," the demon agreed. "Very mad. But I very small demon, not strong. Shoveling shit not need strength, just be able do it long stretches no rest."

"You have to have endurance, you mean," Hector suggested.

"Yes. Endurance. That right word, Hector," Trevor said, nodding enthusiastically. "Not all demon have endurance like that, just strong. Strong not same at all."

"So, you're saying that the demons will suffer more harm than you think they deserve because they're not designed to endure tough conditions?"

"Dead demons not suffer anymore, but demons left here will suffer long time before my Lady decide they not need suffer more. Is fair? I not sure, Hector."

The demon's insight, fragmented though it might sound, seemed impeccable to the human, who wordlessly poured the demon another two fingers of bourbon.

Another sip before continuing.

"Been thinking about that since happened," Trevor said. "Want to talk to my Lady 'bout it, but not want make her angry."

"Would you like me to bring it up to her for you?"

"No," the demon replied, his voice firm. "Should come from demon who has dog in race—I think humans say—right?"

"Horse in this race, but close enough, Trevor," Hector corrected the idiom. "So, you want to talk to her about it yourself since this is something that is sort of related to what you went through?"

"Yes, that," Trevor agreed. "Knew you understand, but not know how to ask you 'bout it."

"When did you want to talk to her, Trevor?"

"You leave for next place in three days," was the reply. "I talk with my Lady day before."

"Three days left in Hell? Really? I had no idea!"

"Oh, thought you knew," Trevor apologized. "Sorry."

"Not a problem, my friend," Hector assured him. "It will give me a chance to plan ahead."

"You want dinner, Hector? Is getting late," Trevor asked, carefully putting his half-full glass down on the coffee table before he stood up. "Not got lot in kitchen, but can make do."

"Tell you what, Trevor, do you have some of those cold cuts, a bit of bread, olive oil, and any of that lovely baklava?"

The demon nodded.

"Then how about you grab those, and bring them here, and we can have them together. How does that sound to you?"

"Can Gil come eat and drink, too?"

"I don't see why not," Hector said. "Jeffrey, come here!"

The demonic feline thing came slinking out from under the couch, where it had been listening in on the conversation as only a feline can do. It jumped onto the couch and went to Hector's outstretched hand, accepting a little bit of petting on its misshapen head.

"Would you mind taking a message to Gilrabin for me?"

The little demon made a noise that sounded like an assent, and Hector got to writing a short note of invitation. When he was finished and had folded the paper into an envelope of sorts, he handed it to the feline, who took the note in its mouth, careful not to puncture it with any of its innumerable fangs.

"When you're done, Jeffrey, if Gil comes, you can have some of those cold cuts, too."

The feline did something decidedly un-catlike, sort of like a four-legged dance, then it slipped out the door at a dead run. Much like terrestrial felines, this one appeared almost magically capable of slipping out any door, even if it seemed to be closed and locked. Not for the first time, Hector wondered if it had been a deliberate design choice by the Devil, or if all felinoids naturally possessed the ability.

Once the little demon was away on its errand, Trevor reappeared from the kitchen, overburdened with a tray that held all the things Hector had asked for, and more. In addition to the meat, bread, and dessert, there was also a bowl of fruit, most of which he recognized, some nuts, and what appeared to be some sort of head-on roast bird about the size of a duck, but no duck Hector had ever laid eyes on had fangs.

He decided not to ask about its origin. He had long ago learned that the demon would never bring him anything he was unable to consume without distress. Whatever it was, he decided it must be delicious, and that was the thought he was determined to keep.

"That's a lot more than I expected, Trevor!"

"If Gil come, gotta have lotta food fill her belly," Trevor explained. "She got nice big belly."

The demon seemed impressed by the other demon's considerable charms, and Hector wondered if demons had anything like romantic relationships. Anything was possible, he supposed.

It was not long before the feline was back, Gil tagging along behind. She had brought someone else with her, and Hector was not very sure how he felt about that, but he did not want to appear to be an ungracious host, so he swallowed his unhappiness and welcomed them both to his quarters.

"Well, hello, Gilrabin! Great to see you," he enthused. "Who is your friend?"

"This Nasbornath," Gil replied. "Nasbornath put out hand and shake hands with Hector."

The newcomer, showing a bit of wisdom, extended one enormous paw carefully, never breaking eye contact with the human. Taking a cue from what he was seeing, Hector extended his own hand, closed his fingers around as much of the huge paw as he was able, which wasn't much at all, and then shook it gently.

"Pleased to meet you, Nasbornath," he told the demon. "That's a very big name. Would you be insulted if I called you Nas, for short?"

Gilrabin snorted with laughter.

"Nas for short? Big Nas? I like!" She chortled, her delight infectious to the others in the room. "You okay with Nas, Nasbornath?"

"It's up to him, Gil," Hector told the gleeful demon.

"Nasbornath is her, Hector," Gil giggled. "You bad with telling boys and girls apart!"

Hector flushed a deep red, and Gil whistled appreciatively.

"Hey, pretty red! You not stay that way all the time?"

"Humans turn red like that when they get embarrassed, Gil," Hector explained, once he regained his composure. "I'm usually my normal pasty pale pink."

"Pasty pink not bad, Hector," Gil replied. "Better than orange. Why you embarrassed?"

"I'm embarrassed that I thought Nas was male. And Gil, your color doesn't matter," Hector remonstrated. "I don't care what color anyone is. What matters to me is what kind of person they are. Color doesn't have anything to do with that."

"You call me Nas, is okay," the newcomer told them, her voice soft and even a little bit shy. Her private personality was very different than the one she presented when she was on duty. "Good name."

Gil stepped forward and jovially pounded Nas on the back with an enthusiasm Hector knew would probably cripple, if not outright kill him. He was gladdened once again that Gil was familiar with the frailties of mortal humans, and counted his blessings that Nas was the one getting all the attention.

"So, what has Gil told you about our merry band of lunatics, Nas? You sure you want to become involved with us?"

"Gilrabin say she learn new stuff from not-dead human soul. I ask what, and she say must come to find out. So I come to find out," Nas replied. "What you teach me?"

"Not-dead human soul? Is that how you described me to your friend, Gil?"

"Friend?" the newcomer asked, her faced twisted in confusion. "What 'friend'?"

"Friend what we are, Nas," Gil began before Hector could open his own mouth to explain. "Like each other. Like do things together. Have fun."

"So, not-enemy? What different?"

"No, not same thing, Nas," Trevor broke in after a glance at and a nod back from Gil. "Much better. Know friend have back. Keep you safe. Not like not-enemy, always looking for better thing."

Hector watched the demon turn that over in her jet-black head. All four eyes squinted as she considered what she had been told, a slight frown on her face. He was, he found, a bit touched at Trevor's explanation of what a friend was, and it made him feel even more connected to the funny-looking creature.

And then he wondered when the little demon had gone from being horrifying to look at to simply "funny," and then realized it did not really matter, now did it? Trevor was his friend, as was Gil, and appearances meant nothing. It was all about what they were like inside, in whatever passed for a demon's soul.

"Friend do stuff like this, and other not worry about why," and Gil wrapped all four of her arms around Nas to give her a hug. Hector watched the demon stiffen momentarily, then visibly relax as her *friend* whispered something in one tiny shell-shaped ear. A few seconds later, Gil released Nas and stepped back, although she left one hand on the other's shoulder.

Hector was amazed that Gil had picked up on what friendship was so very quickly and was then able to explain it, albeit in the direct way most demons seemed to express themselves. He was glad the unexpected embrace had not ended in unintentional combat.

"So, that is 'friend'?"

"Kinda. You learn more over time," Trevor explained. "Got something for you. Have this."

Nas took the sticky square of baklava from the plate upon which Trevor offered it and stared at the tasty treat.

"What this?"

"Put in your mouth, chew, and swallow it," Hector told her. He smiled as Nas did just that.

He had not expected the demon to fall to her knees, but she did exactly that. He started forward, and Nas waved him away.

"I fine. What that?" she asked Trevor.

"Baklava," he replied. "Is food."

"Food?"

"You know. Like humans have."

"Humans eat that?" The demon seemed a bit nonplussed. "Is—need good word."

"Wow?" Hector suggested.

"Yes. 'Wow' is good word, Hector," Nas agreed, getting back to her feet. "Is wow."

"I'm glad you like it, Nas," Hector continued, pointing at the coffee table. "We've got a few more things for you to try since you're here."

He went to sit down again and beckoned everyone else to join him. The feline seemed about to resume its station beneath the couch, but the human patted the cushion beside him, and the creature jumped up to sit there. Looking at the tray in front of him, he selected a slice of what appeared to be ham and offered it to the feline. After some judicious sniffing, it ate the offering then sat up, obviously waiting for more. Hector laughed. He did not know if the similarity to a cat was deliberate on Luci's part, but it was indeed there.

It was probably a good thing that Hector liked cats in the first place. He'd named the demon "Jeffrey" in a moment of desperation, but somehow, the name seemed to fit the creature. Hector was not sure where the name had come from, but in that split second where he'd needed to come up with something, the name had come to be quite easily.

The "cat" seemed to decide that it did not want to hide under the couch and instead decided to plant itself on Hector's lap. In what must have been an unconscious response, Hector began to stroke the creature.

Demons, for eons, had been created with a specific purpose, but this one had no designated task. This was something so very new and different. With every small thing that Hector did, that served to help define what the demon was and what it did.

Cats were something that had never before been a part of Hell, although there were likely at least more than a few theologians who might disagree, although their opinions were based on scanty evidence. They were a species far too capricious to be easy residents of the netherworld, as they were not well-suited to obedience.

"Was there something you wanted, Jeffrey?" Hector asked the pseudo-feline in his lap. The creature opened one glowing green eye, stretched lazily, and then went back to sleep. "I suppose not."

"You make friend many different kind demon," Gil noted as she swallowed whatever it was she had grabbed from Trevor's smorgasbord of delicacies. "You not like other humans."

"I didn't think you'd had much experience with humans other than ones who were already dead," Hector said.

"My Lady bring some humans here over centuries, but you first not run screaming," Gil said, licking her lips. "You more strong than other humans. More accepting demons."

"What's to accept, Gil? You seem fine to me. You laugh at my jokes, anyway."

"Jokes? Hah. Being polite," she chortled, mirth dancing in her eyes.

"Polite."

"Anyway, not sure why, but you talk to demons. Other humans try stay away," she said. "Not seem afraid. Not try magic charm keep demons away."

"Now that's just stupid. What sort of 'magic charm' are you talking about"

"Pray stuff," she continued. "My Lady Parent not pay attention, I think. Not you. Not all humans smart like you."

"I'll take your word for that," Hector replied. "There are times I wonder about the choices I've made in my life."

"All beings have question about things they do," Gil said. "Not just humans."

"Even demons?"

"Yes. Even demons do stupid things. Sometimes the stupid things get demons ended."

"I've learned something new today," Hector said. "Thank you for sharing that with me."

"You have question, ask. I do best to answer," Gil told him. There was a chorus of agreement from the other two demons present. Jeffrey just gave him what he had come to think of as "The Look."

"Okay, then, for example, Jeffrey here doesn't speak. What do you do when you have to communicate with a demon who is unable to communicate back with you using speech?"

"You have hard time with that, I think," Gil replied. "You need learn communicate with Jeffrey best way you can. No right way, I think. Try be patient. He try please you."

The demon in question transferred The Look to Gil, who reached down and patted the creature roughly.

"It be fine, Jeffrey," the demon told the diminutive creature. "You learn to let Hector know what need."

It gave a snort, shook its head, snagged another piece of meat from the table, and then sauntered off to a corner to consume its bounty in peace.

"I'm not sure that I'm ever going to be able to figure that thing out," Hector commented. "We had cats when I was a kid, but they were more my Mother's than mine. It didn't matter that I was nice to them, they only seemed to be interested in my opposable thumbs, from what I was able to tell."

"What is 'cat'?" Trevor asked. "Not see one before."

"Ah, I'm sorry. I thought I had explained cats to you before, Trevor. Think of a hairy version of Jeffrey there, but even more aloof," Hector explained. "Some people love cats and some people hate them. I'm not sure why that is, though."

"You like cats?" The demon continued to appear confused, but then, as a being with a limited range of experience, it was like trying to explain the internet to a person from the Dark Ages. That human kept that thought firmly in mind as he sought the proper words for his explanation.

"Very much," Hector replied. "I like how they aren't usually noisy, and they tend to be quite tidy, overall."

"Hairy Jeffrey?" Nas laughed, spraying partially-chewed food out of her mouth as she did so. Although he might sort of resemble a cat in shape, Jeffrey the demon was lightly scaled, with not a hair in sight on his entire mottled hide.

"Nas, it's considered good manners to swallow your food before you start laughing," Hector told the newcomer as he wiped food fragments from the front of his shirt. "People don't normally like having it shared with them in this way. It's rather like not talking with your mouth full of food. Most people don't like to see chewed up food all that much."

Nas froze, her expression becoming stricken.

"Don't panic, Nas," Hector reassured her. "Everyone has to learn manners when eating. This is just one of those things you learn."

"I sorry, Hector," she mumbled and pushed her plate away from her.

"It's all good, Nas. Enjoy your food," and pushed her plate back in front of her after adding a bit more chocolate and baklava to it. "People bond over food."

"Bond?" Naz and Gil asked in unison.

"Get to know one another and become better friends," he explained. "Eating can be a very social occasion."

"We be social, then," Gil said and grabbed something else from one of the platters of food. "You good cook, Trevor. You make more?"

## Twenty-Five

"Trevor said something about our leaving sometime in the next few days," Hector said to Luci. She had called him to her quarters, requesting that he arrive as soon as he was able, no explanation given, but he had discovered early that this was par for the course with the Devil. "Is what he said correct?"

"I may have said something about it to him, but there isn't anything hard and fast about it, Hector," she replied. "It all depends on if I get my work here finished on schedule."

"What else do you have to do?"

"Nosy, aren't you?"

"Oh, I'm sorry," he apologized. "Forget I asked."

"No, it's all right," Luci told Hector. "I've got to get a few more things taken care of, including figuring out how to handle the demons, now that you've taught them about the concept of friendship, rather than being natural backstabbers."

"Shouldn't I have done that?"

"That's not the problem here, Hector," she elaborated. "I could have stopped you from doing that when it first began, but I was interested in seeing how it all would progress. Sort of a sociological experiment, I suppose. I'm glad that they appear capable of learning and change. You're not their overlord and master, so you're someone they don't need to feel threatened by."

"I'm not sure how to take that last bit."

"It's not a bad thing. Not in the least. You're teaching them to think about their actions, instead of doing things on impulse, and that's an excellent lesson,"

Luci continued. "The only problem I can see is that it might make them more accomplished in their plotting."

"Then it might actually be a problem, then," Hector decided. "Is there anything you can do to change what I've wrought?"

"Hector, I'm saying that I don't want to do that," she corrected him. "I think you know that I don't like having to periodically wipe out large numbers of demons when they become monumentally stupid."

"I know it takes a lot out of you to make new ones," Hector noted. "Your recovery time from creating just Jeffrey was notable. I can't fathom how long it takes when you've undertaken the effort of creating even more at once."

"That's not the issue, Hector. Not at all," she disagreed. "I don't like that their being stupid forces me to do things like that. I don't want to be like my Parent, wiping out entire populations because They are pissed off about something. Believe it or not, I prefer not to rule using fear and terror."

"You want them to love you? That's a surprising suggestion, knowing who you are and what you do," his disbelief colored his tone. "Is that really such a good idea?"

"Well, that might be a bit much," she agreed, "but something a bit less than outright fear and hatred, perhaps. I have an easier relationship with my Parent than my demons have with me, and they're not the ones who are being punished. They are doing the job they have been designed to do."

"So, you'd like to be more of an employer they like working for, then?" Hector suggested.

"Perhaps. An interesting description, anyway," Luci agreed.

"I'm curious to see how you'd work something like that out," Hector said, his expression thoughtful. "I wonder how long it would take to accomplish something like that?"

"Unlike my Parent, I'm not omniscient, so I'm as in the dark as you are on that thought."

Hector gave a soft snort and a smile quirked one side of his mouth. He snorted again.

Luci looked at him, eyebrow raised in unspoken query. What was it about this human that made her care even minimally about what he had to say?

But care she did, so she waited.

"I suppose if you start now, you've got enough of a lifetime ahead of you to see it accomplished," Hector said. "Eventually, anyway."

"Are you telling me that I'm old, Hector," she asked with feigned haughtiness.

"No, I am saying that you are eternal my Lady," he replied, doffing an imaginary cap, then rising from his seat to perform an intricate bow that ended in feigned reverential genuflection.

"Oh, go screw yourself, Professor," the Devil said, expression sour as she glared down at the glee glittering in the human's eyes. "I'm sure there is something you could be doing while I'm finishing up around here."

Hector looked up at her, mischief still playing across his expression. Then all the mischief dashed away, to be replaced by slight embarrassment.

"Yes?"

"Would you mind giving me a bit of a hand here," he asked, something that might have been contrition in his voice. "My knee appears to have decided it doesn't want to behave itself just now."

"Oh, you humans and your built-in frailty," Luci sighed and stepped forward, extending her hand, and pulling him to his feet.

"Too many years not paying attention to how fragile a human body can be, no matter how well one cares for it," Hector told her as he settled himself back in his chair.

"Yes, a *human* body," Luci agreed. "Not something I have to worry about, being a Celestial."

"Lucky you."

"Being an immortal has its perks, yes. Now get out of here. I have work to do and you are entirely too accomplished at distracting me," she said, waving her hand at the door. "Scat!"

"Wasn't there something you wanted to speak with me about," he reminded Luci. "You were the one who called me here."

"Ah, yes," she acknowledged. "Thank you for reminding me."

She poured two glasses of bourbon, then picked one up and sat back in her chair. Hector reached out to grab the remaining glass, but paused to look at Luci.

"Something serious?"

"It could be," she replied. She took a long sip of her drink. "I've been thinking about some things that ultimately have to do with you, my friend."

She considered the word as she spoke it.

Friend.

It had become a powerful word in Hell these days. Trevor, Gil, and Nas had been introducing some of the other demons who populated Hell to the concept, with varying degrees of success.

The more common local concept of not-enemy was something they could understand, but with demons, there was always the potential for double-dealing.

"With me? I'm a ridiculously small dot in a vast landscape."

"I know you've heard of the so-called Butterfly Effect, Hector."

"Of course," he replied. "How every action that occurs, no matter how small, ultimately affects the world around it."

He sipped at his own drink. He noted that whatever the origin of that bourbon might be, it packed quite a wallop, but not in anything like a bad way.

"Yes, that," she nodded.

"What is it that I've done, Luci?"

"You've introduced an entirely new concept to the demons, Hector."

"I have?" he asked, registering confusion. "I don't understand. What concept?"

"Friendship, Hector."

"I know they had 'not-enemy', but I wasn't aware that friendship was such an alien concept."

"Hector, my demons are the result of concentrated evil, so they aren't geared to understand the concept of friendship," she explained. "You made Trevor the first demon to have a friend. He, in turn, has bestowed that appellation onto two other demons of whom I am currently aware."

"Gil and Nas, yes."

"Gilrabin and Nasbornath, indeed. In addition to friendship Hector, you have also introduced the idea of nicknames."

"I find that difficult to believe, Luci. How could there not already be nicknames in Hell? I mean, when you deal with others so often, wouldn't such things just come to be, out of hand?"

"Hector, you need to understand that except in specific cases, such as the one that created your Jeffrey, when I create a demon, I give it a name as I do so. That aids in binding the demon to me."

"Sort of like naming a cat makes it yours?"

"Well, never truly yours, but a name at least creates a link between human and cat, yes," she agreed. "The concept of a nickname creates a situation where demons can create their own relationship between themselves and others. A secondary bond, as it were."

Hector nodded his dawning understanding.

"Sort of like how Trevor, Gil, and Nas are with me."

"Exactly, Hector," she agreed. "Those three now interact on a level much removed from 'I must do as the Master says' and shifts it to something more along the lines of 'I wonder if Nas—for example—might like doing this?'. I'm not necessarily going to be part of what they consider when they think that."

"Does that bother you?"

"I can't say that 'bother' is really the right word, but it concerns me a bit," Luci replied. She refilled their glasses, then paused, the bottle still in her hand. "You know, Hector, I'm amazed at the sheer quantity of alcohol you are able to drink and still conduct a sensible conversation."

"My physician has expressed continued amazement that my liver enzyme tests always seem to turn out beautifully. I was stealing sips of ale when I was a kid and began drinking hard liquor when I was in my late teens," he told her. "I'm sure I was drinking entirely too much, but that was a time when it was what one did at the end of a long workday. It was normal. European society, is, as I'm sure you know, very different in its attitude toward alcohol consumption than American society. The Americans are still much more puritan in their beliefs about such things."

"I have found this to be true, Hector," Luci replied. "It's silly, but every society has different morals about all manner of things. from what I can tell, it has been this way since the beginning of human societies."

"I know I seem to have a considerable capacity for alcohol, but I doubt I'd be able to drink you under the table, Luci," he said with a fond smile. "I've seen at least part of your potential capacity, and it's daunting."

"Not even a distillery full of high-octane bourbon could make me so much as slur my words," Luci said. "I believe I would have more than an unfair advantage in such a contest."

"That's a bit sad to think," he observed. "When I drink, it's usually to relax and let my mind wander. Getting a bit drunk has its benefits at times, I must say."

"Yes, it would be nice to become intoxicated sometimes and be able to relax that way," she agreed, "but then, that might lead to other bad habits, such as alcoholism."

"I don't even want to consider the possibility of an alcoholic Prince of Darkness, Luci," Hector continued. "Sounds like too many possibilities for things going terribly, awfully wrong. Even beyond what you're accused of so far."

"You and I both, Hector," she agreed. "Also, I think my Parent might actually put in an appearance to stage an Intervention, and that's not something I care to contemplate."

They shared a shudder of dread at the thought, then both burst into hysterical laughter.

After a few minutes of laughter, Luci sobered.

"As I said, I'm concerned about what the idea of friendship is going to do where my demons are concerned, but I don't want you to try to nip any of that in the bud," she told Hector. "I just wanted to bring it to your attention. I'm not in any danger from them, and they are limited in what they are able to do to *me*, although I am concerned about what they would be able to do to *you*. This could potentially put you in some danger. Does this possibility concern you?"

Hector thought about the Devil's question. He knew that in the event he was attacked, he stood little chance of survival, but that did not concern him. He had known when he applied for the job that there was the potential for death from one angle or another.

"No, it doesn't, Luci," he said. "I knew when I signed up for this job that there was some degree of danger facing me, and I knew that I would have to accept that possibility."

"You seem rather matter-of-fact about this, Hector."

"Do I have any other choice? I mean, really? When I came to you, I knew there was always a chance that you would have reacted badly when I first let you know that I knew who and what you were, but you didn't."

"I'm still not certain why I didn't throw you out on your ass, Hector."

"I think I amused you, to be honest," the human replied. "I think you're used to playing with humans, and maybe you thought I was just another toy for you to play with."

Luci did not answer, but of course he had hit the nail on the head with his suggestion. She was not sure if this was related to her being predictable at all, or if it was some sort of gift the human possessed. It made her feel a bit nervous about allowing him to leave once the trip to Hell was completed. This Hector Rhoades could be a serious issue for her security, and that was something that could not be blown off without thoughtful consideration.

"I admit to having enjoyed playing with you the day we met, Hector," Luci told him. "But as I played, I also discovered that there was far more to you and I began to look forward to the possibilities of our association, and that's why I ultimately invited you along."

"I'm glad that you did, Luci."

"Remy approves of you, too."

"Remy? Really?"

"Indeed. Remy gave you her seal of approval after your meeting at your flat. It seems you impressed her, but she did not share with me what it was that did so."

"I have no idea what I might have done to earn her good favor," Hector confessed. "Although I think I did a great deal of babbling while she waited for me to write my note."

"She implied there was more to your discussion than mere waiting, but I'll not pry."

"Well, if you somehow find out what it was I did to impress her, please let me know. Maybe I can do it again sometime."

The Devil sat back in her chair and laughed. Hector noted that laughter from the Devil was a common thing, but it was nothing like what had been suggested in religious texts. Lucifer's laugh was filled with almost pure mirth with a soupçon of pure joy thrown in to flavor it.

Another bit of misinformation was thrown onto the mental bonfire he'd been tending since their meeting. There had been quite a lot of that going on in the time since their introduction.

"I imagine you'll have a lot to write about once you return to Earth," Lucifer said, watching the human carefully. "You've experienced many things here in Hell that run counter to everything you have been taught. I'm sure your findings would make excellent fodder for discussion, theological or otherwise."

Hector was silent for a time, but Luci could see him biting at the inside of his lower lip. His expression was concerned but more thoughtful than worried.

"It would be nice to be able to write down what I've seen, to be able to read through it every so often to remember things more clearly," he said a few minutes later, looking her in the eye, "But then, I wouldn't want it to perhaps fall into the wrong hands."

"Wrong hands?"

"Someone who might try to use it to hurt you or anyone important to you."

"I'm immortal, Hector, no one can hurt me."

"Yes, but Ms. Sheffield isn't immortal, and I know you care about her. You care about her a *lot*."

Luci stiffened and her expression changed to something very ugly. If Hector did not know the Devil at least liked him, he would have been frightened for himself.

"If anyone lays a finger on her—"

"That's sort of my point, Luci," Hector interrupted her. "And trust me when I say that if anyone tried to hurt her, you'd have to get to the bastard before I did, and good luck with that. She's sweet and delightful and she matters to *you*, so she matters to *me*."

"Why, thank you, Hector!"

"It's friendship, Luci," Hector continued. "You and I are friends, at least I'd like to think we are, so your happiness is important to me."

"You're saying that friendship has both good and bad aspects to it, but you're focusing on the positive," Luci replied. "So, you're saying I should accept that there will be both good and bad results to your introduction of the concept of friendship and deal with it as necessary?"

"You've extrapolated quite a lot out of what little I've said, but yes, that would be my suggestion," he said. "I wanted to ask you something, Luci, and of course, you don't have to answer me, but I'm curious about how many actual friendships you think you've had during your existence."

"Not many, at least, very few I would consider to be a real friendship. Most have just been close acquaintances."

"I imagine it's hard getting into relationships with creatures whose lifespans are like the blink of an eye to you," Hector suggested. "I couldn't bring myself to get a mouse or a hamster as a pet when I was a youngster, since their lifespan is so very short."

"An interesting comparison to make, Hector," she said. "I had not made the same one myself. I'll have to use that one sometime, with your kind permission. You modern types certainly have come up with some creative descriptions."

"Of course," Hector replied, smiling. "Always happy to lend a hand."

"Realize that I may have to come to you with an 'I told you so' at some time in the future, Hector."

"I'll take that chance, Luci. You're in a unique position to do that just about anytime, after all."

"Very true, my friend," she agreed. "Even if I have to visit Heaven to poke you with a finger."

"Would your Parent be okay with you doing something like that?"

"They wouldn't care in the least. I can go wherever I like, as long as I get my job done," Lucy replied. "It's not my preferred place to be, as I don't get along well with my siblings. It's sort of like a family holiday dinner ending up in conflict of one sort or another."

"My wife and I tended to avoid those whenever possible," Hector mused. "My mother wasn't very fond of her at all. She had hoped that I would marry the daughter of an old friend of hers."

"Seriously? Your mother tried to set up an arranged marriage?"

"Nearly that, but it didn't work, especially once my father discovered her lunatic plan."

"I'm sure that didn't go over well at all."

"I think it may be part of what eventually caused him to pack up and move out."

"Your parents were divorced?"

"Oh, no, neither believed in divorce, so they simply took up the own residences," Hector explained. "If they had relationships outside of marriage, I remain gratefully unaware of that."

"You were raised Roman Catholic then?" She knew his answer from what she had read in the information Remy collected for her, but pretended ignorance to see what his response would be.

"No, Anglican. While the Church doesn't prohibit divorce, my parents still felt that marriage was something reflecting a lifelong commitment," Hector said. "They fought so much while I was growing up, I think they should have at least separated many years before that. I'm sure it would have made my childhood at least a little bit happier."

"I would suggest, Hector, that your childhood, as you experienced it, helped to form you into the person you are today," Luci suggested. "That's not a bad thing, when you come to think about it."

"I'll take your word for it," the human replied, making a face. "With only one Parent, you wouldn't have had the yelling and the anger that I did in my own childhood."

"You're right, we didn't," Luci said. "We came to be as mature beings. There was no childhood, but we fought then and continue to do so until today. Our familial relationship is difficult."

"You aren't close to any of your siblings?"

"No, I'm not. There is something about each of us that makes us uncomfortable spending much time at all in one another's presence," Luci said. "It seems to increase our antagonism toward one another."

"Have you ever tried to work through all of that and perhaps at least become amiable toward one another?"

"I've lost track of everything I have tried over the millennia, Hector. Nothing has been successful. I'm beginning to think it's something our Parent did to keep us apart."

"I can't imagine why They would do something like that."

"They were just learning about families and relationships when they made us. Perhaps we were sort of an experiment before They put Their efforts into creating Substance and then Life."

"I'll take your word for it, Luci," Hector said. "I've got so much to think about now, I can't keep up."

"Well, we've chatted long enough and I really do need to get some work done here, so get your shapely ass out of here and let me get started."

"I hear and obey!" He gave her a jaunty salute.

"Oh, just get out."

"Yes ma'am!"

## Twenty-Six

Hector had found some favorite places to explore in his time in Hell, and he had decided to introduce some of his new friends to them. At first, he had considered that this might be boring to them at this point in their very long existences, but then, they likely had never explored for the sheer fun of it.

"Why we go on long walk, Hector?" Trevor asked when the subject was first broached. "Everything we need right here."

"That's not the point of hiking, Trevor," Hector had explained. "You do it to get some exercise and maybe have some fun while you do it."

"Exercise?"

"Uh, well, I guess demons wouldn't have to worry about that, but living things often do well doing it," the human adjusted course. "But it's always good to have some fun when you can, right?"

"Is true, Hector," Trevor allowed with a nod. "Where you want to go?"

"I'd like to explore the places I've not visited before and thought you might like to come along with me."

The demon appeared to consider the idea, making a face, which Hector only recognized because of his long association with Trevor. Then Hector recognized a decision being made.

"You like climb?"

"Well, as long as I have at least a chance of coming back alive, anyway. I don't think that's something you have to take into consideration, as a demon."

Trevor laughed his naturally sepulchral laugh. If one did not know it was genuine mirth, they might think it was indicative of evil intent. Fortunately, Hector had known the demon long enough that he knew the creature harbored no ill intent. Trevor was, inherently, a very good person.

"I keep you safe, silly human!"

"I certainly hope you do, Trevor!"

Hector found that it felt good that the demon was comfortable enough with him to say such things. It felt more like the banter between friends than that of master and servant, which, officially, their relationship was when it came right down to brass tacks.

"When you want go?"

"I was thinking perhaps tomorrow, after an early breakfast."

"What is early breakfast to you, Hector?"

"Before that awful sound starts the first time in the day," Hector suggested

"Okay, Hector, I make breakfast for you then. Big or little?"

"I expect I'll be expending a lot of energy, so maybe something in between? Too much and I'll just want to go back to bed again."

Trevor laughed.

"I make you good breakfast, Hector. I know you like it."

"I'm certain I will, Trevor," Hector agreed. "I have absolutely no doubt of that, my friend."

"Are there any maps of Hell I could take a look at?"

"No map," the demon shook his head. "No need, really. We be here long enough to know everything."

"So, you'll serve as our map, so to speak."

"Guess so, Hector. That okay with you?"

"As long as we don't end up getting lost, it's all fine with me."

"Good to hear, Hector. I look forward to it."

"I'm going to hit the sack early, so a little light supper would be nice before I do."

"Something simmering on back burner for you, Hector. You get comfortable and I go get it."

Hector was privately glad that Trevor had insisted upon bringing food and drink along with them for their trek across Hell. Yes, water and some dried meat would have been fine, but there was something more than a little satisfying about dining on something that resembled grouse and wild rice whilst sitting on the edge of a high precipice. The wine the demon had chosen was excellent.

He had had to remind himself more than once during the course of the day that the demon was well-nigh indefatigable, so there was no need for him to offer to carry the bulging backpack full of supplies Trevor insisting upon bringing along.

"We not know what need, so being safe and brought all."

"All?"

"Silly Hector," the demon laughed. "You make good joke."

"Trevor, I've learned that you're not necessarily joking when you say things," Hector replied. "Remember the garlic jerky?"

The demon laughed so hard his entire body began to shake with mirth.

"Nas make fun faces that day! May not have nose, but still taste garlic good," Trevor chortled. "I make more for you before you and my Lady go on next trip."

"Trevor, I appreciate the thought, but I think that if my breath was anything less than springtime fresh, she'd throw me out of Hell bodily."

"You not know that sure, Hector," the demon protested with a grin. "Have more and see."

"Alas, my friend, I lack your sense of certainty in this. Let's just not and say we did."

"You right bastard, Hector."

"At your service, Trevor," the human said, tugging at his forelock. "I aim to please."

Hector looked around, surprised at the sheer amount of ground they had covered during the day's expedition. He could see familiar landmarks dotting the landscape from back the way they had come.

Hell was pretty uniform in its landscape when it came right down to it. When pressed for more information, Trevor had admitted that the most variation was present in the miniature Hells that served as torture chambers for damned souls. Of course, they were not designed for those souls to enjoy them, so it was not as though they were vacation spots.

There were plenty of tall rock formations and cliffs to climb where they walked, but no spectacular views to be had. Hell was designed to be ugly after all, with the Divine Architect being the one who had created it so. The closest it came to beauty was yet another torture: A pristine Heavenly-appearing city that used bars as a barrier between itself and Hell.

Trevor explained that the city beyond the bars was not real, but was indeed yet another torture for condemned souls. The place known as "Heaven" was in yet another reality other than the one Hell occupied and it required literal Divine intervention for a soul to pass from one to the other. No one could escape from one or the other without the Divine Parent making it so.

"You know a lot for a work-a-day demon, Trevor," Hector said once the demon had finished his explanation.

"I read a lot when can, Hector. Sometimes not a lot to do when soul is doing what must do. Not like be bored. Is why I can cook now."

"Can cook? You're a genuine chef, my friend!"

"Is nice to say, Hector, but I not have kitchen of own. Maybe I ask my Lady someday, but not now."

"You want to be able to cook for more than just we few?"

"I like cook, Hector," Trevor said. "I like sharing food with others and teach them 'bout good foods. Is way to make friend."

"The key to a man's heart is through his stomach, they say," Hector murmured.

"Demons not men."

"We can always modify the saying, Trevor," Hector said.

"Demons not have hearts."

"Trevor, you are making this unnecessarily difficult, you know."

"Sorry."

"There is nothing for you to be sorry about, my friend," the human corrected the demon. "You just have to learn not to be quite so literal about things."

"I not understand."

"It's how even though words may seem to mean one thing, you can also read or hear them to mean something else," Hector explained. "We'll work on that, okay?"

"You teach many new things, Hector," the demon said after some thought. "Sometimes hard to understand, but I try anyway. Is good to learn, even if from human."

"So, who's the right bastard now, Trevor?"

A giggle came from behind them. It was an ugly sound with no real humor in it.

Demon and human spun to see a dainty-looking creature observing them from a nearby rock. It was humanoid in appearance, but the size of a spider monkey, including a delicate tail that was curled around the base of the rock upon which it stood.

"Pirippa! What you do here?"

"I saw you coming this way, so I followed," the creature said in a high-pitched voice. Its bright red eyes had yellow slits for pupils. Against the jet black of its black skin, the demon's appearance was more than a little jarring. Its entire substance radiated ill-will so substantial Hector felt he could almost touch the negative emotions the creature possessed. He determined to do his best to deescalate things and deliberately put a smile on his face.

"Pirippa? My name is Hec— "

"I know who you are, human," the creature interrupted him. "I don't think I much like your being here. You upset the ways things should be."

"I'm the guest of your lady Lucifer," Hector reminded the grating little creature. "I don't think your opinion possesses much weight in this conversation."

"I don't much care, human," the creature continued. "With you so far away, why anything could happen to you and you would end up either in Heaven, or here in Hell, but you would no longer be wandering around making trouble."

"I? Making trouble? I have no idea what you're talking about!"

"My lady Lucifer has more important things to worry about than shepherding your weak carcass here and there," the angry little thing said. "She has far more pressing concerns."

By this time, Trevor was shaking with rage. Hector could see the muscle under his skin rippling as the demon did his best to contain his anger—no—rage. He had never before seen the demon as angry as he appeared to be now.

"Pirippa, I'm sorry that my presence here upsets you, but it is what it is," Hector said. "For now, I'm her traveling companion and my job is to make things easier for her. I consider myself quite honored to have been given that position."

The little demon cocked her head to one side and seemed to see the human for the first time. The anger was still there, but it had softened a tiny bit, and Hector saw his opportunity.

"Have you ever had the opportunity to try food, Pirippa? I mean, real food?"

"Food! What is so special about food?"

"Trevor, do you still have some of what we had for lunch on hand?"

Without a word, the demon produced a small metal platter of leftover grouse and what was left of the wild rice. He handed it to Hector, who in turn, offered it to the imp.

"Have a taste of this, Pirippa. See what you think," and he gestured to Trevor to pour a small amount of wine into a glass which he also offered over.

Putting out a tentative paw, the demon picked up a piece of grouse and brought it to her nose, sniffing at it carefully. A moment later, seeming to have satisfied herself as to its safety, she took a small bite of the treat and began to chew it.

Hector watched with interest as Pirippa's face relaxed and her lips shifted from a glower into a smile as the tasty juices from the meat were released by the vigorously chewing demon. At a certain point she finished the piece tried the rice, and found it, too, to her liking, and finished that off as well. At that point she swallowed down the wine in a single motion.

"You learned this from the humans, Trevor?" She asked, once food and drink had been dispensed with. "This all had to do with this human here?"

"If not for Hector, Pirippa, I still be torturing and not cooking," Trevor agreed, handing her a chocolate truffle from his carefully curated collection. "You like food?"

"Yes, I like food," the creature said, nodding. She sniffed at the lump of chocolate in her hand. "You make food like this everyday?"

"I try make different things for different meal, but yes, in way I make food like this every day."

The newcomer put the candy in her mouth and bit down on it. Chef and human watched with satisfaction as the demon seemed to lose herself in the olfactory orgasm that resulted. For some reason, demons all seemed to react the same way with their first taste of the stuff.

"Would you like to join us for dinner tomorrow night, Pirippa," Hector asked the creature once she had finished the rich, dark chocolate candy. "When we're done, we could play some cards."

"Cards? What are cards?" The demon demanded, her face bristling with suspicion.

246

After the demon was certain his human charge slept, he crept off to visit Lucifer. Once he arrived knocked politely at her door.

"Come!"

Entering, Trevor found the Devil sitting on her couch, drink in hand. She gestured for him to come forward.

"So, is our guest settled for the night?"

"He snoring loud, my Lady," Trevor informed her proudly. "Put thing you give me in soup he have for dinner. Hector fall asleep quick."

"I hate doing that, but I wanted the opportunity to speak with you without interruption," she said. "You are never to tell him that you gave him a sleeping draft, Trevor. That would make me more than a little annoyed at you."

"No worry, my Lady. I not tell. You the big boss," he assured her with no trace of insincerity. "What you need, my Lady?"

"I wanted your opinion of the human, Trevor," the name sounded odd in her mouth, considering that was not the name she had given him upon his creation, but it had become his name since Hector arrived, and so it would remain.

"Hector good human," he opined. "Not sure why I have him when he come, but glad I do, my Lady."

"Why is that?"

"Hector teach me things."

"Oh? Such as what?"

"He teach me be strong. Not let other demons bully. Stand up for self."

"Couldn't you learn that from other demons?"

"Other demons not friends, my Lady. Just not-enemies or enemies. Hector is friend, which different. He not do things for self. He do things for everyone he like, and sometimes, even, for those he not like."

This surprised Luci. She was not aware of whatever that last bit might be. She asked the demon to elaborate.

"He meet Pirippa on hike other day. Pirippa not like having loose alive human and say so. I afraid I have to call you to help," he explained. "Hector keep me from doing stupid thing by try to fight."

"Indeed. It would surprise me more if he had not. And then?"

"Hector apologize for getting in Pirippa way and invite to dinner and to play cards next night."

Luci knew the demon Pirippa very well, and knew the demon was not the most tolerant of her minions. Small she might be, but inside that roiling manifestation of concentrated sin, she possessed a rage that could only be quailed by the greater rage and power of her Lord and Master.

"What did Pirippa say when he offered?"

"Pirippa not understand at first, so she have me explain cards."

"And…"

Trevor grinned beatifically, which was quite the accomplishment for a demon.

"Pirippa favorite card game be Bridge."

"Bridge."

"Yes," the demon replied firmly. "Bridge."

Bridge was a game where one had to play with a partner and be able to work well with that partner. That was something Luci would never have thought possible.

Until now.

It made her consider her feelings on the entire "friend" subject. Was it good or was it food for disaster? In this instance, it appeared it could be a vehicle for positive things.

"When not have foursome, she like Gin, too," the demon continued.

"You don't say."

"I do say," the demon averred with a decisive downward jerk of his lumpy chin. "She making new deck of card art now. Not know she could art. Surprise me."

"'Draw', not 'art'," Luci corrected absently, lost in thought and equally surprised. Her old and familiar world seemed suddenly to be very far away indeed.

Luci was startled to hear that yet another demon was displaying previously unknown gifts. Cooking, cooperative competition, and who knew what else? And now, her demons were discovering actual art.

It seemed Hector was introducing far more than friendship to her minions. He was creating a society of sorts. One that had time for more than work. One that had the desire and time for things that existed just because they could. What did that mean for the future of the world she had ruled for so very long?

It was probably a good thing that Hell was developing. With so very many individuals being a part of it, it would be natural that things would grow and develop, but was that good or bad?

"You need more, my Lady?" The demon was asking her. "Need to go back before Hector wake up. Sleep stuff only last so long."

Luci was brought back to the present and looked at the demon. There was deference, and perhaps even concern on the misshapen face.

"You truly like Hector, don't you, Trevor?"

"Hector good friend, my Lady," he replied stoutly. "Like him lots."

*Like him lots.* What a thing! In her very long experience, demons did not like much of anything.

"I'm pleased to hear that, Trevor," she said. "I hope you two stay friends for a very long time. Friends are a good thing, I think. You can head back to him."

The demon turned to leave, stopped, and turned back.

"Yes, Trevor? Was there something else?"

"My Lady, not want to make mad, but I like you, too. Lots. Maybe even friend."

"Me? Your friend?"

"Boss can be friend, I think," Trevor said. "Different kind friend, but still friend. Is okay?"

Luci thought about it. Was it okay? She was friends with Remy, her beloved Myra, and now, the curious Hector. Were those friendships okay?

Yes. Yes they were.

"It's fine, Trevor," she told him with a genuine smile. "I'm glad that you consider me to be your friend. I don't think I've got very many of those at all."

"You maybe have more than think, my Lady," the demon said. "Demons just not know that what they think. Hector help me understand feeling. Hector make me know feeling is good to have."

"We're going to have to have a conversation, one of these days, Trevor," she decided. "Things are becoming very different around here, I think."

"Conversation?"

"Yes, a conversation. You, me, and Hector."

"Okay, my Lady! I go now!"

"Scat, Trevor!"

The demon did not move. She should see him screwing up his courage and wondered what new surprise he had in store for her. Finally, he spoke.

"You got plan for dinner my Lady?"

What in the world?

"No, why?"

"I make roast tonight. Veg. Big choc'lat dessert. Got plenty. You come have, too. Drink, laugh, play cards, have fun. Jonny bring special cask in morning. Drink and laugh more."

So now Jonny was sharing her beer with others? The sneaky little bastard!

"Is this an invitation, Trevor? Did Hector ask you to do this?"

"No, my Lady. I like to have you there."

Friendship producing further unexpected results. It gave her a shiver of dread, but she did not feel like bursting Trevor's tenuous bubble of satisfaction.

"Of course I'll come, Trevor. I should be done here in a few hours. Does that fit with your dinner plans?"

"Of course, my Lady! I see you then!"

The demon nearly seemed to dance out the door, he was so happy. Bemused, Luci watched as Trevor gently closed the door behind him. Such a different creature now than the incurious one who had been assigned the care and guarding of an unexpected living visitor.

The interview over, Lucifer rose and went to grab a cup of strong black coffee. Then, eschewing her comfortable couch, returned to her well-appointed desk to drink it. Might as well get at least a little more done, after all.

But then, her thoughts returned to Hector, Trevor, Gil, and Nas. These days, they were never far from her thoughts, if she was being honest with herself.

She sat back in her high-backed black leather chair, put her stocking-clad feet atop the corner of her desk, and laced her fingers together behind her head. Luci's cup of coffee sat atop her desk, cooling and forgotten, as she considered everything she had just learned.

"Hector Rhoades, against all odds, discovers who I really am, and comes to me with a proposition," she mused to the bust of Dante that rested on her desk. "I agree to consider that request and ultimately do, despite the poor outcomes of previous living human incursions into my domain."

Dante kept his silence, as he always did. He had always been an excellent listener.

She brought one hand forward and nibbled at her impeccably varnished index fingernail before remembering herself and returning it to its previous position at the back of her head. The Lord of Hell she might be, but it was still a pain in the ass to make time for her manicurist. There was no sense in damaging Rae's excellent work if there was no pressing need to do so.

"My assistant decides, quite unlike her, that she not only approves of, but likes the human in question. My girlfriend seconds that notion. So, I decide that I will accede to his request and I invite him along for the ride. Hell, it might even be fun!"

"Then, despite all previous experience on my part, the human appears completely unflappable once we arrive. No unconscious drawing back. No wide eyes. No stink of fear," she continued. "He seems to take it all in stride, even when I assign what I truly believe to be the dullest demon I have to be his caretaker."

"What does this paragon of humanity do then? He bestows a name upon this hapless creature and not only that, a real name, rather than something ugly and mocking. He develops an actual friendship with the creature, and then extends that boon to other demons who have never before known such a thing could exist."

"The human's interaction with Trevor the demon enables me to discover that it has talents about which I had been completely unaware. This bothers me, as I should know everything about my demons."

The otherwise empty chamber offered no answers to Luci's commentary, keeping her secrets close to its hollow heart. There is nothing more loyal, after all, than an empty room, when talking to oneself.

Lucifer wished she could have discussed all of this with Myra, but that would require her to take a short trip back to Earth, which could not happen for another month and a half at the very least. She wondered if she would have even that long before discovering some new twist to her current situation.

Thinking of Myra, she wondered if the young woman would be able to not only survive but also thrive even half as well as Hector had. The girl had shown remarkable self-possession when she had seen Luci's "true" self, but would such an unshakeable attitude persist in a Hellish setting?

And then Luci marveled that she was even considering the idea that Myra would agree to come with her on such a journey. A part of her said that of course the young woman would come, while her innermost self reminded her that the human woman had the right to say No to any such suggestion, and that in her own best interests, she should.

"Get hold of yourself, Lucifer!" she admonished herself. "You've got work to finish up and then you have to start planning for the next segment of the expedition. No time for silly, romantic thoughts!"

She picked up her laptop and made a show of going through the spreadsheet pictured on its faintly flickering screen. A few moments thereafter, Luci began to work in earnest.

After all, even with the potential chaos brought to Hell by the addition of a living, breathing soul, work still would not complete itself. That alone kept Lucifer from throwing up her hands and giving up entirely on her day.

The chamber listened in its enigmatic way, its response only audible to ears far more supernatural in nature than the Devil's. Those ears noted the exchange and filed it away for future consideration as it took another sip of its seventh Mai Tai of the day.

## Twenty-Eight

When Luci arrived at Hector's place, as she had come to think of it, she found the party in full swing.

The human was holding court at the bar he'd set up in the main room, pouring drinks and regaling four demons she had not known he was acquainted with with stories of his adventures in the Army, while Nas, Gil, Pirippa, and another demon, a guard from the dungeons, appeared to be playing Bridge, pointedly ignoring the giddy madness as they did. Amidst all of this merriment, Trevor was running around making sure that hors d'oeuvre trays were kept filled with tasty treats.

"Where does a girl find a drink," she asked Jeff the demon, who greeted her at the door. The creature promptly escorted her to the bar, jumping up on it and nudging Hector's elbow with his nose. "Ah, thank you, Jeff!"

The otherwise voiceless demon chirruped what sounded like a polite reply and then jumped back down to oversee the card game, which appeared to be becoming a bit heated. Luci watched for a moment as the little demon employed a judicious claw to remind them to behave themselves. There was a startled yelp and then things calmed down considerably. Satisfied at the development, she returned her attention to her host.

"Welcome, my Lady," Hector said, grinning broadly. "What can I get you while we wait for dinner to be served?"

"Your best bourbon, my man!"

Putting on a show, Hector searched through the bottles arrayed on the shelves behind him before pulling out a familiar-looking bottle.

"Now, where did you get that, Hector?"

"Remy must have slipped it into my bag before we came here, my Lady," he replied. "I only found it in there recently. There was a pocket in there I hadn't discovered previously."

Lucifer laughed.

"Keep looking. She has those things made with more pockets than you would ever think possible. Knowing her, she's got a horse stashed in there, complete with an enormous stack of hay and choice of tack!"

"You don't mean--?"

"Yes, I do. The hard part was talking the horse into climbing into it. I found that blindfolds were my best option there."

"You blindfolded the horse? That actually makes sense."

"No, I blindfolded myself and let Remy do the dirty work," she said. "It was just too much to contemplate watching."

"That bad?"

The Devil just stared at him, daring Hector to continue. He took the hint and relented.

"Doesn't the horse run out of hay and water in there or something?"

"I have no idea how she does it, Hector. All I know is that I had two horses in my bag at one point in the 1700s, and because of certain unavoidable circumstances, they were in there for six to eight months and did not require attention. She most likely shoved an imp in there to act as a groom. I have no idea."

"I thought imps couldn't leave Hell."

"Different kind of imp. Magical summoning sort of thing," Luci explained. "Remy was a sorceress when I first met her. Any imp would be bound to the bag."

"Sort of like a genie in a lamp."

"Indeed. Just that," Luci agreed. "It's just that 'the genie of the bag' lacks flair. So—imp."

"Ah, so that's why she provides the bags!"

"Exactly. They're her thing. She's made a couple hundred of them over the centuries. I keep them stored securely in a storage room attached to my office. Anyone found in there would have a lot of explaining to do, and they'd have to explain quickly."

"I have absolutely no need or desire to do any investigating of your sanctum sanctorum, I can assure you of that, Luci."

Lucifer looked at her empty glass, then up at the human, and then back down into the void of her glass.

"You're a lousy host, Hector. Where's my refill?"

At the appointed time, Trevor asked all of the guests to take their places at the table. The demon had even taken the time to create nameplates for each guest. Luci suspected Pirippa had had something to do with them, as they were ornate things decorated in lilies and skulls.

Pirippa was nothing if not a classicist when it came to all things related to Hell. Fortunately, she had gone with a Day of the Dead theme for the skulls, so they were much more colorful than they might otherwise have been.

"Who designed the nameplates? They're— lovely," Luci asked, picking hers up and looking at it closely.

"I did," Pirippa answered, verifying the Devil's educated guess. "The first ones were all black and white, but Hector suggested adding color. He was right. They look much better than they would have otherwise."

"As you're the artist, Pirippa, you might consider signing them," Hector suggested. "Let people know who did the work."

"Sign? I don't write, Hector," the demon replied, making a face.

"If you don't write, then come up with some sort of picture that is unique to you and put it somewhere on all of your work."

The demon seemed to consider his suggestion, brightened, and then nodded.

"I'll work on something, Hector," she said, bestowing a rare smile on the helpful human. "Thank you for the suggestion."

Luci marveled that once again, the human had managed to tame one of the more violence-prone denizens of Hell. And once again, he had managed it without having to resort to violence.

The first course was an amazing French onion soup that appeared to have been babied and carefully managed from the very beginning. Each serving came in its own miniature brown and cream French onion soup tureen.

Dipping a cautious spoon into the bowl, the Devil took an experimental bite. Yes, Trevor had shown himself to be a good cook, but this was the sort of soup one did not treat carelessly.

Any negative thoughts vanished as the flavor of the soup exploded over her tongue, hitting all the correct notes. Hell, not simply the flavor, but everything having to do with the offering.

The broth was thick and rich, teeming with caramelized onions, then topped with lightly toasted sliced baguettes, topped with plenty of thick shreds of mozzarella cheese, which was all then put into a broiler so the cheese could melt and then brown nicely.

It surpassed anything Myra's temperamental chef could have created, Luci realized. Even that miraculous soup of his paled in comparison. What was it about this single human that caused her demons to excel in things they might otherwise never have even considered?

Conversation died out as the guests devoured the soup, with the only sound in the room being the smacking of lips and the eventual sound of spoons scraping out every last bit of onion and cheese from their hiding places.

"This soup is absolutely amazing," Hector said, voicing what seemed to be the universal opinion of all the guests, judging from the nods and smiles that resulted from his words. "I'm pleasantly stunned."

"As are we all, I think," Pirippa commented. "Thank you for inviting me, Hector. I had no idea what I was missing."

"I'm just glad you were able to come, Pirippa," the human replied. "You're always welcome in my little corner of the world."

The demon looked surprised at the open invitation and murmured a polite thank you in reply. Luci noted the exchange and reconsidered her opinion of the creature.

Conversation resumed, Trevor removed the empty bowls from the table and return to his kitchen, promising to return soon with the second course. Luci kept to herself the knowledge that as an appetizer, a soup would have been a lighter one, as their host did not yet know better. There was no point in making the demon feel bad.

"Well, Hector, was this anything like you expected when you decided to come visit me?"

"Not in the least, Lucifer," he replied. "I was still in that whole Dante frame of mine, I think."

"Dante," she snorted. "Now that one was more than a little too creative, I think."

"I've looked for multiple levels of hell, and I haven't been able to find them."

"That is because they're not necessary, Hector," she laughed. "That's because each chamber is tailored to the specific damned soul. Hell is certainly more than large enough to handle countless souls without having to add even a second floor!"

This time, the laughter came from all around the table.

At that point, Trevor emerged once again from the kitchen carrying a heavy covered silver platter. It looked as though he had spent quite a long time getting it shined to mirrored perfection, and that had likely been the case. He placed it on the table, admonished his guests to leave it be, and then disappeared back into his food-driven domain.

A few minutes later, he returned with more covered platters. They were distributed artfully around the table, but he took his place directly in front of the large platter and with a flourish, removed the cover.

An enormous roast of what smelled like beef was revealed, the aroma almost maddening in its perfection. There was just the right amount of char on the outside, and Lucifer felt her stomach beginning to tumble with greed at the sight and smell of the thing.

"That looks absolutely amazing, Trevor," she told the demon. "I can't wait to try it."

"How you like roast, my Lady," he asked her politely "What cut you like?"

"Ah, well, I would like a piece about an inch thick, on the rarer side," she told him and waited to see what he would do.

Producing a dangerous-looking knife, the demon very carefully cut into the roast at a particular point. Slicing downward, it was easy to see that the meat was quite tender. When it fell into two pieces, Luci could see that the meat was done to perfection. The center was red and juicy, with an appropriate amount of fat distributed throughout.

"Oh, my word," she breathed as she beheld the minor miracle before her. "I'm looking forward to my first bite, Trevor!"

The demon preened a bit.

"You get soon, my Lady. Few other things to add to plate."

With that, he uncovered the other platters to reveal what appeared to be mashed potatoes, green bean casserole, something like sweet potatoes, carrots, and some less identifiable but no less enticing side dishes.

Each guest was presented with the cut they desired, although if they did not state a preference, Luci could see that Trevor took care to offer only the very best of the remaining slices after having served his Master and then Hector. At least a spoonful of each of the side dishes was added to each dinner plate, and then the plates were delivered to their intended dinner guest.

Lucifer looked down at the contents of her plate with undisguised greed. She could not remember the last time she had been presented with such a sumptuous repast in Hell. Every bit of the food she addressed looked as though it had been perfectly prepared.

The rest of the dinner party waited until Luci rook her first bite of the beef before they tucked into their own.

It was immediately clear to her that Trevor knew about allowing the meat to rest before slicing into it. The juices had been pulled back into the center of the meat, allowing it to remain juicy and tasty. The little bit of fat she had included with her first bite gave a sweet, rich accompaniment to the roasted muscle.

She suspected that the roast was actually from one of the aurochs she kept in a far corner of Hell. Its sheer size certainly suggested that was a distinct possibility. No Earthly cow had ever boasted a prime rib of this size. She also suspected that Trevor would be creating every beef dish he could think of until the rest of the carcass had been disposed of. That left her looking forward to the possibility of marrow bones, which was something she always enjoyed but rarely had the opportunity to have over her past century on Earth.

Humans could be entirely too hidebound at times for her comfort. Such things as marrowbones, oxtails, tongue, and tripe, which had once been normal inexpensive so-called "peasant" food for humanity, began to be disdained in favor of more rarified items as human societies became less rural in nature.

The Devil decided she would have to make certain that Trevor knew those items would be welcome on her dinner plate. She wondered if the demon might have found his gifts sooner if he had not spent so very long shoveling the end product of feasts such as the one he was now serving.

After an untold period of time, Luci realized that all conversation at the table had come to a halt. Coming back to herself, she looked around to see what might have occurred.

Trevor had placed a magnificent dessert in the center of the table. It appeared to be some sort of enormous tiramisu, delicately layered, and glistening with the alcohol that had been carefully poured over it.

"It seems nearly a sin to cut into thing," Hector remarked, eyes wide with appreciation for the magnificent creation that graced his table. "But cut it we must, if we are to do justice to our most splendid chef!"

Said splendid chef bowed as low as his own stature allowed, the tentacles atop his head waving merrily. Luci wondered if the demon was aware that his emotions were telegraphed by those tentacles, when he otherwise worked so hard to appear as disinterested as possible.

"Would you please do the honors, my Lady," Hector asked Luci, extending the cake blade, handle first, to her.

Taking the blade, Lucifer moved to the side of the table, where it would be easier to address the cake and cut it properly. She looked down at it and gave a sad smile.

"Thank you, Trevor, for preparing this most sumptuous meal, and also for taking the time to create this most wonderful-appearing dessert," she said. Then she cut into the thing, the cake blade slicing cleanly through it, leaving behind cut marks that suggested surgical precision.

Placing the first piece on a dessert plate, she handed it to the demon, who took it with surprise and then something resembling reverence

"You sure, my Lady," the demon asked. "I just cook."

"Trevor you have done a splendid job here, and tonight everyone else has eaten before you," she replied, her voice soft. "I think that, for dessert, you deserve to have the very first piece. You have more than earned it."

With that, she cut a piece for each of the guests, ending with a dainty piece for herself. She went back to her seat and took a tentative bite of the treat.

"Once again, surprised, but not surprised," she said to the room at large "I don't know how Trevor will ever manage to outdo himself, as this seems to be as close to perfection as one might come."

There were murmurs of approval from the others as they savored each bite of the fabulous dessert. Cappuccinos accompanied the final course, with the demons taking their lead from the Devil and the human as to how to address it. Well, all the demons except for Pirippa, who had not yet learned to pay attention.

Ever the considerate host, Trevor replaced the empty cup with a fresh cappuccino. The small demon looked confused, but then the ghost of a smile, a real smile, blossomed on the hideous little face.

"Thank you very much, Trevor," she told him, her voice soft and even a bit shy.

"Glad you like, Pirippa," the blue demon intoned in his own insanely deep voice. "Drink up. Make more if want."

Was that something like flirtation, Luci wondered, as she watched the by-play between the two. That made for an interesting development. It appeared to be something deeper than lust, certainly. The idea of romance between demons was a little disturbing to her, as Hell was not one of those places that had ever been considered in conjunction with such a thing, especially when one of those demons was spiky little Pirippa.

Lucifer remembered the day she had coalesced the demon.

She had been irritated that day, after having had to bring some other idiot demons up short. At least she had discovered their disobedience before it had spread very far at all, but she had still been required to make a few examples, and that always left her in a bad way. The anger and resentment she had felt about the whole thing had, it seemed, been infused into her newest demon. If she'd realized what she had done, and been thinking clearly enough, she would have thrown it back into the pool and created a different one, instead.

Pirippa had been an object lesson for her, and she had never made such an error again. Ever since that fateful day, she had made it a point to ground before reaching into the glowing pool of sin and evil.

With that thought, she wondered how coalesced sin and evil could develop decidedly different aspects once made solid. One would think that such creatures would be the exact opposite of compassionate, but she was lately finding that was not the case at all. She came to a decision.

"Trevor, Gil, I have some questions for you," she announced. "In fact, I have questions for you all."

All eyes turned to regard Lucifer, all other discussions forgotten or abandoned.

"Yes, my Lady," Gil asked respectfully. "What you need?"

"I know that some of you have developed friendships," she told them. "Before our esteemed Hector came to visit, did anyone here have friendships?"

Trevor made a face, sucking at his upper lip as he cogitated. Then his eyes brightened and he took a deep breath.

"Hector teach me friend," he mused. "Before have not-enemies, but not same thing as friend."

"As I recall, yes, Trevor," Lucifer replied. "What is the difference?"

"With not-enemy, demon know not have to worry too much 'bout watching back," the demon explained. "Friend different. Friend someone demon can depend on for help. Friend someone to do things more than work. Have fun."

"Can you not have fun with a not-enemy?"

"Not feel safe enough, my Lady," Trevor admitted.

"How does a word make that any different?"

"Hector showed us, I think, that we can be nice to one another without expecting anything in return," Pirippa piped up. "No quid quo pro in sight. Just kindness."

"Kindness," Lucinda replied, her voice flat.

"Be nice just to be nice," Gil officially joined the conversation. "Not want something in return."

"Yes, Gil, that's what 'quid pro quo' means," Lucifer agreed.

"It do?"

"Luci, I think these three have just proven that it's a valid concept here," Hector broke in. "Each has described the same thing, but in different words."

"What problem," Nas asked. "Something wrong?"

"Ah, no, Nas," Lucifer assured the confused demon. "I'm just trying to figure something out and decided that it would be best to ask you all about it, as it has to do with you."

"Is good to ask first, not just guess," Gil interjected. "No questions that way."

"And where did you learn that? Did Hector tell you that?"

"No. Make sense when getting to know someone. Ask question, get to know better," Gil explained with a gentle smile that looked strange on her otherwise frightening fanged face. The gigantic demon patted Nas on one massive shoulder. "Learn all sort new stuff."

Nas grinned back at Gil and gave her a peck on the cheek.

"I see," Lucifer murmured. "Learn something new at least once a millennium, I suppose."

Even Hector appeared surprised at the revelation, which gave Lucifer a feeling of reassurance. At least there were something things he had not entirely turned on its ear, although she was sure the blossoming relationship had something to do with the new concepts the human had introduced to the Hellscape.

"You two a couple then," Hector asked the two demons.

"Yes," Nas replied. "Very very good friends."

"Just friends? It looks like more than that," Lucifer suggested.

"Not friends?" Nas looked confused.

"It sounds like love, Nas," Hector suggested. "That's a whole lot more than friends."

"More than friends?"

"It's a special kind of friendship, Nas," Lucifer explained, her thoughts spinning in mental chaos. "You like spending time with Gil?"

"We sleep in same bed," Gil supplied. "Like touch, kiss, feel good."

"How long has this been going on," Hector asked playfully. "I had no idea you two were sweet on each other!"

"Been few weeks now, I think," Trevor interrupted. "All they talk about!"

"You didn't say anything about it to me," Lucifer commented.

"Not my business to say, my Lady," the demon replied. "Keep my big nose out of it."

The ghost of a chuckle escaped Hector and Lucifer glanced over at him. She could see the barely-contained mirth in his eyes. He had one hand clamped over his mouth as though that might help to keep everything in. She almost felt sympathy for the man, but not quite.

"See, Hector, this is part of what I was worried about," Lucifer said a short time later, when they were alone at the bar. The demons had started a game of Monopoly, which Hector had introduced to them a few days previous. It would keep them occupied while the 'grownups' had a chance to speak. "Keeping secrets isn't a good thing."

"Are you telling me you want them to spy on one another and then tattle?"

"Well, I— "

"That just brings back the distrust and the hatred, Lucifer," Hector opined. "I don't think you'd really like that, now would you?"

"It's what I've grown used to since my Parent sent me down here to keep things running."

"I'm not saying you have to be friends with them, Lucifer, but if they can look at you as someone who doesn't necessarily have to be feared, that's not a bad thing, either."

"You've said something like that before, Hector, and I'm not convinced," she replied. "They must respect me or I'll end up having to do more wholesale slaughter when they inevitably misbehave all over again. It's exhausting to replace their numbers, as I've told you."

Trevor wandered over with a platter full of snacks, so the Devil and her pet human changed the subject to something less personal. This was something Lucifer preferred to discuss when there were fewer beings around to listen in.

"Everything has been excellent this evening, Trevor," Lucifer told the demon as she took a pair of tasty-looking nibbles from what was on the platter. "You have certainly outdone yourself!"

"Thank you, my Lady," the creature responded with a smile. "Pirippa help."

"Pirippa."

"Yes, Pirippa," Trevor confirmed. "I give her good knife and she chop up meats for appetizers."

Both Hector and Lucifer looked down at the delicately constructed nibbles. They appeared to be and tasted beyond reproach.

"These are really quite good, Trevor," Lucifer enthused. "Was it difficult to convince Pirippa to help you?"

"No! She ask to help and I say okay," Trevor said. "Was good to have help."

"Did it take long to get her to understand what you needed?"

"She fast learner, my Lady," he said. "Pirippa say she want make meringue next."

"You've created a monster, Hector," Lucifer said flatly. Hector laughed.

"He was looking for something to do, and when you gave me into his care, I guess he decided that if he was going to cook for me, he might as well experiment."

"Is that what happened, Trevor?"

"Guess so," he said. "I know humans eat meat, fruit, grain, but not sure what to do, so I talk to souls who remember how to cook. One say that steak good, but beef bourguignon better."

Well, Lucifer *assumed* the demon meant beef bourguignon, as the creature nearly slaughtered the sixty-four-thousand-dollar word while trying to pronounce it. His oral design had a difficult enough time processing short words without putting it to the additional labor of tackling more exotic terms.

"He has a point there, Luci," Hector remarked. "I love a good slab of grilled beef, but what Trevor can do with a random piece of cow is incredible!"

"So I have just experienced, my friend. It was truly beyond my wildest expectations, I must say."

"I can't argue with you there, Luci."

"What soul did you learn the recipe from, Trevor," Lucifer asked. Would it be worth letting up on some torture if such treasures were to be learned?

"He called Careme," the demon supplied. "Very haughty. Call me many names. Took many blows to get respect."

"Ah, yes, him," Lucifer mused. "Splendid chef, but a downright nasty bastard. He certainly beat enough apprentices and journeymen in his kitchens in his day."

"Sounds like a French chef," Hector said.

"Indeed he was. Considered to be the father of fine French cuisine, in fact. Just like every other chef of his time, though, he thought nothing of beating his underlings for both real and imagined mistakes."

"Really?"

"He beat the wrong apprentice and it ended very badly for the young man," Lucifer said. "That added to his roster of sin. Unacceptable behavior with young women who did not deserve such behavior sent him here."

"So then, even if it was acceptable during the time it happened, it still counts as sin?"

"What part of 'Thou shalt not' did you miss, Hector," the Devil asked, her expression a mite exasperated. "That sort of garbage has happened since the beginning of Time, itself, but it has never been celestially acceptable and there have always been consequences for such things. Much like that former pastor who you encountered when you first arrived, they are always very much surprised when they get here."

"I would imagine so."

"This idiot was so full of himself upon his arrival that for a time, his personal Hell was being the underling of a cruel taskmaster."

"Seems appropriate, but you're suggesting that he didn't remain there?"

"I try to vary tortures in order to keep damned souls from becoming numb to whatever is happening to them. As I recall, right now his personal Hell is being able to see piles and piles of the foods he used to create, but he cannot reach them. He is always an inch too far away to be able grab any of it. It's like he's starving in the center of a cornucopia."

"Oh, that's just—awful," Hector breathed.

"I'm very well aware of that, of course," Lucifer said. "Unfortunately, that's how things work here if we are to make any sort of impression on the souls that have been imprisoned here."

"You'd know best, I'm sure," Hector said. "After all, it's your sandbox."

Lucifer laughed.

"To say the least!"

"So, do you plan to have this chef help Trevor out?"

"I haven't quite decided as yet. Yes, it would be helpful, but he's here for punishment, after all. It would negate that very thing to remove him from that torment. He does deserve it, after all."

"How long has he been here?

"Over two hundred years in your time, but far longer in the twisted version of time that exists here in Hell."

"What does that mean?"

"That means that for you and I, it's been around two hundred years, but for him, it's been a few thousand years."

"A few thousand years of constant torture?"

"Indeed, Hector. That's how it works."

"How does that help things?"

"Isn't that what you would expect in Hell?"

"I suppose so, but—it seems so endless."

Lucifer gave Hector a look he could not interpret, but he felt he should have been able to do so.

"You can't have it both ways, Hector Rhoades," she said.

"It seems that after a certain amount of time, that torture would be meaningless," he suggested. "At some point, it's just about the torture and not benefiting in any way from it."

"Benefiting? What's that supposed to mean?"

"Wrong word, perhaps. Learning, maybe?"

"So, then someone Pol Pot or his ilk should get a pass?"

"That's not what I'm saying at all!"

"Then what *are* you saying?"

"I'm saying that the torment should end at some point. You can't torment them to teach them a lesson, but then not give them the chance to show that they have indeed learnt it."

Lucifer did not reply. She just looked at the human.

"Does that apply to your sister in law, then?"

At first, anger flooded Hector's face. Raw, raging anger. And then his expression changed.

"How long has she been here in her own time?"

"Several thousand years, Hector. The passage of time is different for everyone."

"So, she's relived what happened countless times a day for several thousand years now?"

"At the very least."

Hector's face went pale and he stood very still. Luci reached over the bar, grabbed a random bottle of something quite alcoholic and poured a significant amount of it into the human's glass. He drank it down without even glancing at it.

"I had not thought of that."

"What did you think, then?"

"I'm not sure what I thought, really. I've been so very angry about all of it."

"What do you want to do, then?"

"What can I do, Luci? She's here."

"Do you want the chance to talk with her?"

Hector grabbed his glass and the half-full bottle of gin and wandered over to the sitting area in his quarters. The Devil moved to join him there.

"What would I say?"

"You can ask or say anything you like, Hector," Luci told him. "You'll have an unprecedented opportunity to speak with her."

"Can I think about it?"

"Well, we're supposed to leave here in the next two days, but if you can bring yourself to do it in that time, yes, you may."

## Twenty-Nine

It had been almost a full day since Luci had laid eyes on Hector. It bothered her more than she might have thought possible, but she knew he was thinking about her suggestion.

"It seems you have addressed the vast majority of important issues that needed your attention my Lady," the demon said, interrupting her ruminations. "Is there anything else I might do for you?"

"Do you have any friends?"

"Friends? Ah, yes, that concept that Mr. Rhoades has introduced us to here in Hell," the demon replied. "Indeed, I have been exploring the concept."

"What is that supposed to mean?"

"I seem to have developed a friendship with a certain demon who handles the care and feeding of the sentry demons on the south wall."

"Derenus? Whatever do you two have in common?"

"As a matter of fact, it seems we both enjoy reading."

"Reading."

"Yes! I confess to have taken the liberty of reading some of the items you have in your open literary collection."

"You have."

The demon was not entirely sure if that was a question or a statement, but he determined to push forward.

"Indeed, my Lady. Rather than outright loan things to Derenus, I have taken it upon myself to read aloud to him."

"You're reading aloud to him? Seriously?"

"Well, at this point, there are several demons who seem to appreciate the opportunity."

"Several? How many is 'several'?"

"At last count, I believe eight demons are interested."

"What, exactly, are you reading to them?"

"We just finished Little Women and have begun Alice's Adventures in Wonderland."

Lucifer sat back in her chair, too stunned to say anything.

"Have I done something wrong, my Lady?"

"Ah, no, I suppose," she replied. "As long as it does not interfere with anyone's work."

She watched as a certain stiffness disappeared from the demon's body. He had, she was sure, been terrified that she would react badly to the news that her minions were seeking some manner of recreation.

"Thank you, my Lady," the creature breathed. "I would hope that if there was any problem with this, you would instantly let me know."

"You can be sure of that," she replied flatly.

Taking the hint, the demon excused himself, but not before asking if he could choose another book. By the time he left her office, she had given him carte blanche for all of the books that openly lined her shelves in her quarters.

He thanked her effusively, his expression showing a happiness she could not recall ever having seen before on his gaunt, pockmarked face. She felt unexpected pleasure at the experience.

"Get your ass out of here," she said, waving a hand at him. "I have work to finish."

All was quiet for at least a few hours, and then Lucifer was interrupted by the sound of a tentative knock at her door.

"Enter," she responded.

In walked Hector. His expression was troubled.

"May I sit?"

"Of course you may, Hector," she said. "There is no need to ask!"

"I've been thinking about what you've told me, and I'd like the chance to speak with her, if that offer is still on the table."

"It is," she replied. "When would you like to do it?"

"When would you have the time?"

"Hector we can go and do it right now," she said. "Is that what you really want?"

"Yes, I think it is."

"Then let's go." She stood and suddenly those amazing wings appeared out of what seemed like nowhere at all.

"Really?"

"It will get us there as quickly as possible," she reminded him. "Does that bother you?"

"No, not really," he admitted. "It's still a bit odd to look at, though."

"It is what it is, Hector. Now let's get moving."

In what seemed like no time at all, they were standing outside the entrance to Pernille's private Hell.

"You're certain now? This is your last chance to back out."

"I'm sure, Lucifer," he assured her. "I think I need to do this."

"Very well, then. Follow me."

She opened the door and they entered the nightmare that was Pernille's eternal torment. Lucifer moved to the edge of the lake and waved a hand. In an instant, the damned soul was transported from her confinement in the drowned vehicle and onto the shoreline.

Pernille's once pristine holiday party clothing was covered in algae and mud, which seemed odd, considering its origin in Hellish illusion. She tried to brush the filth from her clothing and skin, with no success.

"What's going on? Where am I?" Then she seemed to notice her brother-in-law for the first time. Her eyes went wide. "Hector? I thought you were on assignment in Sydney?"

"Hello, Pernille," he said. "Sydney was a very long time ago."

"I don't know what's happened," she said, tears beginning to overflow. "The last thing I remember clearly is leaving the party with—oh my dear God!"

"That was many years ago, Pernille," Hector replied. "You both died that night."

"Died? But I'm here! I'm alive!"

"No, Pernille, you're not," he corrected her. "You both died that night because you both were stupid and drove off while you were drunk."

The damned soul dropped to the faux sand and clutched herself in despair. It was an emotion Lucifer had become quite familiar with over her time overseeing the torture of humans. A string of stricken profanity spilled from the girl's lips. Lucifer was a bit surprised to see Hector fall to his knees beside her and wrap his arms around her.

"I forgive you, Pernille," he told her, his voice soft. "I think you've suffered enough."

"It's been a terrible nightmare," she sobbed. "It seems like I've been reliving this forever."

"It has been forever, in a way," he said to her. "I was very angry about it for a very long time."

"I deserve whatever punishment I get for what I did, Hector! I killed my own sister!"

"I think you've suffered enough now, Pernille," he replied. "You don't deserve to keep going through this nightmare."

"I can't—wait! What's happening to me?"

As Lucifer watched, she saw the damned soul beginning to fade. From what she could see, the soul was losing cohesion but was brightening at the same time. The spectral filth of sin was being burned away, replaced by what appeared to be pristine, untouched flesh.

"What's happening to me, Hector?" Pernille gasped, staring at her hand and arm in shock. "What's going on?"

"She seems to be moving on," Lucifer noted as Hector stared at the transformed soul of his sister-in-law. "Perhaps your forgiveness has allowed this to happen."

"My forgiveness?"

"I really have no idea, so I'm guessing here," Luci explained. "It is possible that your strong hatred was what was keeping her here."

"I forgive you, Hector," the now-pure soul said, and brushed her lips against his cheek, bestowing a ghostly kiss before vanishing entirely.

The stricken expression returned to the human's face. And something that might have been shame was there as well.

"I—I can't believe that," he stammered. "I did this to her! How could she *ever* forgive me?"

"You said not all that long ago that she should suffer forever, as I recall," Luci reminded him. "You seem to have forgiven her for *her* part in your wife's passing."

Hector's face flushed red, but not with anger. It looked more like shame to the Lord of Hell.

"I don't deserve forgiveness," he moaned. This was a far cry from the man who only a few days earlier had exuded an almost tangible hatred for his own relation. Luci bit her tongue to avoid pointing this out to him, which was difficult for a Being who normally did not care whose feathers were ruffled by what she said or did. "I put her through all of that!"

"You should, I think," Luci replied, kneeling beside the distraught human and putting a hand on his shoulder. "You said you forgave her and now she seems to be leaving Hell. The only thing I can think of that might cause that is the forgiveness you gave her."

The human was silent for a long time, his face hidden in his hands. Not knowing what else to do, Luci gently stroked his back, then shifted to making small circles with her fingers along his spine. Only the barest shuddering passing through his frame alerted her to the fact that he was crying.

"Hector, this isn't a bad thing," she began. "It gives the possibility of forgiveness and redemption."

"I've hated her for so long, and when I saw her here, I was happy to see her suffer," he moaned. "But I didn't think of what that really meant with her in Hell."

"She's no longer in Hell," the Devil pointed out. "I'm in a position to know when a soul leaves and I can tell you unequivocally that she is no longer in residence."

"Are you sure?"

"Hector, I've been doing this for a very long time now," she reassured him. "I know she's not here any longer."

"So, this has happened before?"

"No, I can't say that it has, but it seems that it is indeed possible. That's not a bad thing, really," she said. Then she noticed that something was wrong.

"Hector?"

"My chest hurts, Lucifer," he said, his face suddenly pale.

"What's going on," she asked him, suddenly concerned. The last thing she needed was a medical emergency involving a human in her realm. It was hard enough getting pizza deliveries here, much less concierge medical assistance when necessary. "Has this happened to you before?"

"No, it hasn't. I don't know what it is," he admitted, his lips now tinged with blue. "All I know is that it doesn't feel right."

"Is it just your heart, or are you feeling discomfort in your arm or does your chest feel as though it's being compressed?"

"It's hard to say, Luci. All I know is it hurts and I can't catch my breath."

"Damn you, don't you dare fall over now, Hector Rhoades," the Devil muttered, gathering the human up in her arms. "Unlike my brother, I'm not a miracle worker. This was not the way I wanted to get you back to Earth again."

"I don't want to go back to Earth, Lucifer," Hector whispered, his voice weak. "Just let me die."

"You're not going to die, Hector," she said. "I will not permit it."

"I don't think that's up to you, Luci."

"Don't you dare tell me what I can and cannot do," she snarled, eyes flaming. "Now shut up, close your pretty eyes, and try to rest while I get you to someone who can help you!"

She ignored the human's weakening protestations as she leapt into the air, her wings making a thunderous downstroke that put considerable distance between herself and the surface of Hell in the blink of an eye.

"Luci, just let me die."

"Oh, just shut up, Hector! Not another damned word. Stop talking and we'll be back on your Earth as soon as I can get us there."

Hector must have lapsed into unconsciousness, as he did not reply. Although it bothered her a bit, Lucifer was pleased that he would not be arguing with her.

But then she realized how very much she would enjoy being able to argue with him and increased her speed. By this time, she was going just short of fast enough to kill the unconscious human. As it was, there was a chance he might not emerge from the experience unscathed, but she truly hoped that would not be the case.

"Would you mind helping this poor dumb bastard survive," she muttered to her Parent, wherever that Entity might be at the moment. "He's a decent guy and doesn't deserve to pass away just yet."

As always, there was no response, but Lucifer did not really expect one. She could only hope that today They were paying attention and would intercede on behalf of her human friend.

There was that word again.

*Friend.*

It presented a burden she had done her best to avoid for her entire existence. Yes, she had had her paramours over the millennia, but this was something different. It wasn't romantic love in the least. It was a connection which was something between that and the connection she had with her siblings.

It puzzled her and piqued her curiosity, but there was now a very real question as to whether or not it would continue. Whatever would she do with Hector Rhoades, providing he survived his current situation? She hoped to have the opportunity to figure that out.

## Thirty

Hector slowly became aware of his surroundings.

There was the unmistakable sound of medical equipment beeping and humming away, all of it sounding much closer than it should. The last thing he remembered was his chest hurting, then some back and forth conversation with Luci that he could not quite recall.

"Did she fly me out of Hell?" His voice was a mere whisper, weak from disuse. His sore throat suggested that he had only recently been extubated.

"Indeed she did, Hector," said a familiar voice. "I'm pleased to see that you are once again awake."

Hector opened his eyes to see the smiling face of Remy hovering over him. She put a cool hand on his brow and smiled.

"Your fever seems to be declining."

"Fever? I thought I was having a heart attack."

"You did. The fever showed up later," she explained. "For some reason, humans have a bad habit of picking up other maladies while they are in recovery. That's the reason we took you out of the hospital and brought you to my Lady's home."

"Later? How long have I been out?" Hector was very confused by all the information he was getting. "Is Lucifer okay? And why is my room blue now?"

"My Lady is fine, Hector. Between you and me, her focus has been returning you to health ever since you fell ill," she replied. "And I thought the change in decor might make you happy."

Hector recalled his thoughts when he had first arrived at Luci's home and could not help a chuckle. The majordomo was right; it gave him a warm and happy feeling inside, and not simply because the room now reminded him of a happier part of his life, a very long time ago.

"How long has it been, Remy?" Despite the happy surprise of Remy's "gift," Hector's irritation was getting the best of him. He had never been the world's most patient patient.

"It's been about two weeks now," she said, her mouth quirked in a sideways smile. "I imagine you'll be happy to get real food in your belly and not have to be tube fed anymore."

"Tube fed? Shouldn't I be intubated, then?"

"You were until this morning when Doctor Runyon extubated you and took you off the sedative he had you on to keep you from pulling the damned thing out of your throat."

"Sedative? Was I that bad?"

"Probably your military training kicking in, my friend," said another familiar voice from the general direction of the doorway. "Glad to see you're awake now. It hasn't been the same without you."

The human shook his head, still weak from his enforced confinement to his bed.

"Tired?"

"More than I'd think I'd be after resting for all that time," he murmured, eyes heavy. It was all he could do to keep them open.

"Then you get some rest," Luci told him, her voice soft. As he began to drift off, he felt her lips bestow a soft kiss on his forehead. "The world will continue to spin while you sleep, my friend. Don't worry."

"I keep safe, my Lady," said a gravelly voice. "I make good easy soup for Hector's stomach. Help him get better fast."

"I know you will, Trevor," Lucifer replied, her tone certain. "You know how to find the kitchen. It's yours, for the duration."

"Thank you let me come here, my Lady."

"Trevor, your connection with our dear Hector is what has allowed you to follow along," she told the demon. "I thought you knew that."

"No, not know, but glad all same," the demon replied. "I make dinner for you tonight?"

"If you like, Trevor, but I'd like something maybe a wee bit more substantial than soup, if it's all the same to you."

"I have more things to play with in kitchen here. I surprise you, okay?"

"I'm sure you will, Trevor, and I am sure I will enjoy it."

"Me, too, my Lady," the demon enthused. "Thank you!"

"Scat, you little shit," she told him, a smile taking any implied insult from her words. "Jason has been told that he is not to molest you while you're in the kitchen. He doesn't like it much, but he loves his job more."

"I make friend with Jason," Trevor assured her with a fanged grin. "Will be all good. No fight. No argue."

"I'll take that as a promise."

"Good, my Lady!"

"Jason doesn't stand a chance," Luci muttered as the demon's backside disappeared out the bedroom door.


The next time Hector awoke, it was to the aroma of something delicious in the vicinity. Opening his eyes, he was greeted by a familiar and very welcome distorted face.

"Trevor!"

"Hector!"

"How are you here? I didn't think we were in Hell again."

"No, not in Hell," the demon told him.

"Then how are you here, Trevor?"

"My Lady say it because we friends, Hector," Trevor explained. "Help us stay together."

"Yes, I suppose friends do stay together at that," he replied. "Whatever the reason, I'm really glad to see you, my friend."

The demon laid a massive hand on Hector's forearm and gave it a companionable squeeze.

"You hungry?"

"Famished."

"Good. I make soup for you."

"For the love of God, Trevor, I don't think I could do French onion soup right now."

The demon laughed.

"No, not heavy soup. I do chicken soup. Chicken, carrot, celery, onion, little salt, and pepper. Do dark meat chicken. Thigh. White meat too dry, even in broth. Clear broth. Easy on stomach. Good for you!"

"A true connoisseur of fine comestibles you turned out to be."

"Connoisseur mean cook?"

"No, actually someone who is discerning in what they eat or drink," the human explained to the demon who was currently adjusting the hospital bed to raise Hector to a sitting position before rolling a hospital table over.

Atop the synthetic wood table was a deep tureen full of the soup Trevor had described. A deep inhalation resulted in Hector's mouth beginning to water in anticipation of the relative feast to come. His stomach growled and the demon grinned.

"You way hungry, Hector," he chuckled. "Sit back, I feed you."

"I'm a grown man, Trevor, I can feed myself."

"I let you argue with my Lady," the demon declined. "I want live some days longer."

The next thing Hector knew, he was being spoon-fed by his demonic nursemaid. The rounded soup spoonful of broth slid over the top of his tongue, just cool enough not to burn the tender taste buds that reveled in the rich flavor that was transported over them.

"Is good?"

"Perfect."

Four spoons full of the excellent soup later and Hector was once again exhausted. It amazed him that the simple act of eating could reduce him to yawning and a deep desire to go back to sleep. He said as much to Trevor.

"Is normal, Doctor Runyon tell me," the demon replied. "You get more sleep. You feel better when wake up again."

"I need to get back to Lucifer," Hector began. "I can't be in bed— "

"You do as my Lady Lucifer say, Hector," the demon said, his voice firm. "You naughty boy to her grown-up. Not like her spankings."

"You're a bastard, Trevor," Hector mumbled, his eyes at half-mast. "A right bastard."

"Happy be your bastard, Hector. Go sleep now."

Hector opened his mouth to respond, but between one breath and another, fell back to sleep. Trevor, careful not to let the drugged soup touch his skin, removed both it and himself from the room. The human might be on the road to good health, but sleeping would be more helpful in achieving that goal than being restless in bed.

Doctor Runyon had instructed the demon most carefully on the proper dosage of the soporific. He had also noted that since it was unknown what affect the drug might have on demon flesh, that it was best to avoid contacting entirely.

Jason was waiting on the demon to continue teaching him how to make the French onion soup that had become the talk of the house. The human was currently tending the baking pan full of tasty auroch marrow bones that were gently roasting in the oven.

Trevor knew the way to just about anyone's heart was through their stomach and Jason knew it as well. Thus, yet another friendship was in the process of being forged.

## Thirty-One

"Lucifer, it's been three weeks! It's time for me to get out of here! I know as well as you do that you had more places to go before my unfortunate incident."

For what seemed like the hundredth time, the Devil squared her shoulders and did her best to stare the impatient human down. How was it that her demons took her seriously, but this ridiculously mortal human thought he could argue with her?

And why did she tolerate it?

Because her regard for the man was genuine, and that stubbornness one of his more endearing qualities.

"Unfortunate incident? It was a bloody heart attack, you ridiculous man!"

"I'm better, Lucifer! I'm good to go. Just give me the chance to prove it to you!"

"When Doctor Runyon says it's okay, then you can," she replied. "He's supposed to be by this afternoon to examine you."

"Where did you find that quack," Hector grumbled. "When I got hurt when I was in the Army, they didn't have me abed this damned long, even when I--," his fingers brushed across the shocking scar that marred his forehead.

"That's because to the military, you are useful cannon fodder," Lucifer reminded him. "And you are *not* useful to me if you are either incapacitated or dead. Runyon said it was close with you."

"Close? Why didn't you say anything about that before?"

"Because I didn't think I'd have to, Hector, but you're making things difficult for me and for everyone else here," she said, her expression angry. "I shouldn't have to have someone keep a constant eye on you to make sure you stay put!"

"I was almost out the front door, too."

It felt like a point of pride to have pointed that out. It was not his fault that every step had felt as though he were slogging through field of deep mud, and he would die before he admitted that out loud to anyone.

"What is it with human males that makes them think they've got to prove they're fine when they clearly are not?"

"That's just a stupid story," Hector protested. "It's not true!"

"How long have I been around, Hector? I've been around human males for a very long time and as a gender, you've been that way the entire time."

There was not anything Hector could reply to Luci's statement. He knew he was guilty of that same accusation.

"If you ever try that nonsense again, I'll have Gil sit on your foot!" Luci threatened. Only the barest hint of a smile took the anger from her words, but the human knew he was walking on thin ice if he crossed her. One did not screw with the Devil.

Of that, he had no doubt.

The demon in question winked at Hector from the doorway. He hated that there seemed to be a monstrous conspiracy against him and said so.

"No conspiracy, Hector," Gil told him, grinning hugely. "We care about you. Not let you make yourself sick again."

"I'm not sick!"

"You lot sick, Hector," Gil corrected him. Trevor nodded his agreement. "So sick my Lady bring me here keep eye on you. You know she not like demons out of Hell."

That reminder brought the human up short. He knew the Devil kept her minions in Hell unless she absolutely could not avoid bringing them out, and for excellent reasons. Getting angry would not solve anything and only antagonize those who sought to help him recover.

Hector took a deep breath, then let it out slowly, doing his best to exhale his anger and frustration along with the carbon dioxide from his lungs. He knew he had lost this argument and that he was probably just a hair short of insulting his friends.

"I'm sorry," he managed to say, once he got hold of himself. "I'm not used to being stuck in bed like an invalid. I shouldn't be taking my frustrations out on you."

"Is okay, Hector," Gil said, coming over and patting him on the head. It was like being smacked in the head with a Virginia smoked ham. "Friends forgive, right?"

*Forgive.*

The word hit Hector like a sledgehammer and the tears began to flow. Stricken, Gil dropped to her knees next to the human's sickbed and put an awkward right lower arm around the him, doing her best to bestow a hug, oh-so-gently. She knew from what she had been told that the creatures in their mortal, living state were especially fragile in contrast to her own substantial self.

"I sorry, Hector! What I say? How I make right?" The demon's eyes were wide with distress and she looked around for some sort of cue as to what she should be doing next. There was none.

"Gilrabin, you have made him remember something he had perhaps forgotten. Something he might *prefer* to have forgotten," Lucifer said so quietly only the demon could hear her.

"I sorry, my Lady," Gil blurted, distraught. "Send me back home I not bother you more."

"It's okay," came a muffled voice from inside the improbable comfort of the blue-scaled arm. "It's okay."

"You sure, Hector? Not want hurt you more."

"No, please, just no," Hector extended his arms as far as they would go around the demon, in the space between both sets of massive arms, which wasn't very far at all, but he did *try*. "Please stay."

Responding to an emotion she had never before experienced, the demon wrapped her other lower arm around Hector and held him as closely as she was able without hurting the human. Lucifer stood close, but not too close, watching as everything transpired. This was something equally as new for her. Who would ever have thought a demon might feel moved to comfort someone feeling distress?

In her millennia of creating and ruling demons, Luci had found the creatures responded only when they had skin in the game. In this case, Gil had nothing tangible to gain from this interaction. What potential did this portend for demondom as a whole?

Luci watched as the demon's normally roiling personal blue cloud settled down, seeming to pool on the ground at her taloned feet. Tentacle-like extensions of demonic smoke would occasionally reach out to make contact with the human's body, then retract again, much like a curious amoeba testing the waters.

The Devil was shaken when she realized the smoke was attempting in its own way to *stroke* the human in a comforting manner, but it seemed it did not know how to do it. Was the "smoke" self-aware? More questions to consider at another time.

The demon's embrace was awkward, but the Devil did not doubt that the concern behind it was genuine. She watched as Gilrabin whispered something into the human's ear and he pressed his face against the demon's muscular shoulder, and then the demon's embrace became something that looked downright protective in nature.

The human drew in the caring and comfort the demon offered him at that moment, and it calmed his heart and soothed his thoughts. The *friendship* they shared helped to make that happen.

It was clear that nothing physical would be permitted to get through, and knowing Gilrabin as she did, Luci knew her demon would go down fighting if anyone tried to interfere. The demon was fierce enough when fighting for her King. What would she be like in the instance she had to fight for the puny human she seemed to have decided she needed to watch over with more sincere care than Lucifer had ever seen a demon show?

Not even Luci wanted to witness that contest.

"Doctor Runyon should be here very soon," Lucifer said, her voice quiet but firm. "We'll proceed from his recommendation."

"I stay till he here," Gil announced. She did not release her hold on Hector. "Keep Hector safe."

"I'm certain that you will, Gilrabin," Luci replied. Perhaps the demon did not realize the threat to Hector was emotional and not physical but now was not the time to correct her.

"Whatever the doctor says, I'll do it," Hector announced, raising his head to look the Devil in the eye. "I promise you that."

"Glad to hear that, Hector," Lucifer said. "I'd hate to have to become upset with you."

"I'd hate it, too."

"Good."

"I meant what I said when I first met you, Lucifer. I want to travel with you, whatever the outcome."

"You've not had the best outcome where all that is concerned. Are you certain this is what you want?"

"Luci, if I wasn't sure, I wouldn't be such a stubborn bastard about all of this."

"Oh, Hector, I'm certain you're a stubborn bastard in all aspects of your life," the Devil told him. "After all, it takes one to know one."

# Epilogue

After a bit of fumbling, the door to Hector's quarters in Hell squeaked open and a furtive figure slipped inside.

"I find it and no one know, is all good," the intruder muttered to itself. "Must go fast. Eyes not distracted forever."

A bit of general ransacking ensued, with various personal items thrown higgledy-piggledy. After all, the intruder reasoned, no one was in the room to see who was doing it.

A short time later, it was behind the bar, tossing bottles of very expensive liquor out of the way when a deep, terrible growl surprised it. The intruder looked up to see a pair of glowing eyes moving forward amidst a roiling swirl of angry blackness.

A snarling mouth opened to reveal what seemed like a cavern filled with innumerable needle-sharp stalagmites and stalactites.

There was a scream. Then a crash.

And then the shrieks began.

They went on for an awfully long time indeed.

## About the Author

Anna Rose has been writing for what might seem to her to be her entire life. Countless spiral-bound, college-ruled notebooks filled with rambling stories, fan fiction, and whatnot. It's probably a very good thing that they were misplaced over the years, because they would be entirely too embarrassing to see the light of day.

That said, she did not publish her first novel until 2012 with the vampire novel Siofra, which came about because, when looking for non-romance-related/monk vampire novels and finding none, she decided she probably was not the only one looking for something different. She wrote two more novels in that universe, Fiach Fola and Droch Fola, with one more planned as the conclusion to that story.

The lesson here is that if you can't find what you want, then perhaps you need to do it for yourself and not rely on someone else to do it for you. That doesn't just apply to writing. That idea works with a lot of other things in one's daily life.

During that time, she also developed the Tales of the Dragonguard series of novels, which begins with Aya's Dragon. Its second novel, Sara's Fire was released in mid-2018, and the third novel, Kal's Heart, is still in development.

She is the mother of a brilliant daughter, the spiritual Mom of a beloved and gifted son-of-the-heart, the besotted caretaker of a sweet Chihuahua furkid, an amateur photographer who has spent far too much money on photography equipment, an unrepentant beach bum, and an avid traveler. (Take her advice and if you decide to travel, make sure to take lots of pictures when you do. Memories are dicey things. You don't need the fancy-schmancy stuff, either. Your smartphone's camera can do a pretty damned good job of recording these once-in-a-lifetime memories.)

Each year she tries to attend at least the San Diego ComicCon and WonderCon, the latter of which is held in Anaheim, California. Both are put on by the very esteemed nonprofit organization, ComicCon International.

She currently lives in the sleepy, sunny Southern California beach village community of La Jolla. Who needs weather extremes when one can live in the most perfect climate in the world?

Luci: Rhoades to Hell is the first novel in a planned series.

What else would you expect? Right?


## About the Cover Designer

Geoff Edwards is a not-so-innocent bystander who was foolish enough to play with a proposed cover image and make it much nicer than the original proposal.

He's also allergic to shrimp.

The rest is subject to change without notice.

9 780985 096854